But who | Caroline?

BY
Mike Healey

But who killed Caroline?

Dedication

This book is dedicated to Liz and Mark Elliott

Copyright

Mike Healey has asserted his rights under the Copyright, Designs and Patents Act, 1998 to be identified as author of all six works

All rights reserved. No part of this publication may be reproduced, stored in a retrieval system, or transmitted, in any form or by any means, electronic, mechanical, photocopying, recording, or otherwise, without the written prior permission of the author.

While most of the locations are real, the characters and the events of this novel are entirely the product of the author's imagination. Any resemblance to actual persons, living or dead, is entirely coincidental.

© Copyright 2013 - Mike Healey

But who killed Caroline?

Profiling

Profiling is the identification of specific characteristics of an individual committing a particular crime by a thorough, systematic observational process and an analysis of the crime scene, the victim, the forensic evidence, and the known facts of the crime. The profiling technique has been used by behavioural scientists and criminologists to examine criminal behaviour and to evaluate, as well as possibly predict, the future actions of criminals.

Although all investigators who deal with violent crime are experienced with criminal profiling, there are behavioural psychologists whose sole job is to profile the criminal mind.

Criminal investigative analysis, or profiling, is currently neither a widely accepted law enforcement practice nor a conventional investigative process, but there is some evidence to support its usage in the investigation of certain types of crime. Furthermore, profiling as a science or as an art is not meant to be a law enforcement panacea or even a replacement for conventional and traditional investigative police work. However, law enforcement agencies are beginning to realize the benefits of this technique as a viable investigative tool.

Within the past two decades, there has been increased use of profiling, although it remains a controversial tool. Not everyone believes that devising a hypothetical portrait of a suspect makes a contribution to solving crimes, but some profiles have been surprisingly accurate. The problem is that it's extremely difficult to know when you're working with a good one until the suspect is caught and compared against it.

Dr Elspeth Grant PhD and Fellow of All Souls, Oxford is a criminal psychologist and Profiler. This particular case is an example of the complex and at times highly speculative work of a Profiler, dealing with dangerous and unpredictable individuals.

1
Friday, 20th April

When Georgina left the pub that afternoon and headed for the beach she could not have known that she would be dead within the hour. No one could know that, except perhaps her murderer.

Within minutes of leaving the car park she was in sight of the sea. She paused momentarily to take in the view.

Saffron sunlight on grassland stretching to the water's edge. Coarse sea-grass, in tufts. Brittle shells and sea wrack. Bleached wood, half buried in the sand. The white skeleton of a gull, one sightless eye-socket star-gazing, blindly.

Then she saw him.

A man - standing alone on a spur of rock, some three hundred meters away. He is holding his binoculars up to his bearded face. He is staring at her!

She turned away, momentarily disturbed by his effrontery but then turned back, raised her own binoculars and resolutely stared back at him.

'There!', she thought. 'Now its my turn!'

He immediately averted his gaze, lowered his glasses, turned and stared out towards the horizon. The waves - wind-blown, troubled - turn a bruised blue as the sun is momentarily obscured by a cloud.

She has won but the idea that he had been watching her still disturbs her somewhat. How long, for example, had he been following her progress along the beach? How long had he watched her? She looked back the way she has come, her footsteps still clearly visible in the wet shingle behind her.

Forward or back? She must chose for his presence on the beach -

her beach - has changed everything.

He is middle-aged - as far as her brief glance had shown. Maybe she knows him? Someone from the village, perhaps? Has she seen him before, in the street or in the post office? He looks vaguely familiar. No. He is a complete stranger. A visitor to the island. English, probably - with his Sassenach ways. His English airs and graces!

She stepped forward, boldly, and headed off down the beach towards him. He is still standing, facing out to sea. His sandy hair, for he is hatless, blows in the wind.
Would he see her? Would he move?

She left the beach and headed inland slightly until she had reached the nearest grassy knoll. Here the grass is short, encrusted with brine. It almost cracks beneath her tread. Some kind of plant covers large areas of the slanting rock, hugging its surface, flattened against the wind, supine, each red-coloured leaf fringed with a crust of salt.

Now, on the upper rim of the knoll, she made good progress, moving closer and closer towards the stranger.

Suddenly (has he heard her? No, impossible at this distance, surely?) he glanced over his shoulder, sees that she is moving towards him then turns and moves off down towards the water's edge, momentarily disappearing from view behind the rocky outcrop on which he had been standing.

She found his abrupt disappearance disconcerting but, as she moved higher towards a spur of rock partly buried within the shale, she saw him once more. Now he is squatting at the very edge of the sea. With a stick he is prodding what appears to be some creature. Crab? Stranded jelly fish? From where she stands it is obscured from her view by the man's body. Then he stands up, steps back slightly and continues to stare down at the object at his feet.

She pauses, astride her rock and raises her binoculars.

What he has found, there at the water's edge, is an arm, severed at the shoulder and now rolling back and forth as each tiny wave hits the beach.

* * *

Earlier that morning she had posted her letters, bought carrots and fresh parsley and filled her somewhat battered Corsa with petrol from the garage behind the post office. At the butcher's she had bought four sausages and a single lamb chop which the young man behind the counter had cut for her. She noticed how carefully he first wrapped it in grease-proof paper before placing it in newspaper, even though it was late. In London they would have refused to serve you, so close to closing time.

Then on impulse, she had driven to the pub three miles south of the village and within sight of the sea loch.

She had first come to the Isle of Skye for holidays when she was a child. Now, twenty years later, she lived close by the pub, in a cottage that her father had himself restored many years before. She is happy in her new life on the island, far from the rat race that had been her lot in London for so many years.

She always craved anonymity and here she finally found it. That and absolute privacy. She has her lover, her books and her 'Mission'. She feels secure in her anonymity. Her 'Mission' is almost complete. There is satisfaction in that. They have prepared for any eventuality. They are ready and soon her new book will be published. She feels happy and secure.

She parked her car and entered the pub. This was only the second or third time that she had been inside, even though it was so close to her cottage and she had lived on the Isle of Skye for two years. She was never particularly fond of country pubs. Never very sociable, really.

The pub that Friday morning was relatively quiet. A few hill-walkers in the public bar were its only customers. She moved to the empty saloon bar and sat by the window, gazing out at the bay. She ordered a glass of red wine and a cheese sandwich. There were two gulls perched on a wooden table in the garden. They seemed enormous, close to. They were intent on consuming the remains of a scampi lunch that had been left on a paper plate on the table. She clapped her hands and they flew off. It was oddly satisfying, to startle these great birds so easily. Ugly creatures! She tucked into her sandwich and sipped her wine.

Perhaps a walk on the beach? Yes. A breath of fresh air. That's what she needed after lunch.

When she had finished her meal she rose, paid her bill and wrapped her red scarf about her throat. She took her binoculars from the boot of her car. She carefully hid her handbag under the driver's seat and locked her shopping and jacket in the boot.

* * *

The man glanced round at her as she scrambled down the dune towards him. To her now he appears awkward, almost embarrassed at what he has found lolling obscenely at his feet. He steps aside as she arrives at the water's edge, casually casting his stick into the sea.

She stared at the severed arm. She had once seen a dead body but never a severed arm. It is unnerving, to say the least!

'I reckon it's been there a day or two', he says, after what felt like a long silence. 'Look, it has a watch on it. Three-thirty. Maybe that was when she died or when she were thrown in the water.'

True enough. On the wrist there is a woman's watch. Three-thirty.

'Reckon it were cut with a butcher's knife. Clean as a whistle, that cut. Mind you, fish may have nibbled at it since then.'
She turned and stared at him - this man with the casual, somewhat unfeeling manner of describing some girl's severed arm. He looks vaguely familiar. Maybe she knows him? Someone from the village, perhaps? Has she seen him before, in the street

or in the post office? His accent is strange. Difficult to place. Is he English or Scottish?

'How did you find it?'

'Through my binoculars. It were there, right below me. Couldn't believe me eyes. There it was, large as life and twice as dead.'

His laugh sends a chill down her spine. Has he no feeling for this dead girl, this sad creature on the beach? Or at least, all that is left of her?

'We must call the police. We must do something.'

'Already have.'

He takes from his jacket pocket a mobile phone and waves it at her.

'Should be here soon, I reckon. Touch nothing, they said.'

'Who was she, I wonder?'

'No idea. No one I knows, anyway.'

'How can you be so sure? From just an arm?'

'Never seen her in me life.'

She turned away, unable to stare any longer at the severed arm, nor indeed listen to this cold, indifferent man.

The police arrived twenty minutes later, in a battered blue Land Rover. It dropped down from the rolling grassland that ran the length of the shore and stopped right at the water's edge. They stared, dumbfounded, at the severed arm. The man had vanished but the body of a young woman was also discovered, partly covered by shingle behind a rock some yards up the beach. She was fully-dressed but she had been strangled with a red scarf.

One arm had been severed at the elbow. There was blood everywhere but Georgina's arm itself had also vanished.

2
Preliminary Enquiries

Detective Inspector John White arrived in Portree later that afternoon from Inverness and took charge of the investigation.

He went first to the scene of the crime on the beach. Although the morning had been bright and sunny, the weather had taken a sudden turn for the worse. It was now cold and blustery. Storms were predicted. White's priority was therefore to protect the crime-scene from imminent bad weather and to get Forensic examiners there as soon as possible. He managed, with the help of the local police, to cordon off a large area of the beach on either side of the body and the severed arm and to rig a makeshift tent over the body itself.

A small team of Forensic Examiners arrived two hours later and began a close inspection of the arm, the mutilated body and the surrounding area. They took numerous photographs. They also had a look at the dead woman's car . According to the owner of the pub, it had been left in their car park when she set off for a walk at two-thirty that afternoon. Forensic forced an entry and examined the car's interior and boot. They found shopping and an overcoat in the boot and her handbag hidden under the driver's seat. It contained her purse, driving licence, Gold credit card, a few receipts and a shopping list.

There was no mobile phone nor iPad. Neither her mobile phone nor her car keys had been found on the beach. Whoever had murdered her that afternoon had presumably taken these away with him or thrown them into the sea. There were no car tracks or obvious foot prints near the body, nor within a fifty-yard radius of where the woman lay, partly hidden.

Once Forensic had completed their examination, Georgina's body and the arm were taken immediately to the SPSA Forensic Science Laboratory in Aberdeen for more detailed examination.

* * *

The name of the murdered woman was Georgina Cousins. She was an attractive thirty-two year old with long, blond hair held in a tight pony-tale. She was five-feet eight, with blue eyes. At the time of her death she was wearing an expensive knee-length tweed skirt and Fair Isle sweater over a white blouse. Her shoes were quality, dark brown brogues.

Her only jewellery was a gold ring on the small finger of her right hand.

According to two elderly neighbours up the lane from Georgina's cottage, she had been living on the island quietly for about two years. Her cottage was only a few hundred yards from the pub. Her parents had for many years used that cottage as a holiday home. Now, presumably, it was their daughter's.

But who had rung the police?

Detective Inspector White was particularly anxious to discover who had rung the local police in Portree and given them the exact location of the arm on that beach. No mention had been made of a body - just a severed arm at the water's edge. The man had not given his name and the duty officer, WPC Deborah Saunders, at the small police station in Portree who had taken the call at exactly three-thirty that afternoon, had not recognised the man's voice either. It had, she said, a 'distinct northern twang' to it. They had so far been unable to trace that call. What was interesting, perhaps, was that the man had rung the Portree police station's own number and not nine-nine-nine. That probably meant he had local knowledge. He had also given the police an *exact* location.

Since Georgina Cousins had been last seen at the pub only an hour or so before she was killed, it was there that DI White began his enquiries.

The pub owner first described the woman he had served and then gave White the approximate time of her arrival and departure. He had no idea who else had been in the pub that lunchtime. They were all strangers to him - visitors, mostly hill-walkers probably.

No, he did not know the dead woman although he had an idea she lived close by. He might, he thought, have seen her in her car from time to time. She was definitely not a regular customer. What he did remember, however, was that he served her a cheese sandwich and a glass of wine.

White did not normally jump to conclusion but on this occasion he had taken an instant dislike to the landlord of the Cross Keys. Apart from being from Birmingham he appeared to be enjoying the 'notoriety' the woman's gruesome death was giving his pub.

'You say there were some customers in the other bar but did anyone follow her out to the car park?' asked DI White.

'Nope. Well, not as far as I remember.'

'Thank you Mr Turnbull. I will need to speak to you again later but that is all for now. WPC Saunders here will take a preliminary statement from you. I will want a description from you of everyone in the public bar this lunchtime. And names, if you have any. Debbie.'

'Yes sir.'

Detective Inspector White turned to leave, crossed the saloon bar then paused at the door.

'By the way, why did she not order hot food this lunchtime? Your menu here lists a wide range of options. Why no hot meal?'

'Simple answer to that, Inspector. The chef is off. Cold food was all we had, what with me being short-staffed and all.'

'So where is he?'

'Well might you ask', replied Turnbull. 'Haven't seen him for a day or two. Mind you, he often takes off when the fancy suits him. Very unreliable. I have no idea where he is or when he might come back. Maybe he's your man. Maybe he killed her, eh?'

* * *

From the shopping in her car and the shopping list and receipts found in her purse, it had been fairly easy to trace Georgina's movements that morning. This John White did, starting with the local butcher's.

He began with the butcher only because he had to start somewhere. Besides, his wrapping paper was the most distinctive - old copies of the *Racing Pink*. By early evening this same young man had become DI White's chief suspect - even if, at this stage, the evidence was entirely circumstantial.

The reason for this was that not only had he served Georgina that morning but that he had gone off for his lunch at exactly the same time as she had driven to the pub. He had, according to the butcher's lad, virtually followed her out of the door. Although that in itself was hardly conclusive evidence, it was his accent that put him in the frame. This particular butcher was from Nelson in Lancashire. That was a 'northern twang' if ever there was.

But there was a problem.

The problem was that he had also been seen that lunchtime at the betting shop in the village. The betting-shop clerk swore that he had been there for the larger part of an hour. Sometime around two-thirty he had placed a bet on the four-o'clock race at Kempton. He left soon thereafter - too late to get to the beach and back before three when he was next seen at the butcher's shop. If that were not enough, his mobile had not been used that afternoon.

Either there was something wrong with the time of death or the butcher was definitely not the murderer.

When the two local police officers had arrived at the beech in response to the mysterious phone call, the body was without any sign of rigor mortis - or so White had been informed. Indeed, PC Rawlinson had even claimed that the woman was still warm when he turned her head slightly in order to try and identify her. Rigor mortis usually took about three hours to occur.

That means that she must have died between two-thirty, when she left the pub, and three-fifty when the police arrived on the scene.

Very puzzling! If the butcher was not our man, thought White, maybe the missing chef could provide an answer?

* * *

White spent the rest of the afternoon tracing Georgina's steps through Portree. The two local bobbies, under White's supervision and with the help of Sergeant McGregor of the Portree Constabulary, spoke to anyone who might have seen her in each of the shops she visited. Although some recognised her description, few knew this woman. She was, it would appear, something of a recluse and seldom talked to anyone. Nor did it appear that she had been followed wherever she went that morning in the village. No, nothing suspicious whatsoever.

White did not go back to Inverness that night. It had been a long day but there was till much to do. Instead, he checked into the Royal Hotel overlooking the bay and settled down to an evening mulling over the day's events.

But first he phoned his wife, Poppy.

'Hello, darling. I'm staying over in Portree. Nasty murder.'

'OK. Take care!'

'Of course. I'll phone you tomorrow, when things have settled down. Love you.'

'Love you too, John.'

White then broke open a box of peanuts and a beer from the small fridge in his bedroom and settled in for the evening.

His bedroom was on the first floor. From his window he could just see the row of coloured houses that lined the harbour wall. By now the threatened storm had arrived, rattling his window panes. It was, he mused, going to be a very rough night indeed!

He sat at the edge of the bed and examined his notes carefully for an hour or so but his reverie was eventually broken by a phone call from Aberdeen. He glanced at his watch. Eleven-thirty. Someone else was working late.

'Hi John. Its Jim. I think someone there in Portree owes you an apology?'

'Apology? Why?'

'Why? Because that arm they sent me does not belong to the dead woman, Georgina Cousins.'

'What?'

'You only have to look to see that it is a right arm, severed at the shoulder. The one missing from Georgina's body is her *left* arm, severed at the elbow. No match, I'm afraid. By the way, I have just emailed you a preliminary report. More details to follow tomorrow. Sweet dreams, Detective Inspector!'

With that Consultant Pathologist James Ledbetter rang off. 'Fuck!' said John White, under his breath. He fired up his laptop and checked the email containing Ledbetter's short, preliminary report.

As the red scarf indicated, Georgina Cousins had indeed been strangled. There were, however, no signs of any kind of obvious struggle nor evidence of sexual assault. Close examination of Georgina's elbow showed that the removal of her left arm had been done with a very sharp knife of some kind; the cuts were not only clean but well executed. This was someone who knew how to use a knife - or perhaps a scalpel. 'Professional expertise', was the phrase the Consultant Pathologist used. 'That', he added somewhat facetiously, 'would probably help narrow your search, John.'

Detective Inspector John White turned off his light, climbed into bed and closed his eyes. 'Fuck you, Ledbetter.'

Outside, in the dark, a mother of all storms raged.

3
Saturday, 21st April

The storm raged all Friday night, battering the island with gale-force winds and high seas. The broad, open harbour at Portree sustained the worst damage. So strong were the waves that the iron balustrade on the harbour wall ended up bent and twisted. Two lamp-posts and a telephone-booth on the quayside had simply vanished. Locals, even the eldest amongst them, could not remember a storm as violent as this for years.

To add to Portree's woes, sometime that night three fishing boats in the harbour broke their moorings and were swept out into the Sound of Rassay - a treacherous stretch of water at the best of times. In such a storm as the one they experienced that night, plus a high Spring tide and gale-force winds, it was probable that all three boats has sunk. If they had survived the storm, then it was likely that the rocks to the north of Staffin would finish them off - leaving only a tangle of splintered wood, broken spars, ropes and torn fishing tackle.

For a small fishing community like that in Portree, the loss of three working boats was absolutely devastating.

* * *

George McClure had been a fisherman all his life on the Isle of Skye. His father and his father before him had fished these waters as far back as anyone could remember. Now in his late sixties, George had stopped fishing. He supplemented his state pension by taking tourists to remote parts of the island, either to go sea-fishing or to gawp at the seals that plagued these waters.

It was a modest living but at least it kept him active. Besides, he loved the sea and intended to sail around his beloved Hebridean islands until the day he dropped. Because he did not wish to pay what he described as the 'exorbitant' harbour tolls, he always moored his boat a mile or two further south of Portree - in an inlet in the more sheltered waters of Loch Rassay. Because of that his small fishing boat had avoided the worst of last night's storm.

The young man from the Northern Lighthouse Board had been holed up in his hotel since the storm began on Friday afternoon. Now, with relatively calm seas and a brisk, offshore wind, he would be able to reach the lighthouse.

Or so he hoped.

He therefore met George at the quayside that Saturday morning at seven o'clock sharp and scrambled aboard.

* * *

But George McClure was not the only boat out early that Saturday morning. Neil McPherson, whose fishing boat had vanished in the night, was anxious to learn the fate of his only source of income. His future depended on finding that boat - or what remained of it.

The north-eastern corner of the Isle of Skye is a beautiful yet desolate spot. Here, in the Bay of Kimalueg, great waves crash against rugged sea-cliffs frequented only by seabirds. Walkers explore this area at their peril for the paths along the coast here are steep and treacherous and likely to vanish overnight into the sea far below.

It was here, along the rocks at the foot of these sea-cliffs, that Neil McPherson had been searching for the last hour or so.

His was one of the three fishing boats that had been swept out to sea sometime during the storm. This was where, if they had not sunk immediately, they would end up - shattered fragments of wooden hull, fishing tackle, ropes and spars. The only safe way to reach these treacherous rocks was by boat and it was Rob Sinclair - another local fisherman from Portree - who had helped Neil leap ashore and search for any remains of the missing boats.

As Neil scrambled from rock to rock, gathering splintered wood and other debris, Sinclair steadied his boat just a few meters offshore, his engine running. When Neil was done looking one area, Rob would cautiously edge his boat in close to the rocks, allowing Neil to leap back on board and then move on further down the coast.

It was very dangerous stuff but Neil was determined to find out, once and for all, what had happened to his boat - and indeed, those of his two neighbours whose livelihoods had also vanished overnight.

* * *

The remote, rocky island of South Rona lies to the north-east of Portree and at the northern tip of the island of Rassay. The approach by boat across the Sound of Rassay from Skye is spectacular - providing the weather is good.

The island itself is a storm-tossed spot in winter but at other times of the year a haven for walkers and naturalists.

South Rona is very rocky but also contains, somewhat surprisingly, small patches of lush woodland. The glaciated landscape has within its rocky folds some of the oldest rocks in Western Europe and its coast, with pink felspar cliffs dropping steeply into the sea, is wild and rugged. There are some red deer and a small herd of Highland cattle. The island is otherwise uninhabited for large parts of the year. There is one, more-or-less permanent resident. He lives on the far eastern corner of the island. He is, in effect, its caretaker for the island belongs to a wealthy Danish businessman. It has at its northern tip a small lighthouse, adjacent to land used by the Ministry of Defence as a gun range. Submarines operate in these waters although no one is quite sure what they are practicing. Gunnery? Either way, South Rona is a beautiful yet desolate spot.

* * *

George McClure and his passenger reached the battered, concrete jetty closest to the lighthouse on South Rona two hours after leaving Portree. It is now about nine o'clock in the morning of Saturday, 21st April.

Although the storm of the previous night had abated, the waves in the Sound of Rassay are still very choppy. There is a brisk breeze. You can taste the salt in the air and the smell of seaweed on the rocks by the jetty.

On the journey across from Portree, George's passenger had been exceedingly seasick and it is, therefore, with considerable relief that he clambers off George's boat and staggers ashore.

'Shall I wait for you?' George asks, shouting into the wind.

'No. This could take most of the morning. I'll call you when I'm nearly done. No need to hang around, George. See you later!'

George eased his boat away from the jetty and watched the man scramble over the rocks leading to the lighthouse.

* * *

Meanwhile, back in Portree, Detective Inspector White rose early, ate a large breakfast in the mahogany-lined dining room of his hotel, glanced at one or two morning papers and sipped his coffee.

He has spent a rough night, what with worries about this case and a storm to end all storms beating at his casement windows.

John White is forty-three. He has been a policeman since he was nineteen. He skipped university - or rather it skipped him - but won a place at Hendon where he shone. Great things were expected of him but he never - or so his contemporaries claim - quite fulfilled the promise of those early years. Today he works out of the Police HQ in Inverness - generally regarded as a highly competent yet relatively run-of- the-mill Detective Inspector. Anyway, that is how certain of his colleagues in Inverness characterise him. John White is aware of these criticisms. He is hurt by them but battles on, supported by a loving wife who knows both his weaknesses and his strengths.

Perhaps this bizarre case could be the making of him? That at least was one of the more positive thoughts that he had had during a largely sleepless night - while the storm raged and battered the Isle of Skye.

The village woke up to news of a bizarre murder on their doorstep and something of a marine catastrophe, what with three fishing boats missing and a great deal of storm damage to the village itself. On his way to the local police station, John White paused at the harbour. Crowds had gathered, staring morosely into the murky waters of the harbour. Of the seven boats that had been moored there on Friday night, only four now remained. Even some of these had sustained damage to their spars and rigging. It would take some time for the fishing community in Portree to recover. Fishing was a tough profession at the best of times and damage on this scale only added to their economic woes.

John entered the police station on Somerled Square. It consisted of two small offices and a cell that doubled as a stationary cupboard.

'Good morning, John. I hope the storm did not trouble you too much last night. Bloody big one, it was. Have you heard about them missing boats?'

'Good morning, Albert. Yes. Terrible.'

Sergeant Albert McGregor and John White had been friends for many years. Albert was the island's long-standing local bobby and a pillar of the Skye establishment. He was six-foot three, fit as a fiddle for someone in his late fifties and a shrewd copper with a vast amount of local knowledge.

John sat down in front of Albert's desk and waved through the open door at WPC Deborah Saunders at her tiny desk in the next office.

'Morning Debbie. Good to see you have settled in.'

'Yes. Thank you, sir. Sergeant McGregor has been very patient!'

'Well, that will be a first, eh, Albert?'

WPC 'Debbie' Saunders was tall and slim, with a shock of curly, red hair. She was born and bred in Portree, very much a local girl. She had only been in the police a matter of months but was proving an excellent support for Sergeant McGregor and the other two officers under his command. PC Ted Rawlings was Albert's driver and PC Alistair McIntyre was in charge of the police launch. It was they who had found Georgina's body on the beach. Between them - plus two special constables based in Broadford and Uig respectively - Albert McGregor, McIntyre and Rawlins - with WPC Deborah Saunders' clerical support - policed the entire island.

John White was pleased to have Albert McGregor as a friend, particularly one who knew Portree and Skye like the back of his big, hairy hands. John, now comfortably ensconced in his chair opposite Albert, took out his pipe.

'Any news from Glasgow yet, Albert?'

'Yes sir. Came through this morning. Debbie pulled you off a copy.'

He handed John a sheet of paper. John read it carefully, sucking thoughtfully on his unlit pipe.

Following his request sent Friday afternoon, the Glasgow police had put out an alert for a certain chef from Portree, known to have been in Glasgow, possibly since Wednesday.

He had not been difficult to find.

It would seem that since he arrived in Glasgow on Wednesday afternoon he had been on what the Glasgow cops had called a 'blinder'. On Thursday night he had been found drunk and disorderly on Bryers Road and arrested - during which he had picked a fight with a particularly large Glaswegian Police Sergeant. The chef spent Thursday night and most of the following morning in a cell nursing a black eye and two broken ribs. The report ended with a crisp: 'Did we really want him back?'

'Not a bad alibi', mused John White out loud. 'Not bad at all! Now, where do we go from here? Albert, I think this calls for a pipe break. Come on, I'm sure Debbie can hold the fort for ten minutes or so.'

They left the police station and strolled down towards the harbour.

'Albert, we need to nail this case pretty quick. The press will be all over us once word gets out, as I am sure it has already. I may need to call for help from Inverness. Are you OK with that?'

'Of course. Meanwhile, we will help you all we can.'

'Thank you Albert. I think we are going to need all the help we can get before this sadistic bastard is caught.'

* * *

At exactly eleven-thirty that Saturday morning the light from the unmanned, automated lighthouse on South Rona unexpectedly stopped.

All Friday night, as the storm raged, its broad beam had swept across the Sound of Rassay, illuminating sea and land. But now nothing. Its steady, revolving beam had lit these dangerous waters for years, without ever stopping - even during the day. In a climate in which sea fog could descend at any time or sudden squalls cut visibility to yards, that light did its work night and day. Now, suddenly, the inhabitants of both Staffin and Gairloch on Wester Ross, saw that it had stopped. People put aside their Saturday-morning newspapers and went outside their cottages to stare at their now defunct lighthouse.

Someone in Staffin phoned Portree. The Portree lifeboat left at once, not least because a lighthouse failure posed a serious threat to local shipping in the treacherous waters of The Minch. They also had a key to the lighthouse and lighting equipment with them to rig a temporary light. No one at this stage knew that George McClure had that very morning taken an electrician from the Northern Lighthouse Company to South Rona.

For reasons known only to himself, George McClure did *not* offer this information, least of all to the Portree police or even to the RNLI crew as their lifeboat left harbour and ploughed its way north, across the choppy Sound of Rassay. That failure might well prove his undoing.

* * *

The first to land on the small concrete jetty on South Rona that Saturday morning was Coastguard Sector Officer Glen McKay.

McKay had been a seafarer since he first sailed with his father as a young teenager. He was now in his early fifties but nothing, not even his considerable experience of many years at sea, including a stint in the Royal Navy, prepared him for what he encountered in that lighthouse.

The iron door leading to the spiral staircase was wide open. This was surprising, not only for security reasons but because waves often struck the door during the storms that frequented these coasts. He pushed it open and entered. Above him the stone stairs curved up into darkness but it was the intense smell that first struck him - thick and claustrophobic. He then looked down, only to discover that he was standing in a deep pool of blood.

* * *

Detective Inspector White was in Georgina Cousins' cottage outside Portree when the call came from those on South Rona.

It was not good news.

It took nearly an hour for DI White to reach the lighthouse. He got there at one-thirty in the afternoon, courtesy of a local fisherman with a small but fast motor boat. It was now cold and blustery, with rain scudding across the rocky landscape of Rassay and

South Rona. Sgùrr Alasdair - the highest point of the Black Couillin mountains to the west, back on the Isle of Skye - was now permanently shrouded in dark, ominous clouds.

White was met at the jetty by Sergeant McGregor. PC McIntyre's police launch was now moored alongside the RNLI lifeboat.

'Not a pretty sight, Inspector.'

'What is it this time, Albert? Please God, not another young woman?'

'I'm afraid so, John. Her name is Alison Rutherford.'

* * *

The lifeboat crew had rigged a powerful light in the stairwell, pointing up at the body of a young woman suspended from the first floor gallery. She was completely naked and was hanging by her feet from a rope attached to lifting gear above the stairwell. One arm stuck out from her side at an alarming angle.

When, after catching his breath and trying hard not to gag, White again looked up at the body suspended in the luridly lit void high above his head, he saw that the young woman's right arm was missing. It had been severed at the shoulder, leaving a terrible wound from which blood still dripped.

4
Who is Charley Gibbons?

After seeing for himself the dreadful scene in the lighthouse on South Rona, DI White returned to Portree in the local fisherman's motorboat to supervise the police response to this new and disturbing development. He left Albert in charge at the lighthouse until Forensic could be summoned. It would take them several hours to travel from Aberdeen and then across to the lighthouse. The police helicopter would have speeded things up but that was not available at such short notice.

Detective Inspector White now had *two* bodies, not one, and both mutilated in horrific ways. The scene at the lighthouse had shocked everyone profoundly. The idea that there was a deranged psychopath loose in the area was disturbing enough but it was the speed with which this murderer had now struck twice within twelve hours that was really worrying.

Skye was an island that knew little crime, let alone murder but the question that now lingered in everyone's mind was: Could he strike again?

When, later that morning, it was discovered that George McClure had probably ferried the murderer to that lighthouse, White hit the roof. McClure was promptly arrested, questioned for an hour and thrown into Sergeant McGregor's only police cell - surrounded by old files, stationary and boxes of photocopy paper. Perverting the cause of justice and aiding-and-abetting a murderer were charges that McClure now faced. Armed now with a name and a description, a quick phone call to the Northern Lighthouse Company soon established that no such person had been assigned to inspect that lighthouse that Friday. Moreover, nobody there had ever heard of an engineer called 'Charley Gibbons'.

Word was immediately sent to the team on South Rona that someone who called himself 'Charley Gibbons' - an electrician claiming to be from the Northern Lighthouse Company - was now missing. It was just possible that he was still on the island, probably hiding. If found, he should be approached with extreme caution. They could begin a thorough search of the island just as soon as White got reinforcements from the mainland. Meanwhile, they should stay alert. Forensic teams, he assured them, were now on their way.

White then called Police HQ in Inverness and asked for immediate additional support, including armed officers.

These were refused, on the grounds that a murderer was not likely to hang around once he had disabled the lighthouse. There was also a matter of costs. With only one police helicopter in the region, to scramble it and find a team of armed officers at such short notice was just not possible.
'Damn you, you mean bastards!', said White to himself as he slammed the phone down. 'Let's hope you never rue the day you denied me that support, you miserable bunch of fucking accountants!'

White then phoned Sergeant McGregor and told him not to expect any additional support. He was told to search the island as best he could but to take care. Besides, HQ was probably right. The murderer would be long gone by now. But where? And how did he get off that island without McClure's help?

White next commandeered the Community Centre in Portree as his operational base and again informed his superiors back in Inverness of what he was doing and what other logistical requirements he might need in due course - not least some additional manpower. The local police were already stretched and with a second murder he would need experienced officers, preferably from Inverness, the nearest mainland Police H.Q.

Since White did not believe for one moment George McClure's story that he was 'merely taking a lighthouse official to the lighthouse for its regular maintenance', he asked WPC Saunders - still holding the fort in Portree - to check the name and address Gibbons had given the receptionist at the Royal Hotel. It was here, according to McClure, that Gibbons had spent Friday night. Later Debbie went round to the hotel herself to check the room where

Gibbon's had stayed and to ensure it was secure, should Forensic wish to examine it at some time. Gibbons had left no luggage, nor the registration number of his car. If he had not already escaped from the island, then a car belonging to him could still be in Portree somewhere. Special Constable McIntosh from Broadford was summoned to Portree and told to check all the village car parks, just in case Gibbon's had used a hired car that could be traced.

If 'Charley Gibbons' was indeed the murderer - as DI White and the Portree police now assumed - then he had covered his tracks very well indeed. Moreover, the realisation that he had spent Friday night in the same hotel as a dangerous psychopath did not make John White's current frame of mind any easier. It also meant that Gibbons was in Portree the afternoon Georgina Cousins was strangled.

* * *

It took a Forensic team of Examiners nearly four hours to get from Aberdeen to Skye and then by police launch to the lighthouse. They arrived at about five-thirty. It was already starting to get dark.

Even they were shocked by what they saw.

The forensic examination of the crime-scene in the lighthouse took four hours. It was completely dark by the time they finished. Alison's body was then carefully taken down and placed in a body bag. She, and the Forensic team, were taken back by PC McIntyre on the police launch to Portree where an ambulance was waiting to take Alison's body on to the SPSA Forensic Laboratory in Aberdeen for more detailed analysis. Forensic then examined the hotel bedroom Gibbons had occupied on Friday night but found nothing - thanks largely to the hotel cleaner who had been particularly thorough that morning.

Sergeant McGregor secured the lighthouse then travelled back with the RNLI lifeboat to Portree and immediately reported to Detective Inspector White. He found White and Debbie still setting up the new Command Post in the Portree Community Centre.

Already telephone lines had been installed and additional staff summoned from outlying police stations in the region. This, said Inverness, was the best they could do for the time being. The five police officers rapidly assigned to the investigation would arrive Sunday morning.

White, who was now really beginning to feel the pressure, needed all the help he could get so he decided not to complain to his superiors in Inverness. He would have to make do with whoever turned up. One thing had not changed though. There was a murderer still out there somewhere.

*　*　*

When Albert joined him at the Community Centre that evening he found John White sat in a chair, sipping a cup of tea and staring morosely at the faded, somewhat patchy linoleum.

'Rum business, Albert. I have never seen the like.'

'Yes, sir. Terrible.'

'I assume you and the lads found nothing on the island?'

'No. He was long gone.'

'I'm not surprised. I think he may have had a boat of his own.'

'What makes you think that, John?'

'Well, McClure may not be as white as the driven snow but from what I saw of him this afternoon he is not stupid enough to get involved in murder.'

'I agree. I've known George for years. He only gets off his arse in the morning if there's money to be made.'

'This whole thing was meticulously planned, I'm sure. Not George's style. I think our George has been duped. He might have taken Gibbons out to the lighthouse early this morning but he certainly did not bring him back.'

'Which means...?'

'Which means, Albert, that Gibbons probably has an accomplice with a boat. I think we are not looking for one murderer but *two*!'

* * *

However, what happened next was a surprise to everyone, not least to Detective Inspector White.

Later that evening, just as John White, Sergeant McGregor and Debbie were about to go for a spot of supper at the nearest pub, a young woman breezed into the Community Centre.

'Good evening. My name is Dr. Sutherland. I'm told', she added brightly, 'that you have found my arm. If that is true, I would like it back please!'

'When you say 'your arm' what exactly do you mean, Dr. Sutherland?'

The young woman smiled sweetly at Detective Inspector White. She was wearing her coat slung casually across her shoulders. When she sat down and placed it on the chair beside her, White was relieved to see that both her arms were present and correct.

'I am a post-graduate research student at the University of Stirling, currently working in association with the A&E Unit at the Aberdeen Royal Infirmary. My subject is trauma. Two weeks ago a young woman was admitted with terrible injuries sustained in a car accident. The upper part of her right arm had been badly crushed. Surgeons had to amputate that arm and her left leg that was also virtually severed. They tried to save her life but sadly she died on the operating table. I got her arm. Once I had examined it in my laboratory back in Stirling, I incinerated the crushed upper arm and placed the lower part in cold storage for further examination later.'

'Then what, Dr. Sutherland?'

'Early this morning I got an email from your Consultant Pathologist in Aberdeen. When he discovered that Georgina Cousin's arm did not belong to her he contacted a number of departments, including mine, asking us to check our records. It was then that I discovered that my arm was missing.'

'Missing?'

'Yes, Inspector. Missing. Assumed stolen! And that's why I am here. To claim it back.'

'How do you know its your arm, Dr. Sutherland?'

'I don't but I can soon tell you if it is.'

'Did it by any chance have a woman's watch on its wrist?'

'Certainly not!'

* * *

The pub that Saturday night in Portree was largely empty. A sombre mood had descended on the village and no one particularly wanted to sit drinking when word spread that the dead girl found hanging in the lighthouse was none other than Portree's Assistant Librarian - Alison Rutherford.

Few in Portree really knew the other victim, Georgina Cousins. Although Miss Cousins was often seen shopping in the village she always kept herself to herself. Alison, however, was a popular young women, especially with the older folk of the village. She was involved in various fund-raising activities in the region and had recently begun a series of informal workshops that taught pensioners how to use the internet. Following this initiative, a surprising number of elderly folk had recently popped up on Facebook or with blogs of their own. Three elderly gentlemen, once interested only in bowls, now appeared regularly on Twitter to express their somewhat outlandish views on everything from the efficacy of Viagra to the length of some women's skirts recently seen in Portree.

Alison Rutherford, whose shocking death had disturbed the entire community, would be sorely missed.

Alison lived in a small cottage a mile or two outside the village, on a quiet country lane - the same lane that led to the pub Georgina Cousins had last been seen at. Alison had an elderly neighbour called Miss Turner. She had got into the habit of visiting Miss Turner most evenings on her way back from the Library, just to see if she was OK or if she needed anything.

Miss Turner had been questioned by the police that afternoon but had collapsed when told of Alison's death. She was now in intensive care at Raigmore Hospital in Inverness. Doctors there - or so WPC Saunders had gathered that afternoon - thought it unlikely that Miss Turner would recover. This was her third stroke in two years.

* * *

Later that evening, Sergeant McGregor accompanied an exhausted Detective Inspector White back towards his hotel.

The troubled weather of the last day or so seemed now to have blown over. It was a calm, Spring evening with only a slight breeze to ripple the murky waters of the bay. Lights along the promenade, with its brightly-coloured row of houses, sparkled and shone, reflected in the water of Loch Portree with the Sound of Raasay beyond. Above their heads countless stars shone dimly through thin, gauze-like cloud.

Both men were in sombre mood. They walked on in silence.

Rather than head directly to the Royal Hotel on the Green, they took a short diversion down Quay Street. On reaching the harbour, White took out his pipe and lit up. Albert did likewise and for a while both men puffed on their pipes in absolute silence whilst leaning on a balustrade, bent somewhat by the storm of the previous night.

It was John White who was the first to break the silence.

'Albert, I believe we have a major killer or two on our hands. I have never seen such savagery as I saw in that lighthouse or on that beach. He not only kills, but tortures and mutilates.'

'I agree, John. You are also going to have to deal with the press. They are everywhere already. There is nothing like a possible serial-killer out there to attract media attention. God help us!'

'Well, thanks Albert. I needed cheering up!'

Albert grinned. He tapped his pipe on the edge of the harbour rail. Sparks flared momentarily before disappearing into the dark.

'Goodnight, sir. I'm sure you will catch this bastard. Its only a matter of time. At least we now know where that arm came from.'

'Yes. This case gets more and more bizarre. Anyway, I hope you are right about catching him. Thanks for all your help today. Goodnight, Albert.'

They shook hands and went their separate ways - DI White towards his hotel on the Green and Sergeant McGregor towards his cottage on Beaumont Crescent, facing the bay.

* * *

Back at his hotel John White rang his wife. She knew at once from his tone of voice that he was distressed and exhausted.
They had been married sixteen years. There were no children. Perhaps that partly explained why they were still so close, so loving.

'Poppy, I'm not sure I can cope with all this. Its turning into a major investigation. I think they may bring in someone else, over my head.'

'Well, that is their choice, my darling. Meanwhile, you are in charge. I know you will do your best. From what you tell me there is not much else you could have done at this stage. Tomorrow is another day, darling 'Inspector Plod'. Now try and get some sleep.'

'You are right, as usual. Tomorrow is indeed another day. By the way, please stop calling me Inspector Plod!'

'OK. How about Robocop?'

* * *

Twenty minutes later Sergeant McGregor was putting the kettle on his gas stove when there was a knock at his cottage door. He opened it to reveal a rather anxious Neil McPherson standing outside.

'Albert, sorry to bother you at this hour. Can you spare a moment?'

'Of course. Come in.'

Neil entered the cottage. Albert closed the door behind him.

'What is it Neil? By the way, I'm sorry to hear about the loss of your boat. I gather you have been looking for wreckage. Any luck?'

'Not exactly. I found bits from two boats but not mine. Mine must have sunk. But what I did find was this.'

Neil handed the Sergeant a length of rope. Albert took it and looked at it quizzically.

'It's a piece of rope, Neil!'

'Yes. Its rope used to moor a boat. But look at the end. It's been cut. This did not snap in a storm. This rope was deliberately cut with a sharp knife.'

5
Sunday, 22nd April

Wing Commander Duncan Finlayson (RAF, retired) had taken up sea-angling some years ago and was now pretty good. Indeed, he had won a few trophies in his time and landed some damn big fish - marlin, sea-trout, tuna, sting-rays and one great sea bass weighing thirty-two pounds. He mostly fished abroad, taking long vacations in Florida where he would rent a boat and fish at sea. This year, however, having lost a few bob on the gee-gees, he was obliged to cut his losses and fish locally, from the shore.

On Skye, to be precise.

He has fished here before, with some success. The catches were not as big as one could expect off the Florida Keys but big enough to get the old adrenalin pumping. Yes, these rocks might be just the ticket.

He has chosen a beautiful spot to the south of the island, not far from the fishing hamlet of Elgol - a small community of scattered cottages. Here high cliffs overlook rocky beaches. From where he now stands he can see several small white cottages with grey slate roofs. A few hundred yards to the north is a spur of rock falling into the sea. That, he thought, will be an ideal spot from which to fish for sea trout.

Something tasty for tea, what?

Finlayson then clambers over the rocks, moving closer to the sea. Great waves crash against the shore, drenching him with spray. He is well dressed for such conditions and besides, he loves the excitement that pounding waves, strong winds and the lure of the sea engender. He can actually taste salt on the sea breeze that blows in his face.

He finally chose a spot on a flat rock, steadied himself and cast - with consummate skill. His line soared out in a great arc, the bait landing forty meters away in the thick of the churning foam.

Wing Commander Finlayson could never be said to lack confidence. He was sure to catch something but what he did *not* expect to land on the end of his Super PE, ultra-thin yet strong modern lure fishing braid - courtesy of the Japanese line company, Sunline - was somebody's arm.

* * *

Detective Inspector White had not been idle that Sunday morning. Additional police staff - drafted in from Wick, Oban, Tobermoray and Mallaig - arrived separately throughout the morning. Scotland is a vast area and outside the main conurbations is not really equipped to deal with multiple murders, especially in remote areas like the Isle of Skye. Until officers from Inverness and Aberdeen (or even Glasgow, if necessary) could be withdrawn from current investigations of their own, White would have to do with whoever could be scraped together from rural outposts. White knew this but was grateful for any help Inverness could push his way.

White met them all as they arrived, assigned each one an immediate task and generally supervised their overall deployment.

There were five officers in all, two women and three men, including one Detective Sergeant - the most experienced of the lot, relatively speaking. They were all young and keen, even if they had never worked on a criminal investigation of this scale before. On arrival, White had handed them each a document giving both a timeline and whatever evidence they had thus far. It was dry and factual, devoid of speculation. He wanted his young team to know only the basic facts and to at least start with an open mind. Debbie had typed it up for him that morning. It did not look much when written down. No much at all.

Later that morning White gathered his little team round the coffee machine and asked them each to introduced themselves.

'I assume that you have more or less met each other but just for clarity's sake, I would like you to say who you are and where you are from. Could we start with you, Detective Sergeant?'

'Yes sir. My name is Tom Watson. I am from Wick but I now work in Fort William. Mostly community work, car thefts, burglaries. I am also part of the local mountain-rescue team.'

'My name is Charlotte Stephens. I work out of Mallaig. I have been a WPC for two years. Again, mostly basic community policing but I have special responsibilities with women's issues, including rape-management and support.'

'Thank you, Charlotte. Yes. Nick?'

'Yes sir. My name is Nick Fellows. I am originally from Aberdeen but I am now stationed in Oban. I work with Detective Constable Paul Miles here.'

'Paul?'

'Thank you sir. As Nick says, I am based in Oban. My duties involve burglaries and assault - quite common amongst the young hill walkers and rock climbers who frequent our pubs. And that's just the women, mind you.'

This produced a round of laughter. At least, thought White, they have a sense of humour. They will probably need it.

'Finally....?'

'Thank you sir. My name is Janice Ward. I am from Edinburgh but for the last three years I have been based in Tobermoray, on Mull. Very quiet, mostly community work or keeping an eye on tourists. Car thefts, petty larceny, drunkenness and the like - and that's only the men.'

More laughter and a polite round of applause.

'OK. Great to have you all on board. Please attend to the tasks I have already assigned you and read my notes thoroughly. I will bring you all up to speed later this afternoon. Meanwhile Debbie here - WPC Deborah Saunders, that is - will help you settle in. Laptops are on their way but I see most of you have brought your own. We have phone lines and a fax machine. Broadband has been installed and there are, if all else fails, fully-trained police carrier-pigeons at the ready. Only joking, of course!'

Even if these young officers lacked operational experience, their presence there that morning had instantly raised John White's spirits.

After a dreadful night at his hotel, he had arrived at the Community Centre early Sunday morning and had already mapped out the day's investigation by the time the first of his new support team arrived. He had also rung Police HQ in Inverness to ask for clerical support and laptops for his team. There had been some talk of HQ appointing a Detective Chief Inspector from Aberdeen to take over the investigation soon but for the moment, at least, such a senior officer had not materialize.

That meant that Detective Inspector John White was still in charge. For the time being, at least.

There were times, however, when he wished that he was not in charge. Word had quickly got back to Edinburgh, Glasgow and beyond and the island was now swarming with journalists. They were everywhere, including John White's own hotel. Mind you, all the hotels in the town and most of the shops - particularly the off-licence and tobacconist's - were now doing a roaring trade. He had issued the barest press statement earlier that morning but the journalists were already demanding more information. They sensed a major story and talk of a serial-killer on the loose was widespread.

It took, therefore, all of John White's experience to conceal from the press news of Wing Commander Finlayson's gruesome catch, details of which had reached him at about ten o'clock that morning.

The arm had been handed in early that morning by a rather

shaken Finlayson, to a retired doctor who just happened to live in Elgol. He then informed the nearest policeman - Special Constable Tammy McIntosh from Broadford. The arm was then bagged and taken directly by motorbike to the SPA Forensic Laboratory in Aberdeen. After that It took a further hour or two before a preliminary report was faxed back to Detective Inspector White in Portree.

The arm that Finlayson had found - when checked against Alison Rutherford's DNA and blood - proved positive. It was her arm, or so the Consultant Pathologist now officially in charge of the case - Dr. James Ledbetter - assured DI White. Although they still had more tests to complete, it would appear that the arm the local police had erroneously assumed was Georgina's could well be the right arm stolen from Dr. Sutherland's laboratory in Stirling. That meant that Georgina's left arm was still missing.

* * *

It was over a hastily convened lunch that Sunday at the Royal Hotel in Portree that Detective Inspector White got to meet the Psychological Profiler he had been sent from Edinburgh. She had been assigned to this case by someone high up in Inverness and at very short notice - or at least once the second murder had emerged and the police realised they had a major case on their hands. Finally, thought White, Police HQ in Inverness are acting decisively. About bloody time, he added mentally. Perhaps this too meant that they had also assigned a senior officer above him?

No concrete news yet but rumours were already rife back at Police HQ - or so his chums there had been quick to tell him.

Anyway, the Profiler - now sitting in front of him sipping a glass of wine - was a mild-mannered, middle-aged lady called Elspeth Grant who looked more like a librarian or retired school-teacher than a highly qualified, forensic psychologist. This was somewhat deceptive, as White soon realised, because Dr. Grant could be both direct and incisive - not to say abrasive.

'The reason you first suspected the butcher and the chef from that pub was that both used knives. Correct?'

'Yes, but...'

'Both however have excellent alibis, which only goes to prove my point. We all need to think outside the box, Detective Inspector. Stats show that very few convicted murders are either butchers or chefs. Chefs might occasionally go mad and kill their Sous-chef or their wives but it is seldom in cold-blood. Butchers? Never. They mostly lack the imagination. No, you started looking in the wrong place. You should have started with my profession. Medicine!'

'Maybe. But I had to start somewhere.'

White was beginning to feel more and more defensive. Did he really want a Profiler this critical? She was there to help him, surely, not question every aspect of what was already proving a very difficult investigation?

'Sure. But let's take the mysterious 'Mr Gibbons'. He has certainly disappeared and it is not unnatural to assume that he could be the killer but I doubt it. I would say that at best he was a petty criminal.'

'What on earth makes you say that?'

'Instinct, Detective Inspector. Instinct. Gibbons does not feel right. He is clearly up to something but it is not murder. He *feels* like a petty criminal.'

'Funny you should say that. One of my officers has been looking into Alison Rutherford's hard-drive at the library here in Portree. Rutherford's elderly clients includes George McClure. Guess what he has been looking at on the web with his new-found computing skills? Lighthouses! When I told Sergeant McGregor he was not at all surprised. It would seem that our George has been involved in a number of 'scams' in recent years. Maybe he and this Gibbons fellow were hand-in-glove, out to steal something from the lighthouse. Maybe....'

'Copper', interrupted Elspeth. 'They were after copper wire, sure as eggs-is-eggs. I know about lighthouses. Before modernisation and fibre optics and all the rest, old lighthouses were riddled with copper wire. There must be a few thousand quids worth still in your lighthouse. That's what Gibbons was probably after. However, when he entered that lighthouse he walked in, unexpectedly, on something very nasty taking place. That may have cost him his life. In short, I think our Mr. McClure was involved - not in serial murder but common-and-garden theft. Let's hope, for Charley Gibbon's sake, that I am wrong!'

'So where does that leave us? And what about these severed arms? That's all a bit over-the-top, is it not? Even for a deranged serial killer.'

'That, my dear Detective Inspector, is the sixty-four-thousand-dollar question! The best I can say at this stage is that our killer needs to *signpost* his crimes. That phone-call from the beach was merely to start the ball rolling. The murder at the lighthouse? Well, what bigger signal can you give than switching off a lighthouse? This man thinks big. Very big and I'm afraid it's not over yet.'

6
All at Sea

It was at about two o'clock that Sunday afternoon, on his way back from his first meeting with Elspeth at the Royal Hotel, that Detective Inspector John White got an urgent call on his mobile. It was Sergeant McGregor.

'John, I have just had a call from RAF Lossiemouth. One of their jets has just spotted a boat off the island of Soay, moving south-east towards the Strathaird peninsula. They gave it a radio call but got no reply. They were unable to identify it definitively but it certainly fits the description of Neil's boat we gave them this morning'.

'Where are you now?'

'I have just asked PC Rawlings to bring the Land Rover round. We can pick you up in five minutes.'

'OK. But make it snappy. Where do you reckon he could be heading?'

'Probably Loch Eishort. If he spotted that jet he might assume that we are on to him. If he wanted to hide that boat or land then Loch Eishort is ideal. It will take us about ninety-minutes to get there. I have asked the local bobby in Broadford to assist. He's called Tammy McIntosh. I told him to get on his motor bike and head for the top end of the Strathaird peninsular. Find the highest point on the cliffs there and see if he can spot Neil's boat. I told him to stay hidden at all times. If he saw anything, he was to call me immediately.'

'Good. I'll bring Tom Watson with me. He's a climber. So is DC Miles, I think. See you outside in five minute - or less if you can manage it. This might be our only chance to grab the bastard if he's on that boat!'

Minutes later the Land Rover stopped outside the Community

Centre and White and his two officers squeezed in. With Ted Rawlings at the wheel they sped off out of Portree, heading south for Broadford. On the far side of Broadford they turned south, along the A851. The countryside here was wild and desolate, with stretches of bare rock exposed by the weather and coarse grass and heather. There were mountains to their right, partly covered with low cloud. There were many small tarns on either side of the road, the water black with peat.

It was a spectacular route but for the five policemen huddled together in an old Land Rover there was little time to admire the scenery.

'Is there a coastguard station or lifeboat anywhere near where we are heading, Sergeant?' asked DI White.
'Yes, sir. There is an RNLI lifeboat station at Elgol and another at Minginish, further north. I suggest we call Elgol. The wind and tide will suit them better. Its not much more than an oversized rubber dingy but its bloody fast. I'll call them on the radio. Could one of you give Tammy a call?'

Sergeant McGregor then reached into his breast pocket and handed his mobile phone to Tom Watson in the back of the land Rover.

'Sergeant, use my mobile. The number's already selected. Find out where he is and if he has spotted anything.'

While Sergeant McGregor explained the situation to the RNLI officer in Elgol, Tom Watson rang Tammy McIntosh. It took a while to get through but in the end Watson was able to speak to him.

'Tammy, this is Detective Sergeant Watson. I'm with Sergeant McGregor in the Land Rover. We are somewhere on the A851, well south of Broadford. Where are you and have you spotted anything?'

'Aye. The boat's about five mile away, heading towards me. I spotted it twenty minutes ago, heading south-east. I think he's aiming for somewhere on the east coast of the Strathaird peninsular, just north of where I am. Tell Ted Rawlings to leave the A851 just south of Loch nam Dubhrachan. There' a rough road that heads west, following the edge of the forest. Keep going until you come to loch Medodal on your left. When you get there give me another call. I will try and guide you from there. OK?'

'OK Tammy. We also have the RNLI lifeboat from Elgol heading your way. Let us know if you spot them.'

'Oh my God! Bring on the cavalry! There'll be nay stopping them boys. Bunch of cowboys, if you ask me.'

They eventually reached the track and headed due west, with the dense, dark shapes of Braighan uird Forest towering above them to the right. The track here was very rough and those in the back of the Land Rover had a bad time of it. Old police Land Rovers are not celebrated for their suspension - certainly not the way PC Ted Rawlings drove. It had also begun to drizzle.

They were about seven miles down the track when they got a call from Tammy on McGregor's mobile.

'I can see you through my binoculars. In about a mile from where you are now you will find the track divides. One way leads south to Tokavaig. Ignore that. Instead, turn north, heading for Ord. About a mile or two up that road you will pass a wee croft in ruins. Turn sharp left and follow the track as far as it goes. Leave the car there and walk the next five hundred yards, heading due west. You should be able to see me by then. Bring ropes and any climbing gear you have. The cliff below me is a sheer drop of about sixty feet. Very steep, with something of an overhang. I've been looking for a way down but I canna see one yet.'

'OK. Can you still see Neil's boat from where you are?'

'Aye. He's starting to hug the coast so I think he's looking to land soon. He's still heading towards me so I think I will stay where I am. Mind you, the sooner those cowboys on that rubber duck of theirs spot him the better. I am likely to lose him from sight if he gets any closer to these sea cliffs. I'm perched on the very edge as it is.'

'OK. We will be with you soon. Meanwhile, I will check with the 'Cowboys'. Thanks.'

It was Sergeant McGregor who eventually managed to contact the RNLI dingy on his police radio.

'Donald, my man. Its Albert. Where the hell are you when we need you? Not still in that pub of yours in Elgol, surely?'

'Albert? I thought you were dead. Good to talk to you, though. Always pleased to help an old-stager. Especially as I recall it was your round last time you had to rush off - as usual.'

'Sure. Where the hell are you?'

'We are about two miles off-shore heading north up the west coast of the Strathaird peninsula. Where do you want us to be?'

'Keep heading north. We will call you again when we have a precise location. You are looking for a large fishing boat, registration number P54. Its painted grey and white. If you spot it do *not*, repeat, do *not* approach it. The man, or men, on board, could be dangerous. Roger and out.'

Fifteen minutes later they spotted Tammy. They parked the Land Rover and set off on foot, bringing with them ropes and other climbing tackle - fairly standard equipment for police units in these remote, mountainous parts of Scotland. The weather was deteriorating rapidly. A fine drizzle soaked them very quickly while sea fog began to roll in towards the cliffs ahead of them. Visibility was getting worse by the minute. That would make life for the RNLI boys out as sea increasingly difficult.

Tammy was crouching a few yards away from the cliff edge. His motorbike was lying in the heather close by. White and his team were surprised to see that it was not police issue but a motor-cross bike. Tammy was splattered with mud from head to foot. Where his goggles had been his face was a lurid white. Sergeant

McGregor introduced the team. They shook hands. Tammy was a tall, laconic individual - thin as a rake but clearly tough as nails. He had eyes that were as black as a gypsy's - or those of a poacher.

He led them to the cliff edge, where they all crouched.

'He's over there, about three hundred yards to the north. See that spur of rock, well he's moored just to the right of that. When the waves rise you can just see his stern. He's been there about twenty minutes.'

All five men peered over the edge of the cliff in the direction Tammy was pointing, along a spectacular line of rugged sea-cliffs stretching north into the fog and then disappearing. Some sixty feet immediately below them they could see sharp rocks, partially covered with water. Waves continuously crashed against the base of these sea-cliffs, causing a thin veil of air-born spray to slowly rise towards them, carried on the wind.

Occasionally, they caught sight of the boat as it rose and fell on the swell. They could only see the tip of the stern so it was impossible to say if there was anyone on board.

'Look!', said DC Paul Miles suddenly, 'The cavalry have arrived!'

There below them, and about five-hundred yards off-shore, was the distinct shape of a large rubber dingy. It was bright orange. The four men crouched in it were dressed in survival suits of a bright, florescent red. They wore white helmets. The dinghy's powerful engine could be heard, carried towards them on the wind. Behind them, far out to sea, a thin, ominous sea-fog was slowly moving towards them.

It was Sergeant McGregor who called them on his mobile.

'Well. That's a turn up for the books! You actually made it, Alan. About bloody time, I might add. Its cold and wet up here!'

'Not as much as it is down here, I can tell you! Anyway, you know me, Albert. Not one to miss a party! We can just about see the boat from where we are. It looks like he's tucked into a sea cave. What do you want us to do, Sergeant?'

At this point McGregor handed the phone to DI White.

'This is Detective Inspector White. Thank you for your support. We have reason to believe that there is a dangerous man, or perhaps men, on that boat. Our plan is to abseil down the cliffs above them and try and get on board.'

'We could certainly board that boat for you, sir. Shall we give it a try?'

'No. This is a police matter. I want you to stay off-shore, out of gun range and observe our descent. You may be able to guide my men down the cliff face or let us know if there is any activity on board. Stay in radio contact with Sergeant McGregor on the normal police frequency. We have a portable radio with us. That means my men will have radio contact with both you and Sergeant McGregor up here with me. They may not be able to answer but you can let them know immediately if anyone takes counter action. If that boat and whoever is on it tries to make a dash for open sea then we made need to change our plan. Your job, in that eventuality, is to try and keep him penned in. Can you see any signs of movement on board?'

'No sir, none at all. Mind you, they could be down below. I can just about see the wheel-house but its too dark in that cave to see if there is anyone watching us. Let's us know when you are ready to descend.'

The team moved cautiously along the cliff top towards the boat. The plan was to descend about thirty yards to the south of the boat, then move along the rocks at the base of the cliff. That way they would be less of a target if the men on board were armed and spotted them.

Detective Sergeant Tom Watson and DC Miles had volunteered to make the descent by rope. Both were experienced climbers.

It took about ten minutes for the climbers to secure their lines and start their descent. They reached the foot of the cliff in less than two minutes. The radio operator in the RNLI lifeboat kept those on the cliff top informed of their progress down the cliff face and onto the narrow, rocky beach at its foot.

'Right, Paul', said Tom. Follow me but keep your eyes skinned. If you see any movement, hit the ground. OK?'

'Ye, Sergeant. I'm right behind you!'

Slowly, cautiously, the two men edged their way along the narrow rocky 'beach' towards the partially hidden boat.

They were now within yards of the boat, separated from it by a spur of rock sticking out, round which they would have to climb.

'Paul', whispered Tom, crouching low. 'I'll go first. As soon as I'm out of sight, you follow. OK?'

'Yes, but Tom....'

'Just follow me, as soon as I'm off that ledge. OK Paul?'

'Yes, Sergeant.'

Tom stood up and edged his way towards the slippery spur, partly covered in seaweed. Just above water level there was a narrow ledge, sufficient for him to secure a foothold. He eased himself up onto this ledge, clasping dry rock above his head with both hands. He was, he suddenly realised, a sitting duck for anyone on the other side with a gun. Pushing that thought swiftly to the back of his mind, he slowly edged his way round until he had disappeared from Paul's sight.

On the far side of the spur Tom found himself in a vast sea-cave, the domed roof of which towered high above his head.

There was something of a natural jetty, made up of slabs of rock worn smooth by the action of the waves that had formed this cave over thousands of years. There, in the middle of this almost entirely enclosed area, bobbed Neil McPherson's fishing boat. It seemed huge even in this vast cave.

Tom crouched low and waited. It was eerily quiet in the cave, apart from the slap of water against the sides of the boat. There was a slight swell, causing water to regularly cover the slab of rock on which Tom crouched. It was not deep, but sufficient to cover his boots every thirty seconds or so. He could hear Paul behind him, working his way slowly round the spur of slippery rock. After three or four agonising minutes, Paul was at his side, grinning broadly and looking around him in wonder.

'Wow!', he whispered.

'I cant see anyone on board,' said Tom. 'Let's get a closer look but keep your eyes open, Paul. We have no idea who's on that bloody boat.'

Tom led the way, moving cautiously towards the boat's prow. It had been moored to a rock, so close to the back of the cave that the wheel-house was almost touching the sloping roof. There was a rope ladder at the prow, dangling over the side and trailing in the dark, green water within the cave.

'OK. Watch my back. I'm going on board.'

'Aye, aye, skipper!'

Tom climbed the rope ladder, at first peering over the boat's rail before stepping onto the deck. He then leant down over the rail and silently signalled Paul with one hand to join him on deck. Once Paul was at his side, they moved cautiously towards the wheel-house, now only a few yards away. Their only weapons were a pair of police-issue extendable batons which they now grasped in their sweaty hands.

The door of the wheel house was open. There, seated in the skipper's swivel chair, was a figure. Tom saw at once that his hands were secured behind his back with silver gaffer tape and that a rope held him upright in the chair. Tom moved slowly forward and with the point of his baton pushed one side of the chair. It at once spun round to reveal a young man, his legs splayed and with his head thrown back. There was blood all over his chest, staining his sweater a dark brown. His throat had been cut from ear to ear.

7

Detective Inspector White and Sergeant McGregor reached Neil's boat - with the help of the RNLI lifeboat - some fifteen minutes after Watson had called them on the radio and told them what he and Paul had discovered.

The crew in the rubber dingy had spotted a steep path from the cliff top down to the narrow beach - some three hundred yards north of where the two young policemen had made their original descent. Parts of it had fallen into the sea but it was manageable, and better than abseiling down. That was the way White and McGregor scrambled down to the narrow 'beach' and then edged their way back along a narrow, rocky ledge towards the cave and Neil's boat.

Since it had soon become apparent to Sergeant Watson that there was no one else on board, White had despatched Ted Rawlings in the Land Rover and Tammy McIntyre on his motorbike to make an immediate search in the area north and south of where the boat was moored. If the murderer and his accomplice had already made their escape in the mist, then they could not be that far away. Without any additional support near at hand it was the best White could do in the circumstances. Without any kind of description, there seemed little point at this stage in issuing a more general alert.

Once on board, White and McGregor at once examined the wheelhouse. They were shocked at what they saw.

The body was that of a young man of about twenty. He was dressed in jeans and sweater. It was Tom Watson who suggested that he was probably a climber, for his boots were thin and made of rubber, flexible but with ribbed soles. Five Ten 'Hornet' shoe, to be precise - according to Watson. There was no trace of a knife and White and his team were reluctant to explore too much of the boat until Forensic had examined it thoroughly. White had radioed Aberdeen and had been promised a helicopter. This would bring two men from the Forensic laboratory in Aberdeen to the boat and then, on its way back, make a cursory search of the area - just in case they spotted anyone on the run, heading inland.

Two hours later two men from Forensic arrived by helicopter. It took a while to land on the cliff top as light was fading fast and the sea fog seemed to be getting worse. Once the two Forensic examiners were safe on the ground, the helicopter took off and headed back to Aberdeen.

Any chance of spotting fugitives on the ground was looking virtually impossible, such was the visibility now.

The two men from Forensic staggered down the cliff path with their equipment slung over their shoulders and joined Detective Inspector White on board Neil McPherson's abandoned boat.

The police launch from Portree had already set off on the long trip round the island, bringing Neil McPherson. This launch was PC Alistair McIntyre's pride and joy. The Portree police had only had it two years. It was fast and sleek and with its powerful engines could generate four-hundred horsepower. It should make good time, even if visibility was deteriorating rapidly.

The Forensic examiners took photographs and DNA samples from various parts of the wheelhouse and elsewhere on the boat and then cut the body free and put it in a plastic body bag. It was then lifted out of the boat and gently placed on the floor of the rubber dingy. The RNLI crew then took it north to Minginish where an ambulance was waiting to take it on to Aberdeen.

Both DI White, Sergeant McGregor and White's two young officers were glad that the body had finally been removed. DC Miles threw a bucket of water over the wheel-house floor to remove the blood stains - well before Neil McPherson, expected within the hour, arrived in the police launch to reclaim his missing boat and take it back to Portree.

'Albert, if you were the murderer, where would you head for?'

'That's easy, Inspector. Look over there.'

White looked in the direction Sergeant McGregor was pointing. There, far across the dark waters of Loch Slapin and north of the entrance to Loch Eishort, rose the dark outline of a mountain range, now partly shrouded in thick mist.

'He, or they, would need to travel northeast from here. They could then either take the road we came down or head west-north-west, around the entrance to Loch Eishort, and then make for the safety of the Cuillins. Those mountains could hide a regiment, let alone one or two men on foot. 'Even the devil', said Bonnie Prince Charlie, 'shall not follow me here'. Our murderer can not only handle a boat this size but clearly knows this island like the back of his hand. If I were he - God forbid - that's where I would head for.'

'But then, Albert, he must have killed that young man and made good his, or their, escape - probably up that path we came down - within the short time between when Tammy first saw him reach this cave and our arrival on the cliff top? That's incredibly quick. Let's say, at the most, forty minutes. And what was that young man doing there in the first place? It does not make any sense. Do you think he had been abducted earlier?'

'No idea, John. As your DS Watson says, he may be a rock climber who just stumbled across this boat - and died as a consequence. Even if our murderer did cut that lad's throat almost the moment he reached this cave, that still gives him about an hour's start on us. If he wants to avoid the more populated areas near the A851 he has no choice but to head for the mountains further west. That means, if my theory is correct, that he is probably into the Cuillins by now, or at least the lower slopes. We have no chance of finding him there without air support and its both too late and too dark for that. Mind you, the murderer could be in Sligachan within three or four hours and heading for the bridge to the mainland. We may have lost him, I'm afraid Inspector.'

'Look, sir', said Tom Watson, pointing at the boat's radio. 'This radio is tuned into our frequency - the same frequency the police and emergency services share. The bastard has been listening in to us all the time.'

'Then he knows what we are doing even now', added White. 'Albert, call Ted on your mobile and tell him to switch radio frequency in the Land Rover and tell Portree why. Debbie can inform Inverness. This murderer is a clever bastard, that's for sure!'

Thirty minutes later the police launch arrived. Neil McPherson could tell that something terrible had taken place on his boat but, devout Presbyterian that he was, he kept his peace.

He fired the engine up and backed out of the sea-cave, then turned towards Portree. Meanwhile, detective Inspector White and his team boarded the police launch and started out on the long trip back to Portree in the wake of Neil's boat.

It was now getting really dark.

On the journey back they had plenty of time, all four of them, to reflect on the day's events.

* * *

Much later that evening DI White phoned Elspeth, now back at her apartment in Edinburgh. She had returned that same day to Edinburgh rather unexpectedly - to attend to her ailing mother. Anyway, that was her explanation for jumping ship so soon after her preliminary meeting in Portree. For his part, John White felt tired and mentally exhausted by the day's events. The image of that young man with his throat cut had haunted him all afternoon.

'So, you lost him John. That was rather clumsy of you!'

'Not funny, Dr. Gant. What do you make of the lad's murder? Different pattern but same tragic end.'

'It's a statement. Our man knew he was in danger of being trapped and yet he still had time to overpower that young man, tie him up and cut his throat. That takes dedication!'

'But what was the lad doing there in the first place?'

'Going by the your description I would say that DS Watson is right - that poor young lad was a rock climber. He was looking for sea-cliffs to scale. He must have stumbled on that cave and Neil's boat by chance. Perhaps he was welcomed on board then overpowered.'

'Simple as that?'

'Yep. Accidental encounter, I would say. But poor timing. *Very* poor timing, on the part of that unfortunate young man! By the way, John, what do you know about Georgina Cousins?'

'Quite a lot. Thirty-two. Unmarried. Very well off. Lived alone. No known boyfriends or close associates. No brothers or sisters. Both parents dead. Moved up here in 2010....'

'But do you know her real name, John?'

'Real name? What do you mean? Her real name is Georgina Cousins. We checked with Social Security. What are you saying, Elspeth?'

'Her real name is Sara Daniels. It's the name she writes under. Cousins is a pseudonym, to hide from the village who she really is. Its usually the other way round, I know but that's how she kept her anonymity.'

'Don't tell me she's a writer of detective fiction, Elspeth. Spare me the cliché, please!'

'Well, not exactly. She writes psychological thrillers. There's one in particular you should read. I've already emailed it to you.'

'Read? What must I read, Elspeth?'

'A novel by Sara Daniels. Its called *The Lighthouse*.'

8
Monday, 23rd April

Detective Inspector White rose early, grabbed a quick cup of coffee and then left the hotel. He had been summoned to Inverness, with the rest of his team, to meet their new boss.

He got into his car and left Portree, heading south for the Skye Bridge via Broadford. It was now seven-thirty. He wanted to be in Inverness early. The others, in cars belonging to Watson and Fellows, would make their own way to Police HQ. Elspeth had agreed to drive up from Edinburgh and meet up with the team in Inverness.

It was a fine day. The water in the Inner Sound sparkled in the early morning sunshine. There was a light breeze and high clouds, suggesting a break in the weather after what had been, in every sense, a dramatic weekend. White sped across the Skye Bridge then on, via Kyle of Lochalsh. He then took the A87 west, towards Inverness.

He had slept very badly last night. He was still buzzing with the excitement - and disappointment - of the discovery of Neil McPherson's boat and the murdered lad found on board. They had come so close to capturing the murderer and perhaps his accomplice and yet they had escaped. Most of the night White had wracked his brains thinking what else he could have done. With limited resources and such short notice there was, he eventually persuaded himself, not much else he could have done.

Let's hope, he thought, that his new boss shares that view.

He was, though, proud of what DS Watson and DC Miles had achieved. They had been exceptionally brave to abseil down that cliff and approach Neil's boat, armed only with extendable, steel batons. He was proud too of the dedication and hard work shown by the local constabulary in Portree - under Albert McGregor - and what they had done yesterday to assist him in the pursuit of such a determined, ruthless and utterly callous killer. And yet, when

Tammy McIntyre and Ted Rawlings had searched the area and questioned a few farmers living in that remote part of the Strathaird peninsula, they had found nothing. No lonely figures running across the skyline. No fugitives hiding in a barn. Nothing. Even the police helicopter on its way back to Aberdeen that evening had spotted nothing suspicious.

The murderer and his accomplice had completely vanished into thin air - like the three witches in *Macbeth*.

Which meant that they were no nearer capturing them than they had been from the start. Perhaps, if Neil's boat visited Soay, there might have been a sighting. Sergeant McGregor had already been asked to investigate. If that boat had stopped off on the island - for fuel, perhaps - they might at last acquire an actual description of their quarry.

In short, they badly needed a lucky break.

* * *

The entire team, including John White's young officers, convened in the main briefing room at Police HQ in Inverness at ten o'clock that morning. It was now less than three days since the mutilated body of Georgina Cousins had been found on the beach on the outskirts of Portree. For all those involved in that, and the subsequent discoveries, it seemed a lot longer.

Detective Chief Inspector Elliott turned out to be a quiet, efficient and thoroughly likeable man. On entering the room he dispensed with preliminaries and cut immediately to the chase.

'Gentlemen and ladies, I would like to share with you - especially our colleagues working on Skye - some recent information from our Forensic laboratory in Aberdeen and a number of new lines of enquiry that have emerged. The first is that the arm that Wing Commander Finlayson caught on the end of his fishing line definitely belongs to Alison Rutherford, the young woman found in the lighthouse. The one 'missing' arm is that which was taken from Georgina Cousins. I dread to think where that might turn up.

I would now like to hand you over to Dr. Grant. Elspeth, would you begin, please.'

Elspeth stood up and faced the sea of faces - some nine police officers with a smattering of clerical staff and technicians. She spoke, quietly but with authority and without notes, for nearly fifteen minutes. It was very impressive.

'In conclusion', she added, 'while this murderer may well have an accomplice, we are primarily looking for a mature male, mid-forties. He could be Scottish. He can handle boats and appears to be fearless. He is also very bright, can act decisively when required and has a very cold streak. He also appears to be a dab hand with a scalpel. Perhaps, after all, we are looking for a crazed medical man. There are plenty of those about - I deal with them every working day of my life.'

A ripple of laughter ran round the room.

'So far, so obvious. In fact, you are probably thinking why do we need someone with a PhD in Criminal Psychology to tell us any of this? Perhaps you don't but what I will tell you is that this man is desperately trying to tell us something. It is his *message* that we should be concentrating on, and not simply his identity. If we cannot fathom that out and respond then he will surely strike again, and again until we do. That is what really worries me and why we need to be alert to what actors call the 'subtext'. The key to these bizarre murders lies in that subtext and it is up to us to find it.'

She sat down. Silence filled the room. It was a moment or two before Detective Chief Inspector Elliott stood up and spoke.

'Thank you, Dr. Grant. I should add that we have made some progress regarding the stolen arm - the one found on the beach near Portree. It is indeed the one that Dr. Sutherland had in her keeping, taken from a patient called Jenny Chancellor, aged 38 now deceased. She died in the operating theatre in Aberdeen. We know approximately when the arm was stolen from Dr. Sutherland's lab at Stirling University - two days before it turned up on the beach on Skye. What we do not know as yet is who took it.'

A murmur of interest went round the room.

'Exhaustive enquiries have, however, eliminated most of the University staff who had direct access to Dr. Sutherland's laboratory and cold store in Stirling so we are currently working on the theory that it was someone from outside but with inside information. That may mean there is an informant involved. I will let you know how we get on with that part of our investigation. DS Phillips and WPC Nelson here in Inverness are looking into that and saw Dr. Sutherland as recently as this morning. They will liaise directly with Detective Inspector White throughout. John, is there anything you would you like to add?'

John White stood up and cleared his throat. He looked tired and nervous. You could feel the tension in the room.

'Thank you, sir. I would like to endorse what Dr. Grant has said. It was she who also pointed me towards a work of fiction that it seems Georgina Cousins wrote under her real, and much better known name - Sara Daniels.'

This created a buzz of interest in the assembled officers. White waited until it had subsided before he continued.

'This work of fiction by Miss Daniels, published three years ago, involves the discovery of the body of a young woman in a remote lighthouse off the Devon coast. In the story the young woman is abducted, imprisoned in the lighthouse, then mutilated. Her dismembered body is later washed up on the shore where it is spotted by a local farmer.'

An audible murmur of astonishment spread round the room at this startling and unexpected information.

'Before you get too excited, that is as far as the resemblance goes. There are many other details in the story that are unlike anything we have experienced so far. The point, though, is that it is simply too much of a coincidence for one of our victims to have, as it were, predicted the fate of the other.'

'Clearly the murderer knew of Miss Daniel's story and, indeed, knew Georgina's real identity - something which she had successfully kept an entire community ignorant of for two years. We have as yet no idea why Alison in particular was also murdered but there is surely a 'subtext' here. It is part of our job, with Dr. Grant's professional help, to decipher it. Thank you.'

* * *

After the meeting Detective Chief Inspector Elliot took John White aside, away from the rest of the team still talking amongst themselves.

'John, I want you to take a day or two off. Go home, get some rest.'

'But sir....'

'No buts, John. That's an order. You have had a tough few days. We think you have handled a very difficult situation exceptionally well but you badly need to recharge your batteries. My job, over the next couple of days, is to properly resource your investigation. You are still in charge on the island but in my view your investigation is seriously under-resourced. You have not had the support you should have had from the beginning.'

'Well, I would not go so far as....'

'I would, John but that's between you and I. But I will try and change that. Report back on Wednesday in Portree. As you saw a moment ago, I have been assigned two experienced officers here in Inverness to help you and your young team - DS Phillips and WPC Nelson. I will use your absence to get them up to speed. Besides, there's plenty for your lot in Portree to be getting on with for a day or so. Bright bunch, John. I am impressed, and not just with the bravery of Watson and Miles but with the enthusiasm and intelligence of all five of them.'

'Thank you. Sir.'

* * *

It was as Detective Inspector White was getting into his car following the meeting with DCI Elliott that a young woman ran up to him in the car park. It was Dr. Eleanor Sutherland.

'Inspector. Can you spare a moment?'
'Of course. Get in.'

He opened the car door. She slid into the seat beside him, closing the car door behind her.

'Something curious happened a week or so after Jenny Chancellor died. I got a phone call asking where the body was. It was a man. He would not give me his name but he was quite angry, demanding to know where Jenny's remains were. I told him that she had been cremated on her mother's instructions. Because of the very poor state of the body following both the accident and surgery, it was decided that cremation should not be delayed. It was at that point that he rang off.'

'Have you told Detective Chief Inspector Elliott all this?'

'Yes, of course. That's why I am here in Inverness this morning. I spoke to him a few minutes ago. But thinking about it since I keep asking myself why should that man have called *me*? I had nothing to do with the operation, nor indeed with arrangements for the cremation. There was nothing, absolutely nothing, any outsider could know that would connect me to that operation and what happened afterwards. Why then did he call *me*?'

'Could anyone have told him that you had Jenny Chancellor's arm? After all, that was, as it turned out, all that was left of her.'

'No. No one knew, other than Jenny's mother who gave us permission to use the arm for further research. These things are, for obvious reasons, always handled very discretely.'

'Eleanor, why are you telling me all this?'

'Because last night I remembered something else that I had forgotten until now. Something important.'

'And what is that?'

'After the operation a theatre nurse told me that she had had a phone call, only an hour or so after Jenny had been taken to the mortuary. It was a woman and she asked her where Jenny's personal belongings - clothes, jewellery and the like - could be picked up. The nurse naturally assumed that it was a relative. Could they, she asked, be posted on rather than Jenny's mother having to collect them herself? Yes, of course was the answer. The woman then gave the nurse an address, which she wrote down. The parcel was posted off the next day.'

'Is that normal practice?'

'Not always but if the experience has been traumatic, as death of a loved one in surgery surely is, then the nursing staff will lean over backwards to help grieving or traumatised relatives.'

'But I am still not clear why you are telling me this.'

'Because, Inspector, the woman asked if there was a watch amongst Jenny's effects. 'Yes,' she was told 'but it is broken'. 'Never mind', she said, 'post in on anyway.'

'She then asked - and this is what stuck in that nurse's memory - that 'if it was broken, what time was it when it stopped?' 'I'm not sure', replied the nurse. 'Three, four - I can't remember. Why do you need to know?' It was then that the woman rang off.'

9
Home, Sweet Home

John White spent the next two days back with his wife at their home in Dunkeld, in Perthshire where they had lived for most of their marriage.

It was not until he got home that Monday afternoon that he realised just how exhausted and emotionally drained he had become. He therefore slept for a large part of the time during the next day or so - either in bed or slumped in a deckchair in their garden.

Arabella White, ever alert to her husband's emotional state, largely left him alone to rest and recuperate.

Conventional wisdom has it that busy policemen and marriage seldom go hand-in- hand. This was not the case with John White and his hugely intelligent, effervescent wife, 'Poppy'. They had been happily married for many years. Although there were no children in the marriage, they fervently loved each other and always enjoyed each other's company.

On Tuesday evening they went together into Dunkeld for a meal at their favourite Italian restaurant. They were regular customers and were met at the door by the restaurant owner, Mario.

Over a fish supper John told Poppy in outline the startling events of the last few days - of the murder and mutilation of both Georgina Cousins and Alison Rutherford and the latest discovery of the murdered lad on the stolen fishing boat. Poppy had gathered quite a bit from their brief telephone conversations each evening but now she got a clearer, overall picture. She now understood better why, from the moment he unexpectedly arrived home Monday afternoon, he was in such an emotional state and why he had slept most of the time since then. It was as if his body was not only trying to recoup physically but for his mind to come to terms with the horrors he and his team had experienced over that dreadful weekend in Portree.

Poppy was glad John had told her everything about a case that was clearly troubling him. She had always encouraged him to share his deepest concerns with her - even if the subject matter was sometimes of a gruesome nature. She hated it when policemen - colleagues they knew, for example - bottled everything up. The wives in such cases invariably suffered.

They retired to the coffee lounge and ordered a large brandy each. Their taxi was due to take them home in half-an-hour's time.

'Tell me, Poppy. Have you ever heard of a very successful writer called Sarah Daniels? That, it would seem, is the name under which the late Georgina Cousins used to write. Anyway, that's what Elspeth Grant says?'

'Yes, I have. Fairly raunchy, I recall. Often violent but, unlike a lot of chick-lit, rather well written.'

'Tell me, who reads her stuff?'

'Men mostly, I think.'

'Really? But I thought her books were written for women.'

'Maybe that was her intention at first but men get off on this kind of stuff. The men in her books are often victimised or abused. Some men find that exciting. Women, on the other hand, identify with dominant women - or at least those dishing out the punishment. That may explain her broad appeal.'

'But its fiction. Surely readers do not take this rubbish seriously?'

'Some do. Anyway, that's what they say on her website.'

This revelation came as something of a shock to John White. He stopped sipping his brandy and stared at his wife. Was there something else they had missed? None of his team had ever mentioned a web-site. His heart sank into his policeman's metaphorical boots.

'What web-site?' he asked, anxiously. 'Sarah Daniels did not have a web-site. We checked.'

'Well, not specifically under that name but she did endorse one specific web-site and occasionally her photograph would appear on screen. I first came across it when I was with Social Services in Berwick.'

Poppy paused and took a sip of brandy.

'Go on please.'

She put her glass back on the table and looked at her husband. She saw at once that her information was important to him, probably significant. She would need to chose her words carefully.

'It was a website for abused women, endorsed by Sarah Daniels. Her name, as a famous author, gave it a certain allure I suppose. If women were trapped in a violent marriage they could seek help online, tell their story and share their misery. It was meant to be therapeutic. I guess it provided some help but in the end it seemed to us at Social Services less than satisfactory. We felt that it was in danger of becoming a site where men could target vulnerable women rather than a place where such women could seek safety.'

'I see. So what happened then?'

'We refused to support it in any way or give it space or links on our government website.'

'Thank you, my darling. Thank you very much. I think you might just have earned yourself an expensive new present. Something girlie, like a small diamond. My treat, naturally.'

'Oh, goodie. But I won't hold my breath!'

* * *

Meanwhile, Sergeant Albert McGregor had been busy - visiting the less than alluring island of Soay.

McGregor had lived all his life on Skye. Although he knew most parts of both the Inner and Outer Hebrides he had, inexplicably, never been to Soay. When he got there, later that Tuesday morning, he knew why.

Not only is Soay as flat as a pancake - apart from a bump in the middle called Beinn Bhreac - the number of sheep on it seriously outnumber the people who lived there. That did not bode well. It is a dumb-bell shaped island, virtually cut in half by deep inlets that form Soay harbour - such as it is - and the bay called Camas nan Gall. It had achieved a kind of notoriety in 1946, when author Gavin Maxwell bought the island and established a factory to process shark oil from basking sharks. The enterprise was financially unsuccessful and resulted in a serious drop in the number of sharks in the surrounding seas.

Neil edged his boat into the tiny harbour.

Sergeant McGregor had persuaded Neil McPherson to ferry him to the island that morning rather than use the police launch. His thinking was that if he was to find out if that boat had been seen in these waters, then it were best to have the actual boat there to jog memories - if he could find anyone whose memory he could jog, that is.

Neil knew now what terrible things had happened on his boat. Sergeant McGregor had told him, not sparing any detail - no matter how graphic. Indeed, there were still blood stains on the deck close to the ship's wheel that no amount of bleach would remove. At the time Neil had said nothing. He was of a taciturn disposition and seldom showed any emotion to the outside world. Whatever he may have privately felt about that young man's death on his boat, he kept it to himself - as ever, the quiet, stoical Presbyterian Scot that he was.

After waiting half-an-hour or so - in which both men lit their pipes and puffed contentedly in absolute silence - they were joined at the jetty by a young man dressed in faded corduroy trousers, fisherman's roll-neck sweater and waders. He looked suspiciously at the uniformed policeman standing on the jetty with a pipe stuck firmly in his mouth. When Sergeant McGregor spoke to him in English he refused to answer in anything other than Gaelic. Neil had to translate, which rather slowed up the investigation, as far as Albert was concerned.

What transpired was that Neil's boat had indeed stopped off early one evening and someone had bought two jerry cans of diesel fuel from someone else in the hamlet called Mol-chlach. No, the man spoke Scots. Yes, he paid cash. No, he did not give his name. Yes, he only stayed a minute or two. And yes, he did seem to be in a hurry to be on his way.

When asked if he could describe the man, the young man said no. Who could? That would be my father. And no, his father was not here. Where was he then? Oh, he's on the mainland. Did he have a mobile with him on the mainland? Don't know. What's a mobile?

It was WPC Debbie Saunders of the Portree Constabulary who eventually managed to trace the young man's father from Soay. In fact, Murdo MacColl was a distant relative of hers. She simply rang an aunt in Glasgow (where Murdo regularly went to buy fishing tackle - he was a sea angler of some renown) and was able to get an address and a telephone number quite quickly.

However, Murdo MacColl proved almost as intractable as his son. Talking to him was like drawing blood from a stone. But Debbie persisted.

After what seemed an age, she managed to get some kind of description from him of the man to whom he had sold two jerry cans of diesel fuel on the day Gabriel McCallister was murdered.

The information was not particularly encouraging.

Yes, the boat had stopped at the island for fuel. No, he had not recognised or seen it before although he could tell from its registration number that it was out of Portree. The man old Murdo remembered was nearly six foot, slim and suntanned. No, he had never seen him before. Yes, he spoke broad Scots but did not have the Gaelic. He wore fisherman's clothes - green anorak over a roll-neck sweater and dark blue jeans. He also had a beard. No, there was no one else on that boat, only the one man.

At least they now had some kind of description of the man who, like some dark, avenging angel, had brought violence to the Isle of Skye.

10
Wednesday, 24th April

Detective Inspector White returned to Portree early Wednesday morning and touched base with his team at the Community Centre. On his desk, waiting for him, was the Forensic report on the rock climber Watson and Miles had found on Neil McPherson's abandoned boat.

The young man's name was Gabriel McCallister. It was the temporary manager of the Glenbrittle Youth Hostel who had supplied the name of the murdered boy and who had been the first to identify the body. Since the boy was on a climbing holiday for a few days his parents were still unaware that anything had happened to their son. It had, therefore, been Detective Inspector White's very first task on his return to Portree that morning to call the police in Ullapool and arrange for a WPC to break the sad news in person to Gabriel's parents and to arrange for them to travel to Inverness and identify the body of their only child.

Half-an-hour later Detective Inspector White addressed his team gathered in front of him for their first briefing since his return from Dunkeld.

'Forensic have nothing much to add regarding the murdered boy - other than that his throat was cut with a knife with a serrated edge; the same knife, possibly, that the lad carried but which is now missing. I have asked for a local diver to search the sea bed in that cave just in case the murderer slung it overboard there and then. Unlikely, but possible.'

'What about stuff on the boat, sir? Anything there to go on? He - or they - must have left something if they had been living on board since the murder at the lighthouse.'

'You would have though so Nick but there was absolutely nothing left on that boat. I'm sure he dumped anything that might identify him overboard once he realised that the RAF had spotted Neil's boat. This man is meticulous. He leaves nothing to chance and an empty beer can or used toothbrush is not his style. If, as Tom spotted, he had been listening in to radio-traffic between us and the RNLI crew from Elgol then he was always one step ahead of us anyway.'

'Where do we go from her, sir?'

'Good question, Janice. I think our best line of enquiry for the moment involves the two computers belonging to Alison and Georgina which we have been examining. So far we have absolutely no evidence that either women knew each other but their respective computers might show otherwise or even reveal some common online link or connection. Both machines have been sent off to Edinburgh for detailed analysis. Those guys can find things deep inside a computer that would alarm most of us, I suspect.'

'So, sir. How can we help?'

'Your task is to see if we can link both Alison and Georgina to chat-lines, websites or other social networking sites that cater for sexual deviants preying on vulnerable women. Not particularly nice work, I admit but Dr. Grant thinks this could be a fruitful line of enquiry. I agree with her.'

He crossed to the door but then hesitated. Turning back into the room and looking at his small team, he said finally:

'We are moving into murky territory here but all the evidence, such as it is so far, suggests that both women and perhaps even our killer are somehow involved in these unseemly, often dangerous networks. My advice to you all is tread carefully.'

* * *

Alison Rutherford's cottage is small and cosy. It is situated up a narrow lane on the outskirts of Portree, just off the A87. It is within walking distance of the village centre and the library but out of sight of any other cottages on that coast, all of which overlooked the still waters of Loch Portree. Her nearest neighbours, apart from Miss Turner, are an elderly couple from Kirkby Lonsdale, Cumbria. They live about three hundred yards further up the lane. In other words, Alison's cottage - although on a slight hill - is isolated and invisible, even from the lane that runs past it.

It had been Elspeth's idea to revisit the cottage just as soon as John White returned to Portree after his short break at home. Having briefed his young team at the Portree Community Centre, White met Elspeth outside the Royal Hotel and drove her the couple of miles to Alison's cottage.

The cottage and garden had already been thoroughly examined by the Forensic team from Aberdeen. They had found nothing to suggest that there had been a struggle or that Alison had been abducted violently. They found DNA for both Alison and her part-time cleaner but little else. Indeed, the cottage was immaculately tidy and nothing apparently disturbed. Too tidy, one of the crime-scene Examiners had thought.

'What do you think happened here, John? What do your celebrated policeman's instincts tell you?'

'That she knew her abductor. That she let him in willingly and that, in all probability, she was drugged before being taken to the harbour in Portree.'

'What makes you think that?'

'No obvious signs of forced entry and absolutely no fingerprints - other than a few (too few, perhaps) belonging to Alison herself. Alison was not a recluse. She had friends and even a lady that occasionally cleaned for her. The cleaning lady at least would have left prints but there are none. None at all. Which means that the murderer had plenty of time to thoroughly clean the place and remove any evidence of his (or their) presence.'

'Then what happened?'

'If my current theory is right, Alison was drugged and then

smuggled on board Neil McPherson's boat during the storm. She *must* have been sedated. Even with an accomplice to help, it would have been very difficult to carry a lively young woman onto a boat, even if she was bound and gagged. The problem, however, is that the initial toxicology examination showed no discernible trace of any sedative.'

'Unless we are dealing with someone who knows his drugs?. Maybe our man is a doctor? He can sedate patients without leaving a trace and amputate limbs swiftly and in a highly professional manner. 'Jack the Ripper' he is not, but there is something highly professional about this man.'

'I agree, Elspeth. Then there is the matter of her laptop. There is nothing of significance on it. For someone who taught computing skills at her library this is very strange. Someone has wiped it of anything of importance, suggesting to me that he is again covering his own tracks. If his name was on that laptop or if he had had any email communication with her, then it has vanished - along with much else that should normally have been there. This again indicates that our killer was known to her and had communicated with her prior to her abduction and that he does not want us to know that.'

They strolled out into the garden.

Alison Rutherford's garden was small and mostly filled with apple trees, some already starting to show the first signs of blossom. At the far end, on a slight rise, was a low beech hedge - something of a wind break. Over this hedge, if you stood close to it, it was possible to see grassy slopes stretching down to the sea loch. It took a moment for White to realise what he was looking at.

'Oh my God! Look Elspeth! It's the beach where we found Georgina's body. If you stand here you can even see the path leading from the pub.'

Detective Inspector White suddenly held his head in both hands and let out a muted groan of despair.

'Elspeth, why have we been so stupid! He was *here*, on the same day Georgina was murdered. Perhaps he even saw Georgina starting out on her walk. Maybe...'

White moved closer to the hedge, peering once more into the distance. There, clearly visible, was the rock at the water's edge behind which Georgina's mutilated body had been left.

'From here you can easily reach the beach before someone leaving the pub is even halfway there. Better still, if he already knew that Georgina often took this walk then he could have lain in wait, ready to strike.'

John White turned and held Elspeth by the shoulders, staring intently into her pale blue, somewhat startled eyes.

'Elspeth, we have been blind! He was here all the time, planning both murders, including that of the poor girl in whose cottage he was actually present. Maybe he was even living here!'

* * *

From old man Murdo's description it had been possible - in his presence - to create an EvoFIT portrait of the possible murderer.

Unfortunately, he looked like scores of similarly bearded men who regularly visited the Isle of Skye. Still, it was better than nothing.

Despite the lack of any real distinguishing features, the EvoFIT image was then distributed throughout the island and beyond - to Kyle of Lochalsh, Plockton, Fort William, Dormie and other towns and villages in the area.

* * *

Detective Inspector White and Elspeth Grant had lunch together later that morning in a small, private dining room at the Royal Hotel.

The room was closed to journalists so they were able to continue their conversation in peace; a conversation that had begun at Alison's cottage earlier that morning.

'I'm not sure we can say yet that the murderer was hiding out at Alison's cottage before he murdered Georgina but I do think you are right about the significance of that weird website for battered women. Your wife is a clever lady, John. She made the link between Sarah Daniels and that so-called 'helpline'. We missed that connection. I blame you - naturally!'

'Thanks a bundle, Elspeth! But where does Alison Rutherford fit into all this? Surely you are not telling me that she is a battered 'wife'. As far as we know neither woman had a boyfriend or current lover. Certainly there is no evidence that either were in some abusive relationship or indeed that they even knew each other.'

'Precisely. Neither of these women were victims - when alive. If anything, they got off on the suffering of such women, pathetic victims of patriarchal abuse. That's exactly what Georgina wrote about in her books, not as a protest against such violence but as a *celebration* of it.'

'Now you are being bold. That might be true for Georgina but what about Alison? Where is your evidence for her involvement in these sick fantasies? Are you saying that she was a lesbian? That she knew Georgina, or rather 'Sarah Daniels' and shared her enjoyment of vulnerable women being beaten and mutilated, just for pleasure?'

'I don't think they knew each other at all, even though they lived in the same small town. I think they 'met' on the internet or through some deviant chat-line in which both woman mutually indulged their fantasies, neither knowing the identity of the other. Its very easy to disguise your identity online, even conceal your natural sexual orientation.'

'Sure, but...'

'I think Georgina used her 'battered-wives' help-line to identify vulnerable women, extract their stories for her books then draw them into intimate, sexually gratifying exchanges. Remember, many of these 'battered wives' have an innate disposition towards violence. They are natural victims, frequently *drawn* to abusive and violent men. It would not take much for them to be coaxed into more intimate revelations if they thought that the woman listening to them was caring and sensitive to their needs. That is how Georgina got her sexual thrills - that and the recasting of those cries for help in her sordid yet hugely popular books.'

'You have still not convinced me that Alison was of a similar disposition. Where is your evidence, Elspeth?'

'If information *has* been wiped from the computers of both women then it would indicate an attempt on the part of our murderer to cover his tracks. The one computer that he has *not* been able to tamper with is the one Alison used at the library. I'm pretty sure she only used her laptop at home for her peculiar 'hobby' so we are not likely to find any incriminating evidence at the library. What you *will* find, however, is a link or two to the very same 'help-lines' we have been discussing.'

'How on earth do you know that?'

'Because on Monday afternoon, after our meeting in Inverness, I came back here and visited the Portree library. There, with the help of WPC Stephens (charming girl, very bright), we opened up the 'history' tab on the library's PC. And there it was - plain as your face, John. 'Battered Wives', endorsed by Sarah Daniels!'

'Well, I guess that shows that you really are after my job. I should warn you, Elspeth, I will not go easily.'

'Of course that alone does not prove that Alison was into the same stuff as Georgina. However, the fact that her laptop was wiped in *exactly* the same way as Georgina's does suggest some mutual need - by someone - to conceal deviant interests possibly shared by both women. What it does also prove is that both Georgina and Alison accessed the same dubious website for 'battered women'. My guess is that it was for exactly the same reason - the exploitation of vulnerable women and girls for gratuitous, sexual satisfaction. Portree's Assistant Librarian was definitely *not* what the good people here still think she is - a really nice young woman.'

* * *

It was growing dark by the time Rob Tait and his two-man crew docked in the harbour at Portree that Wednesday evening.

They had been out fishing all day, having left Portree at dawn. It was the first time since Friday's storm that they had been able to fish. They had spent the last few days repairing their boat from the storm damage it had received. They were now desperate to try and recover some of their lost earnings.

However, what they now fervently wished was that they had never set out that morning for, hanging from the spar they had just swung out over the jetty, was a net containing not only half a ton of fresh herring but the body of a man, his arms and legs sticking out obscenely through the netting.

A small crowd had gathered and were staring and pointing at Rob's strange catch by the time Sergeant Albert McGregor arrived at the harbour, dispersed the crowd (including several journalists, already taking pictures) and took charge of the task of extracting the body from its net.

Eventually the fishing net was lowered to the jetty. Under Sergeant McGregor's supervision, two men from Macleod's Funeral Directors then carefully extracted the bloated body from the net and placed it in a body bag. They then took it in their car to their funeral parlour on Dunvegan Road where it was placed on a metal table in the mortuary. It was there, in the mortuary, that Sergeant McGregor was joined by Detective Inspector White.

The receptionist from the Royal Hotel was the first person to identify the body as that of the man claiming to be Charles Gibbon's. She took one look at his colourless, distorted face, nodded her head quickly once or twice then turned away in horror.

George McClure, recently released on bail, was also summoned to the Funeral Parlour. George had seen dead bodies before. Colleagues drowned at sea. Men whom he had worked with and known for years.

When Detective Inspector White turned back the rubber sheet covering the body George did not blanch or turn away but stared resolutely at it.

'Yes. That's him.'

'Tell me George, was he carrying a suitcase when you took him to the lighthouse?'

'No, but he had a rucksack with something heavy in it. I assumed it was a laptop. That's what engineers carry these days. No suitcase though.'

'I ask because the hotel receptionist at the Royal was sure that when Gibbons checked out early last Saturday morning he had a suitcase with him.'

'Maybe he left it in his car?'

'Yes, that's what we thought. But there is no car. Well, none that we can find. So, if there is no car, where is his suitcase?'

'No idea, but I tell you one thing, Inspector. When I took him to that bloody lighthouse he weren't dressed like that.'

At this point George drew back the rubber sheeting further, to reveal the whole body spread out on the funeral table.

'He had on a green anorak over a roll-neck sweater and dark blue jeans. This man is wearing a white shirt and a suit.'

11
Motivation?

Unlike John White, Elspeth was no longer staying at the Royal Hotel on her occasional visits to Portree - too many noisy journalists was her excuse. Instead, she was now settled in splendid isolation in a small bed-and-breakfast establishment called 'Dunroamin' on Home Farm road. From her bedroom window on the first floor at the front of the house she had a fine view across the bay towards the island of Raasay.

Her actual bedroom was what hoteliers call 'Period'. In other words, it was stuffed with old furniture. Elaborate Victorian pots and fussy bric-a-brac covered every available surface. There was a porcelain 'potty' under the bed and even a large, 'decorative' brass spittoon in one corner. Both articles were regularly used thereafter (despite the perfectly modern *en-suite* bathroom attached to her bedroom) but it was the spittoon that gave Dr. Elspeth Grant the most wicked pleasure.

She spat into it often and - with practice - increasingly deadly accuracy.

Most evenings now she could be found lying on her bed, with her hair in curlers and a fag hanging out of one corner of her mouth. While there were smoke alarms in her room and conspicuous 'No Smoking' signs everywhere she always ignored them. Indeed, she carried a small screwdriver in her bag for just that purpose and over the years had become a dab hand at disconnecting most types of fire alarms. True, she had been banned from a large number of hotels in her time but there were always fresh new ones to discover.

When relaxing in this manner she usually wore an old lace nightdress and a faded silk dressing-gown covered in an elaborate, Japanese dragon design. She never actually got into bed until much later but simply lay on the top covers, contemplating her poorly painted toe-nails (she was over weight and slightly short-sighted).

This was her way of thinking - and very effective it usually proved.

She was not surprised that the body of Gibbons had eventually turned up. John White had called her an hour or so ago to tell her the news - before she read all about it the next day in the morning papers!

She had always somehow known that Gibbons was one of life's victims and as incapable of multiple murder and mutilation as was, say, her elderly mother. Clearly, Gibbons had accidentally stumbled into something going on in that lighthouse that Saturday morning. That had cost him his life - as the bloated body found at sea now sadly proved.

No, what interested her much more was the possible relationship between the two murdered woman and what was it that linked them to their murderer?

She had puzzled over this for some days now but it was her visit early that morning with John White to Alison's cottage (and John's sudden 'epiphany') that had unexpectedly shown her the way.

What linked these two young women - neither of whom, as far as she could tell, knew each other personally - was books. Alison worked with books; she was, after all, the town's Assistant Librarian. Georgina, although in 'disguise' in Portree, wrote books. Lots of them. Her cottage was stuffed with books - many, it transpired, written by her. Georgina Cousins (better known as 'Sara Daniels') was a prolific writer and Alison Rutherford was a librarian. Bingo!

Or was it? Could it *really* be that simple?

Possibly not. Indeed, as much could be said of anyone in the village who tried to write and at the same time borrowed books from their local library. Maybe even the old couple up the road from Alison's cottage were secret pornographers, publishing their sordid tales globally, casting their smut on the internet or even actively creating an entirely new genre - Kindleporn?!

It was at that point that Elspeth abruptly sat up in bed, lowered her bare feet to the floor and tottered into the next room to pour herself another large slug of whiskey.

But what about motive?

Even sadistic lunatics were capable of killing for a purpose. But what was *this* man's motivation? He was certainly trying to *say* something. If he had an underlying message - the sub-text of these murders, as it were - then it must be predicated on some kind of *rational* explanation or intention. What was motivation after all if it was not the intentional drive or passage towards some darker fulfilment - even if that fulfilment was itself hidden, obscure or unfathomable?

Murder in itself could be fulfilling perhaps - for a psychopath - but was this man really mad?

Some irrational prompting deep within Elspeth's ample bosom immediately, spontaneously said: 'No, he is *not* mad!'

With this alarming thought buzzing round and round in her head, Elspeth swallowed her large slug of whiskey then promptly poured herself another - which disappeared as quickly. Placing the empty glass back on the table she then tottered back to bed - but not before pausing briefly in front of the spittoon and generating a satisfactory 'ping' as her whiskey-flavoured spittle unerringly found its target.

* * *

Detective Chief Inspector Elliott had spent the last two days looking into the road accident that had led to Jennifer Chancellor's tragic death on the surgeon's table in Inverness.

The accident had taken place on the A9, one of the main roads leading into Aberdeen. It would seem, from the two people who witnessed the accident, that she had been driving in excess of one-hundred miles an hour. That speed was nothing for the powerful Mercedes-Benz CL-Class that she drove but too much for a modest, Scottish A road. She lost control, spun twice then ended up in a ditch, upside down.

It was no one's fault but her own. No one else was involved and no one else died. She did it all by herself.

The car was a complete write-off. Indeed, the fire brigade had to take it apart to get the seriously wounded woman out. No one thought at the time to check the brakes. No one suspected foul play. Everyone was too busy trying to save Jennifer's life to think *why* such an accident had happened on an open road with next to no traffic. Had she deliberately crashed? Had she, or someone else, planned it in any way? Was this suicide or murder or just another ugly, entirely pointless accident?

These were thoughts that Detective Chief Inspector Paul Elliott pondered as he examined the accident report.

He and his small team at Inverness had also spent some time trying to identify the man and the woman who had, on separate occasions, telephoned Dr. Sutherland at her office in Stirling and the Royal Infirmary in Aberdeen, seeking specific information about Jennifer Chancellor's personal effects - including the watch that she had been wearing at the time of the crash.

Unfortunately, no record had been kept of the address the woman had given the theatre nurse nor was there any record of the man's initial phone call.

When asked, some days later, if she had received her daughter's effects, the distraught mother's answer had been an emphatic 'No'.

That watch, found on Jennifer's severed right arm on the beach, was therefore the only link between a road accident outside Aberdeen and two known murders on the Isle of Skye. The paramedics had said that it was they who had taken the watch from Jennifer's wrist on their way to the hospital and it was the nurse at reception who had taken charge of it the moment

Jennifer was admitted to the A&E. unit of the Aberdeen Royal Infirmary.

The watch was definitely Jennifer's but what was its importance for the murderer and why had he placed it so carefully at the water's edge in Portree?

Regarding the theft of the arm in the first place, this was proving very difficult to unravel. While the cold-store containing Jennifer's arm had no lock, access to the room itself was by keypad. This meant that whoever removed the arm not only knew *where* to look, *when* the lab was likely to be empty but *what* the access code was. This could only mean one thing - an inside job. However, Phillips and Nelson had now interviewed every likely suspect and all had proved negative. If it was someone inside the department or close to it, then they had been very clever in covering their tracks.

While the press had been crawling all over the island since Friday evening of last week, no one had made the connection yet between Georgina Cousins and a celebrated author called 'Sarah Daniels'.

One reason may have been that the photograph Georgina used on her books was definitely *not* her. No one, not even her publishers, knew who the self-confident young woman on the back cover was. Perhaps she was a model Georgina had found, or a distant relative or even someone picked at random. Since no one had ever clapped eyes of this reclusive but highly successful writer, they would not have been able to add much anyway.

Either way, that photograph had fooled a lot of people for a long time.

When news of her death reached Sarah Daniels' publishers in London they very sensibly agreed to say quiet. They knew the secretive character of their author well enough to know that she would have wanted even her death kept secret. So they said nothing and for many weeks thereafter the press - like the rest of the world - remained ignorant of Georgina Cousins' true identity.

That was exactly how Detective Chief Inspector Elliott wanted it to remain. This was already proving to be a very complex case. To have a famous author involved would only fuel interest in the media - a media already lapping up the discovery of yet another dead body on the Isle of Skye.

Since taking overall control of the investigation, Elliott had issued a number of broad statements for the press and held at least three live press conferences - all in Inverness. He had hoped that way to distract attention from Portree and White's difficult work on the Isle of Skye. Since journalists were now swarming all over the island, his plan was to draw them away from Portree to the Police HQ in Inverness. Here they were better equipped to deal with the press at large, especially the national press who clearly 'smelled' something sensational happening in remote parts of Scotland - not generally known for murder and mayhem.

Talk of a dangerous 'serial-killer' on the loose had already appeared on the front pages of the tabloids - in both Scotland and the English press. Indeed, it was proving hard to contain this story and to prevent some of the more determined journalists from interfering with the investigation itself. The murderer at the heart of this case was rapidly acquiring the status of Scotland's worse 'serial-killer' (if, indeed, he was a lone killer) and that itself made for excellent copy.

Either way, Detective Chief Inspector Elliott clearly had a major public relations disaster on his hands - and one sure to get worse before it got better.

12
Thursday, 26th April

The identification of Charley Gibbons' body had taken place on Wednesday evening, whereupon it was taken to Aberdeen for examination overnight. The autopsy had been swift and thorough. The initial report reached both Inverness and the Community centre in Portree Thursday morning.

Thanks to Detective Chief Inspector Paul Elliott's effective intervention, priority had now been given to White's case at the highest level. At the SPSA Forensic Science Laboratory in Aberdeen measures had been taken to ensure that the examination of cadavers, body-parts, body fluids or DNA samples obtained from at least four specific crime-scenes be given absolute priority. Moreover, Aberdeen's most senior Consultant Pathologist, Dr. James Ledbetter, had now been officially assigned to the case. Since he and John White were personal friends and had once been neighbours in Dunkeld, it was felt at last by White and his team back in Portree that they were being given the resources they deserved.

Moreover, the discovery of Gibbons' body on Wednesday had prompted a full confession from George McClure - Charley Gibbons' 'partner in crime'.

According to McClure's written statement to the police, Charley Gibbons was a scrap-metal dealer from Glasgow whom George had first met at a pub in Perth. When George told him that the lighthouse contained miles of valuable copper wire (Elspeth, as usual, had been right!) they had hatched the plan together. George would ferry Charley to the lighthouse and then collect him and the loot later that day. They would share the proceeds, once Charley had flogged the copper wire to his dodgy contacts in Glasgow.

When Gibbons failed to call George from the lighthouse later that morning George panicked. He hid Gibbons' car in his own garage. When Gibbons went missing and they found Alison's body hanging in the lighthouse, George subsequently hid the car in a barn belonging to his uncle on the mainland.

The boot of the Gibbons' car contained clothes and papers from which it was possible to identify the dealer as one Trevor Burns, a convicted thief and conman. His finger prints on record with the Glasgow police matched those of the dead body now on the examination table at the SPSA Forensic Laboratory in Aberdeen.

What was not yet clear, however, was how exactly 'Charley Gibbons', real name Trevor Burns, had died.

The natural assumption at the dockside was that he had drowned but White and his team knew now that in this case nothing was quite what it seemed. The problem was that rapid decomposition after several days in rough seas had made it difficult to arrive at any immediate conclusion but close examination of Burns' internal organs suggested that he had suffered several massive blows, probably caused by a fall. Forensics' current theory - partly supported by DNA evidence found at the South Rona lighthouse - was that Gibbons had been pushed from the top of the lighthouse stairs and had thus 'fallen' to his death. Ledbetter was pretty sure, therefore, that poor 'Charley' was already dead by the time he was dumped in the sea - probably over the side of Neil McPherson's stolen boat. He also suggested that the 'fall' may have happened more than once, suggesting perhaps that it had taken some time to kill 'Charley'. This was due to the extensive damage done to the man's internal organs plus the fact that he had two broken legs and a shattered collar bone.

This information had sent a collective shudder of horror through the 'Gang of Five' when White read this out to them.

Where Rob Tait and his crew had 'caught' Charley in their net suggested that he had been thrown overboard somewhere in the Minch, off the northern-most tip of the Isle of Skye. Its likely that from the navigational co-ordinates Rob had given the police, that the body was being carried south-west on the tide when Rob stumbled across it. The body, if not eaten by sharks, would probably have ended up somewhere near Waternish Point later that day - had Rob and his crew not saved the police the trouble.

Why 'Charley' was not in his original clothes but wearing an expensive suit remained something of a mystery.

* * *

Elspeth was in a particularly combative mood later that morning as she and John White sipped their coffee in the Community Centre.

'Well John, have you read those books I sent you?'

White's team of young police officers - now known affectionately as his 'Gang of Five' - were already busy, working together in tight huddles in different corners of the large, rather bare room. Their standing in the community had risen somewhat when word got out about the brave assault on the boat. When they had got back that Sunday evening, Detective Sergeant Tom Watson and DC Paul Miles had acquired hero status amongst their peers. The white board at one end of the room was covered in what educationalists call 'mind maps'. There was also a scattering of photographs and squiggled notes in red and green inks, together with a large cartoon figure of Batman and Robin to which had been stuck the photographic heads of Watson and Miles.

'No, not really. I never did like stories about brilliant detectives. Far too depressing. Anyway, chick-lit is not my thing.'

'It may be chick-lit but Georgina's style is very interesting. For example, the men in her books are always the victims. Female domination - not a lot of that about in contemporary fiction, these days. Its usually the women who are beaten, abused...murdered.'

'What are you trying to tell me, Elspeth? That Georgina was a raving lesbian with male-domination fantasies just asking to be murdered? Spare me the clichés, please!'

'You checked her cottage the day she was murdered. The shelves were stuffed with female fiction, much of it of a fairly salacious nature. What is interesting though, is that there was nothing on her laptop to indicate that she had been working on a new book. Nor was there anything in her car which she had left at the pub - apart from that day's shopping. That's how you came to interview the butcher, remember?'

'Less said about that the better, Elspeth.'

'Quite. But it is rather strange, this 'missing' manuscript - not least because her literary agent told me she was expecting a new book any month now. Nor indeed were there any hand-written manuscripts lying about that cottage. Nothing, in fact, to indicated that she had been working on a new novel. Don't you find that rather odd?'

'Very odd, particularly for an author as productive as 'Sarah Daniels'. According to her Wikipedia entry, she regularly publishes two books a year. What is also strange is that her laptop has been wiped in much the same way as was Alison's. There is always the chance, of course, that Georgina downloaded new work onto a memory stick. We haven't found one but she could have hidden it somewhere in her cottage. But that laptop contains neither drafts nor emails, nor indeed anything you might normally find on a working computer. Which means....'

At this point John White carefully replaced his coffee cup in its saucer and looked at Elspeth.

'Which means, Elspeth, that I think that our murderer - clever bastard that he surely is - also had access to Georgina's cottage and that it was he who removed material from her laptop.'

'Yes, but....'

'The question, though, is when? The police were all over that cottage the moment they found Georgina's body on the beach.'

'You mean...?'
'If our murderer tampered with Georgina's laptop it could only have been *before* he followed her to that beach and murdered

her.'

Elspeth rose, crossed to the coffee table and poured herself another coffee. She had added three heaped spoonfuls of brown sugar to her coffee before she next spoke.

'By the way, John - did you know that Georgina was left handed?'

'No. How on earth do you know that?'

As she crossed back towards John's desk she carried her coffee in her right hand and wiggled the fingers of her left hand provocatively.

'Does that not strike you as significant?'

She sat down in triumph at John's desk and grinned at him with a grin that might have made the Cheshire Cat pause for thought. She continued to tease him by drumming the fingers of her left hand on the table in front of him.

'Maybe. Not sure? What are you getting at? And how do you know that Georgina was left handed?'

'How do I know? Because when Charlotte and I went to Georgina's cottage on Monday afternoon, after we had been to the Library, I noticed that the arrangement of objects on her desk in her study favoured a left-handed person. Telephone. Inkwell. Lamp. To make absolutely sure, I checked with her agent in London.'

'And, clever clogs?'

'Do you know that she couldn't tell me if Georgina was left or right handed because they had never met! Not once, in twelve years of representing a hugely successful writer. Talk about secretive! But that's not all. Left-handed people tend to strike a PC keyboard harder with their left, *dominant* hand than they do with their right. This would be easier to see if Georgina used a conventional typewriter. However, if you look closely at her PC you will see that the 'qwerty' keys on her left are more worn than those on the right. Neat, eh? Mind you, you need a magnifying glass to see the difference but its there, all the same.'

'All very clever, 'Miss Marple', but where is this leading us?'

'Not sure but I have a very worrying suspicion that sometime soon Georgina's left arm is going to resurface.'

She took another slurp of coffee then placed her cup on the desk.

'Our killer is nothing if not methodical. He removed Georgina's *left* arm while on the beach for a purpose. Nothing he does is random. Nothing. Moreover, he *thinks* symbolically. His work is marked by flamboyant gestures yet riddled with meaningful sub-text. Remember, I spoke ages ago about subtext? Look for his message, I said. Well, nothing has changed. Except that he still has Georgina's left arm - her *writer's* left arm. That for him is hugely symbolic. Sometime soon I am afraid that that left arm will make an equally dramatic reappearance, you mark my words!'

She was right of course. But no one - not even Dr. Elspeth Grant - could have guessed that Georgina's missing left arm would turn up two days later wired to the face of a church clock in the middle of Portree. What is more is that clock, together with its obscene addition, had been stopped at exactly three-thirty.

13
Saturday, 28th April

The Minister at the kirk in Portree became distraught when it was pointed out to him by one of his parishioners early that morning that there was somebody's severed arm now attached to the face of his clock. He was, moreover, at a loss to know how, in broad daylight, anyone could have done such a ghastly thing, not least to his church. Shocking! Absolutely shocking!

Nor, indeed, could anyone else - although some devout Portree locals did argue that it was surely the Devil's work. Surprisingly, perhaps, they might have found some support for this hypothesis from the small band of dedicated police officers who, for nearly a week now, had been chasing someone who resembled Satan - or so they increasingly thought.

Detective Inspector White, whose hurried press conference that morning outside the Community Centre in Portree had not gone particularly well, might have agreed with those sceptics who believed, on the contrary, that it was God's doing, thereby warning us all of 'worse to come unless we changed our sinful ways'. Worse to come was what White now dreaded for if the murderer was telling us something he was not doing a good job of it. No one, including John White, had the slightest idea what this sick bastard was trying to communicate to the good people of Portree.

'Elspeth, I know you asked us to look for the 'subtext' but what the hell is it? I for one cannot see any 'message' in these grotesque displays. What's he trying to do? Threaten us? Warn us?'

'Steady, old fruit!'

They were standing in the square in the shadow of the kirk. A large crowd had gathered, staring up at the church tower where a mechanical 'cherry-picker', containing an operator and two forensic Examiners, rose slowly up until positioned within feet of the clock face. For the next fifteen minutes or so the forensic photographer photographed the arm from several angles before carefully removing it, placing it in a surgical bag. The 'cherry-picker' then gently lowered them to the ground.

The crowd pressed forward, eager to get a glimpse of the bag as it was carried to a police van.

John White turned away in disgust.

He took Elspeth by the arm and headed back towards the Community Centre. All he could think as they left the square was that the community, with yet another atrocity to cope with, was once more in deep shock. As was Detective Inspector White himself.

'Elspeth, I need answers, not speculation. This has got to stop. We must nail this bastard, once and for all. The press have gone crazy with this last *message*. There are already TV wagons parked outside the Community Centre and print journalists crawling all over the parish. We even have CNN in the municipal car park and France 24 on the school playing-field. Imagine what the tabloids will make of some poor woman's arm wired to the parish church in the middle of Portree! I can just see the photographs. Elspeth, we are beyond damage limitation. We now have a thumping great disaster on our hands!'

'Maybe, but we need to look beyond the sensationalism of that arm wired onto a church clock. He did that simply to get our attention.'

'Well it worked. He certainly has *my* full attention!'

'Calm down, John. We need to think logically. I know you are upset but now is the time for clear, lateral thinking. Let's start with the *symbolism* of an arm on a church clock. Its Georgina's left arm so that must have some deep significance for him but absolutely none for those unfortunate to see it attached to their church. But it its also fixed to that clock face in such a way that it highlights the fact that the clock has been stopped at three-thirty exactly. Is it, therefore, the arm he wants us to see or is it the time?'

'I would say the time. Yes, the time.'

'I agree. Remember, Jenny Chancellor's accident took place at about three-thirty in the afternoon on that road outside Aberdeen. We could perhaps deduce that even without witnesses because the shock of the crash itself probably caused the watch to stop. Our murderer then risks all by audaciously stealing back Jenny's arm from Dr. Sutherland's laboratory in Stirling just so that that same watch can turn up again on Georgina's arm on the beach. Very elaborate. Very elaborate indeed!'

'So, is this all to do with Jenny Chancellor's untimely death on the A9? There must be more to it than that?'

'I'm sure there is. So, if time is important where else has that obsession reared its ugly head? Well, the Portree police got a call from someone on the beach where Georgina was found at about three-thirty. Coincidence? I doubt it. What about Alison's murder? Well, I've been thinking about that quite a lot too. The lighthouse, like the church, is a large structure that is central to any community. One lights the way for mariners, the other lights the way to salvation....'

'Elspeth, really! I thought you said this was a time for clear, logical, thinking and not loony speculation?'

'Yes, but bear with me. If you look at the photograph Forensic took of Alison it shows her suspended by both feet. Her feet have been tied together, with her head pointing straight down the stairwell. However - and this is what caught my eye when I saw that photograph - her left, surviving arm is stuck out at an awkward angle from her body. I don't' think anyone at the time really noticed this, not least because everyone there was so horrified by the overall image. Normally, you would think that that free arm would hang straight down, but in that photograph it is sticking out, almost at a right angle. Not sure *how* but it is. At first I could not work out what troubled me about that picture - until I held it up in front of my mirror at the hotel.'

'Your mirror? But....'

'Think about it, John. The *reverse* angle of that photograph showed a body with its head pointing straight down to 'six' and Alison's surviving arm pointing straight out to 'three'. Bingo! Three-thirty!'

* * *

The rest of the day got worse and worse. A second press conference, this time presented by Detective Chief Inspector Elliott in the ball-room at the Royal Hotel in Portree, was a rowdy affair with the press screaming for information.

It was now impossible to prevent talk of 'serial-killers on the loose'. Elliott wisely did not attempt to do so but what little he did tell the press proved somewhat unsatisfactory. Everyone now knew of the deaths of Georgina and Alison and the bizarre matter of the severed arms. No one yet had any details of Alison's body suspended in the lighthouse, although it was now widely thought that George McClure had been re-arrested - this time for possible murder. He had, after all, been the last person to have seen 'Charley Gibbons' when he took him, allegedly, to the lighthouse.

George's arrest was, frankly, a diversionary tactic of Elliot's part. He was in no hurry to disabuse the press as to McClure's real involvement in this case. Like White, he doubted very much if McClure was capable of murder but at least his arrest might keep the press 'happy' for a day or two. He was, unfortunately, wrong in that regard. It did not take long for the more astute members of the press present in Portree to find out from the locals that George McClure may be something of a scallywag but serial-killer he most definitely was not. Could the police be hiding something, they wondered?

Finally, there was the discovery of Neil McPherson's boat containing the body of the young climber. So far nobody at all knew about that. Even McPherson himself, taciturn at the best of times, had remained resolutely silent - even without police prompting. Thus Elliott had managed to keep that murder secret from the press. One more murder at this stage was a step too far. Elliott knew that he could not keep a lid on that for much longer but for the moment, news of George McClure's arrest was all that he was prepared to reveal to the press.

The local police in Ullapool were co-operating fully and thus far only a handful of close relatives of the murdered lad knew of Gabriel's tragic demise. That too could not last for long but at least the funeral could not take place until the police released the body. Despite the parent's grief, the police had no intention of doing that quite yet.

The press conference therefore ended in uproar and loud calls for the Detective Chief Inspector Elliot's resignation.

* * *

Normally, Sergeant McGregor would not drink in the pub at the end of a day's work, not least because he was not really a drinking man. However, that evening, after perhaps the second worst day of his life, he changed his mind.

It was while he was quietly sipping a glass of stout in a corner of the snug that a man came up to him and sat down in the chair opposite. Without a word he took from his jacket pocket an envelope and slowly slid it across the table towards the policeman.

'Sergeant, I think you should see this.'

Albert opened the envelope and took out a photograph and stared at it. It was obvious from his immediate expression that he was shocked by what he saw in front of him.

'Where did you get this?'

'Off the internet. Its all over the web. Mind you, you have to know where to look but this picture is 'hot' amongst the scum that collect this stuff.'

The Sergeant got up. He seemed flustered. Troubled.

'I need to keep this. Is that OK?'

The man nodded.

'Thank you. What's your name, by the way?'

'Tim. Tim Waterhouse. *Daily Mirror.*'
'Thank you, Mr. Waterhouse. Thank you.'

With that Sergeant McGregor hurriedly left the pub.

* * *

The photograph, when examined closely by Forensic the following day, proved to be not one of theirs. This is what Detective Inspector John White both hoped (and feared) would be the case.

It was true that occasionally photographs of a graphic nature taken by the police or the emergency services had found their way onto the internet. But this was not the case on this occasion. Had it been, then DI White could have begun an immediate investigation to identify and arrest the individual leaking such stuff to the press or other, even more dubious, sources.

However, a far worse scenario even than that was now opening up before them. If it was definitely *not* Forensics' photograph of Gabriel McCallister with his throat cut, then it could only have been taken by his killer. That probably meant that there were other photographs still to surface. If that happened, then the case would be blown wide open and all hell would be let loose.

The sceptics were right. There *was* worse to come. It had just arrived!

14
Sunday, 29th April

The following morning Detective Inspector White gathered his troops at the Portree Community Centre on Park Road for yet another team meeting. White's young 'Gang of Five' were becoming jaded and battle-weary. This was the second consecutive Sunday they had worked. No one complained but White could tell that they all badly needed a break sometime soon.

For the last three days now they had been delving into the murkier side of the internet. Not only had some twelve, state-of-the-art laptops appeared on the scene (courtesy Inverness Police HQ) but for the first time in its one-hundred-and-seventy-three-year history the town's Community Centre had direct access to the Police National Database (PND) in London - with related access to Interpol and certain other international police websites. The PND contains the details of about fifteen million people. Of these, 9.2 million are records of convictions or arrests, but it also covers an unknown number of victims of crimes and others who have come to the attention of the police.

It was time to see what, if anything, they had found. Detective Sergeant Tom Watson was the first to report back to the team.

'Well sir, we now have the report back from the computer experts in Edinburgh. They confirm that both computers had been tampered with, as we suspected. Both had had material removed from their hard drives, but selectively. Much that was left was innocuous but there were what they called 'ghost' traces of files that were either illegal or, at best, highly dubious. They cannot say exactly what they were but it would seem that both computers had been accessing similar material. Please don't ask me how they know this but that's what they say.'

'What about 'Battered Wives' or related material?'

'Nothing, sir. Nothing at all. They thought that odd since Sarah

Daniels' site is legitimate - allegedly. Why would anyone need to remove that? The fact that they probably did could in itself be considered suspicious. What they did confirm was that whoever tampered with these two computers really knew what they were doing. We are talking about a real computer expert. His 'fingers' are all over both computers, suggesting that the *same* person had access at some time to both Georgina and Alison's personal PC's or laptops.'

'Thanks Tom. Charlotte, what did your team come up with?'

'We were tasked to look into chat-lines or other social interfaces that might link Alison and Georgina. There are thousands out there, some more dubious than others. Online 'rooms' where homosexuals of either persuasion can communicate at will are all over the internet. What *is* surprising, though, is that places where lesbians with sado-masochism tendencies can freely communicate are few and far between. In a way that helped our search. Most sites seem to be based in the Netherlands or Belgium. DC Miles was able to narrow these down to thirty-seven identifiable sites.'

'So. Paul, tell us what you found?'

'Yes sir. I started by contacting the Met's Obscene Publications Unit in London. They proved incredibly helpful. Not only did they tell us *where* to look but gave us software that helped us improve our own search engines. Lesbian sites that cater for those interested in violence of one sort or another are highly sophisticated. Although they may appear to be sited in, for example, Antwerp they probably originate in Bangkok or Ho Chi Minh City. This is true of most sites that deal in child pornography, bestiality, necrophilia, rape or torture.'

'Have you been able to narrow it down at all?'

'Yes sir. The one site that best fitted the profile we were looking for showed up in Dubai, of all places. Since most users of these sites hide behind false names, sometimes even disguising their sex, it has proved impossible to say whether Georgina or Alison used the same site, if at all. But then we had a break-through. Nick here discovered a kind of digital 'map' that gave some clues as to the type of global traffic involved.'

'Nick?'

'Yes sir. The 'map' shows which countries are using the site over a given period and, more importantly, how often. Its pretty basic but it does provide some indication of both the number of users each day and where they come from. Scotland showed up as Edinburgh and Glasgow primarily - as one might expect - but the only usage in our area was, wait for it - Portree! That, unfortunately is as far as it goes. It does not tell us *who* is using it, just where they are from. Somebody (could be more than one person, of course) in Portree has been accessing a porn site that caters primarily for lesbians who get off on violence to vulnerable women or young girls.'

WPC Janice Ward raised her arm.

'Janice?'

'I should add, sir, that we also found a link from the 'Battered Wives' site that took you from there to an informal chat-line, called 'Talk&Talk'. While the main website uses trained counsellors, this 'room' means that anyone can talk directly with those women who first told their stories to the official site. Access is one-way, though. It is up to the battered or abused women to make the initial contact. Some do because they see this as another place to seek help or comfort. Others use it because, frankly, they want to show off or because they desperately crave attention. If Georgina or Alison were tapping into this kind of material for their sexual kicks then it was through a site like 'Talk &Talk' that they did so.'

'Well done. Well done all of you. Now, what about the photograph of Gabriel McCallister? How did that get onto the internet? Nick, if you can tell me who put it on, then we may have solved this case and I personally will make you Chief Constable!'

'Thank you sir. Much appreciated but I'm afraid my elevation to CC may have to wait. The short answer is that it is virtually impossible to say where any given photograph originates. Police officers with the Child Exploitation and Online Protection Centre in London face this problem every day. What happens is that someone sells a photograph to a dealer, usually under a false name and via a virtually untraceable site on the internet.'

'Yes, but what about payment? Is that not traceable?'

'Sadly, no. What happens is that any virtual exchange of money happens on day one, usually disguised as some legitimate online transaction. The dealer then releases the photograph onto the internet, often through a site that in itself appears innocuous but to which those in the know have secret access. Once it is out there pornographic or sadistic material rapidly spreads, depending on the nature of the images. Snuff-movies and the like can go global within seconds of their original release. Once out there, nothing can stop such material spreading throughout the internet. If that happens, then the original supplier with even more images or video of the same 'quality' can name their price. Its all a matter of supply and demand.'

'So, if our killer released that photograph, there is as yet absolutely no way we can trace its origins?'

'I'm afraid not. Mind you, it *is* possible to put a hidden tracer on a given image, provided it is digital. This is the digital equivalent of a radio isotope used in medicine. The CEO squad employs this trick on a regular basis. They deliberately release a tagged image, merely to see who picks it up and runs with it. That could be something we could try but much would depend on how graphic the image was and how many sick folk out there would want to add it to their secret porno collection!'

'Quite. Let me think about that one, Nick. What then about Tim Waterhouse, the journalist who gave Sergeant McGregor the photograph?'

'Yes sir. He showed me the porn site in which he found that

image. The site itself was essentially soft-porn and readily accessible. However, it had hidden within it a second, secret site which those in the know and who are willing to pay could readily access. This contained hard-core porn - including snuff-movies and the like. Terrible images. The killer's graphic photograph of Mr. McCallister was amongst them.'

'Is *The Mirror* going to publish it?'

'I doubt that, sir. Its far too graphic, even for them. I got the distinct impression that Waterhouse's interest in that photograph lay elsewhere. I suspect they are working on a story about leaks from within the police. Waterhouse knew from the boat that it was taken in Scotland and that's probably why he gave it to Sergeant McGregor in the first place. I suspect that he also thinks it's a fake. There are plenty of those about, it seems - phoney pornography, designed merely to make money. Once Waterhouse realises that it is *not* a fake he will almost certainly assume that it was leaked by one of our lot. The press do not yet know about Mr. McCallister's murder so Waterhouse has not yet linked it to the present enquiry. I think, however, that it is now only a matter of time before he does. Nothing then will stop him publishing - unless it is an injunction we manage to slap on the *Mirror*.'

* * *

That night, in his bedroom at the Royal Hotel in Portree, John White thought about a great deal, not least his fear that other photographs taken by their killer might surface any day. The alarming idea that this psychopath might also have taken *moving* images - an idea raised by one of his 'Gang of Five' - filled him with absolute horror. Overnight, the entire case had taken yet another, sinister turn.

He rang Poppy, partly to take his mind off the case and mainly because he missed his wife terribly.

'Hi John. I was just thinking of you. How are you, my darling?'

'OK.. What have you been up to?'

'Not a lot. Fiona rang. She wants to know if we are free sometime next weekend for supper. I said that I would ask you, as you were pretty busy.'

'Tell Fiona, 'yes'. If I don't get a break soon I might just top myself.'

'Poor darling! That bad, eh?'

'Don't even ask!'

* * *

John White undressed, showered, cleaned his teeth, put on his pyjamas and sat on the edge of his bed. For a long time he simply stared at the carpet, becoming more and more morose.

Elspeth's theory that Alison's body - suspended within the lighthouse - somehow represented some kind of 'one-armed Vitruvian woman signalling three-thirty' worried him deeply. Frankly, he did not buy it. Elspeth had clearly lost the plot and yet she had been right about most things so far. Could this killer be that sick? The probable answer was 'yes'. He had no doubt now that they were dealing with a raving psychopath who was both vicious and highly dangerous. What is more, the murderer was now releasing images on the internet of his handiwork. That was deeply worrying. Where might that stop, for God's sake?

John White was never the most confident of men, even though he was an extremely efficient police officer with a respectable case record to prove it. He was, moreover, a passionate man who often became emotionally involved - not perhaps the best quality needed for police work. He found the cynical indifference of his colleagues difficult to handle although, deep down, he recognised that cynicism was probably an effective way of dealing with the horrible things policemen regularly encountered.

It was at times like this, alone in his room at the end of a difficult day, that John White felt most vulnerable.

He was grateful that at least he had one of the best Profilers in Europe working beside him. There was no doubting Elspeth's extraordinary intelligence. He found that exhilarating but also something of a challenge to his own powers of deduction. Even the 'Gang of Five' now recognised that she outshone them all, including their boss. That did not do much for his self-confidence. On the other hand, while he had begun to enjoy working with the ebullient Elspeth Grant, he often found her habitual *bonhomie* exhausting, and her jokes distinctly lacking in taste - rather like the abrasive humour of medical students or consultant pathologists.

Was he, he wondered, turning into a neurotic prude?

With that sobering thought burrowing like a worm into his troubled brain, Detective Inspector John White crawled into bed and turned off the light.

* * *

The next morning he arrived early at his desk in the Portree Community Centre and took out his file on Alison Rutherford. It was now Monday 30th April, eleven days since they had found Jenny's severed arm and Georgina's mutilated body on the beach near Portree.

Elspeth was right in one thing. The photograph taken in the lighthouse showed that Alison's left arm was indeed sticking out at an unusual angle. Since the woman was naked, this could only mean that the arm had been fastened in some way to the stair rail or the iron balustrade that circled the first floor level of the lighthouse. But where was the thread? Why had it not surfaced during the forensic examination of the lighthouse?

What else had they missed, he wondered.

The name at the bottom of the Forensic report on Alison Rutherford was Dr. James Ledbetter - the same 'Jim' he and Poppy would be having supper with at the weekend at home in Dunkeld. He had known Jim and his wife, Fiona, for years. They used to sail together in the Inner and Outer Hebrides. On these occasions their respective wives would go on a credit-card jamboree in London while the 'boys' explored the islands in Jim's yacht. At one time they were even neighbours in Dunkeld but now Jim and his wife had moved to Aberdeen to be closer to the SPSA pathology laboratory where he now worked.

It was Consultant Pathologist James Ledbetter who had been assigned exclusively to this case.

Detective Inspector White picked up the phone and dialled Jim Ledbetter's private mobile number.

'Yes, we assumed that some kind of thread had been used to support the arm. I have a photograph in front of me that shows Alison's left wrist. There is a circular indentation that suggests that she was attached to a thread or wire by that wrist. I suspect, John, that if you go back to that lighthouse you will find that thread still attached to the gallery rail. It must have snapped when our guys took the body down. Anyway, all this is in my original report. The moral here, John, is that you should read my reports more carefully in future!'

'Thanks Jim. Up yours!'

15
Thursday, 3rd May

Two days later Alistair McIntyre, at the wheel the Portree police launch, took a very nervous WPC Saunders to the lighthouse on South Rona. The light had been repaired the same day Forensic had completed their inspection and now its revolving beam was working once more.

They entered the lighthouse, found the interior light-switch and climbed the stairs. The bloodstained floor had been cleaned but both felt a chill as they ascended the very same stairs that the murderer and his accomplice had climbed that dreadful weekend when at least two people had met their deaths in the narrow confines of this gloomy interior. Moreover, Debbie had been unable as yet to get out of her head that she had probably spoken to the killer and mutilator of women. It had been Debbie who had taken that call when some man with a false northern accent had called the Portree police to report the discovery of a severed arm on the beach near Portree.

It took ten minutes to find a black, cotton thread attached to the upper rail - as predicted by both Elspeth Grant and Dr.Ledbetter. It had clearly snapped at Alison's wrist and now hung down the stairwell from the upper level rail. In the dark interior of the lighthouse it was virtually invisible. It had clearly been missed by forensic. Elspeth had been right - again.

The positioning of Alison's suspended body, with one arm sticking out, had been deliberate. What had fooled everyone was that Forensic's photograph had been taken from the *wrong* side. But then, how was anyone to know that what the killer was displaying in that grotesque way was a symbolic 'clock' that showed 'half-past-three'?

* * *

'Well, was I right or was I right, John?'

'You were right. I apologise for ever doubting you, Elspeth. It will not happen again. Now, just is case it has slipped your prodigious memory, its definitely your round!'

They had just finished lunch in a small restaurant outside Portree on the Staffin Road, going north. The meal had been excellent but neither had shown much interest in the food on their plates. They had now left the dining room and had retired with their drinks to the covered, wooden veranda outside. They each settled into a comfortable wicker chair with soft cushions.

They had eaten here before. It was impossible now to find any privacy in Portree. There were journalists everywhere. They knew John White by sight but not Elspeth. She was anxious to keep as low a profile as possible - hence their decision to meet relatively secretly, as far as their official duties permitted.

John had joined Elspeth for lunch, having left the 'Gang of Five' finishing up their morning's work before going for a communal 'fish and chips' lunch at Portree's celebrated 'Lower Deck' restaurant down by the harbour. The 'Lower Deck' had become something of a tradition among the young police officers stuck in Portree. It was cheap and friendly and as yet, mercifully free of journalists on expenses who preferred to eat at the Royal.

It was a sunny, May afternoon. From the veranda of their restaurant Elspeth and John could see across the bay towards the hazy outline of the island of Rassay. Beyond that, further north, lay the island of South Rona and the fateful lighthouse.

They were both glad that they could not see that at this distance although the photographs of Alison's suspended body still haunted them.

Elspeth lit a cigarette.

'I wish you wouldn't smoke, Elspeth. You must be on at least forty a day. It cannot be doing you any good.'

'Let me remind you, Detective Inspector, that based on my salary scale I outrank you by a not inconsiderable amount. Please keep your advice to yourself.'

'Very well. Tell me though, what is our killer likely to do next? He's gone very quiet, assuming he is still up here somewhere.'

'Oh yes, he's still here. Every fibre of my smoke-ridden body tells me so. In fact, I would not be surprised if he is not building up to some ghastly climax. He's outsmarted us thus far. Since these people thrive on publicity, he may well strike again but this time I fear it could be spectacular.'

She gave him a very cheesy grin and lit another cigarette.

'I think you have a very morbid sense of humour, Elspeth. I hope with every fibre of my lean, healthy body that you are wrong. Now, you said you wanted to talk about the toxicology report......'

* * *

The fish and chips lunch had been a great success and for an hour or so the Gang of Five had managed to talk of something else other than the case. However, they all recognised that they were exhausted. No one felt that much progress had been made, least of all progress that could lead to an arrest. It was with that thought uppermost in their minds that they dragged themselves back to the Community Centre.

This was a view, it seemed, shared by Detective Chief Inspector Elliott. To that end he had rather unexpectedly summoned the team to a meeting that afternoon in the Portree Community Centre. It was clear from his rather business-like manner that he was looking for answers. Real answers.

'Thank you. I am sorry this meeting was called at such short notice but I am anxious to find out where exactly we are. So, let's start with the suit Gibbons was mysteriously wearing when they pulled him out of the sea. So Janice, Detective Inspector White tells me that that was your job. What have you found out about this suit?'

'At first, very little, sir. Forensic themselves found nothing. The only strange thing was that the labels on both the jacket and the trousers had been removed, stitch by stitch. It was as if our man did not want us to find out where this suit was from or who made it.'

'Perhaps that was his way of challenging us *to* find out?'

'Yes sir, that's what we thought. Anyway, we sent the cloth for analysis to Dundee University. They have a research project there called FABRIC. This is short for 'Fashion and Apparel Browsing for Inspirational Content'. Bit of a mouthful, I know but what it does is - and here I am quoting from their Newsletter - 'develop innovative technology to improve browsing, retrieval, and management of digital images throughout the textile and clothing industry'.'

'How on earth did you come across this?'

'Very easily, sir. My sister, Annette Ward, is FABRIC's Project Manager. She worked in the fashion department at the V&A but moved to Dundee University last year. She was only too pleased to help us.'

'And....?'

'It took FABRIC ten minutes to identify that suit, using their search engine and sophisticated software - courtesy of the Victoria and Albert Museum. That suit was made in America. Gainseville, Florida to be exact. The company - you will never believe this , sir - the company who actually made that suit is called 'Three-Thirty Couture'.'

'Well done. Excellent work. However, that does not in itself explain why Gibbons was wearing an expensive American suit when, by all accounts, he went off to nick several thousand quids' worth of copper wire from that lighthouse. If it is a subtle way for the killer to again 'sign' his handiwork then I suppose it makes sense but it does seem to me highly improbable. What also worries me is that none of us have the slightest indication of this man's possible whereabouts. After his latest escapade with the church he has again completely vanished. I appreciate that we have only a limited idea what he looks like, based on Murdo's somewhat unreliable testimony, but you would have thought that on a small island like this, with its close community, someone would have seen something suspicious, or at best odd. He seems 'invisible' and I find that very disconcerting. Has anyone any thoughts on this? Paul?'

'Yes sir. If he is part of this community then I suspect that he is probably being protected. Its possible people here on the Isle of Skye know more than they are letting on.'

'OK. Tom, what's your take on this?'

'Well, sir, I think we may have be looking for the *wrong* clues. What unconsciously we have been hoping for since the beginning is that someone will remember seeing a lone walker on the run in the Coullins or a stranger scrambling up some rock face or perhaps a bedraggled figure arriving at a small hotel without a suitcase - all the signs of a man on the run. I think now that that is a complete waste of time.'

'Why is that, Tom?'

'Because sir, instead of looking into the distance, as it were, we need to look closer at home. I think he is right here, under our very noses but fully integrated into the community. He is no stranger but known to everyone - not as a killer, of course, but as an accepted part of the social landscape. It is his very familiarity that gives him the anonymity he needs. That way he is free to move around the island without anyone taking the slightest notice or seeing anything odd in that. His camouflage is not that he is a stranger but that he is known to everyone. That makes him exceptionally difficult to 'see'.'

'You may well be right. Thank you Tom. Very perceptive. Now, I know you have all been working very hard but you all need a break. Enjoy your week-end. You have all deserved it but we have to catch this murderer. I know Detective Inspector White here is as determined as you all are to catch this man and his possible accomplice. It is now thirteen days since Miss Cousins died on that beach. We need results. I'll see you all back here Monday. Thank you. Carry on, Detective Inspector.'

With that Detective Chief Inspector Elliott strode out of the room. His message was clear enough. It was all taking far too long!

* * *

When, a few hours later, John White told Elspeth about the suit she merely chuckled.

She and Inspector White were sitting in John's car which he had parked close by the harbour wall, watching the fishermen hosing down their decks. That day's catch already lay in boxes of ice, awaiting shipment to the mainland. The air was pungent with the smell of sea, salt and fresh herrings.

Lost in though, she lit another cigarette, drew on it slowly, then smiled wickedly at Detective Inspector White who was now rapidly opening his window.

'Since that suit was clearly *not* made for the late 'Gibbons' (better known to the Glasgow constabulary as Trevor Burns) we might just have our killer's actual inside leg measurement. That, at least, is far more than we knew before our Trevor stumbled into the deadly plot.'

'Do you mean that it was our murderer's suit? Too obvious, surely?'

'Quite possibly. Remember though, our killer was not expecting Gibbons to barge in on his grisly *soirée* with Alison Rutherford. If he jumped out on him at the top of the stairs and pushed him to his death down the stairwell then it must have happened *before* he hung that poor girl by her ankles and meticulously removed her arm.'

'How do you know that, Elspeth?'

'Because it would appear from Jim Ledbetter's forensic report that there were no traces of Alison's blood on the suit. Seawater might have washed away dust or skin fragments but it would not have removed dried blood embedded in the fabric. No. Gibbon's arrival was wholly unexpected. I think, realising that here was yet another chance to leave his 'signature' on a dead body, he swapped clothes with our Trevor then dumped the body in the sea, knowing full well that it would eventually turn up somewhere.'

'OK but my worry is that the 'three-thirty' signature was prompted by the chance encounter with Jenny's watch. Why would he also have a suit from Three-Thirty Couture? He may be clever but he cannot read the future, surely? Did he buy it especially. He could hardly know that Gibbons was going to stumble into his gory activities on Rona?'

'No idea. Lucky coincidence?'

She took another drag on her cigarette then flicked the stub through her widow towards the harbour, narrowly missing a fisherman coming up the harbour steps.

'Either way, thanks to your clever young WPC and her even cleverer sister, we now at least know what size killer were are looking for.'

'Dr. Grant, have you ever though of quitting psychology and taking up conventional detective work instead? You would make a very good copper.'

'Well, thank you, kind sir. I think I will stick to criminology. Its far better paid, even if the hours are shit!'

'So? Where do we go from here? Are you any closer to identifying this brilliant yet horribly elusive psychopath? That, after all is why we are employing you at a salary which, as you tactfully pointed out recently, is considerably larger than mine! Have you the even slightest idea who he might be?'

''Yes, as it happens!'

'What!?'

'I think I know who our killer is. Moreover, I have a little plan that may just prove that my suspicions are right.'

John White stared at her. His mouth had fallen open. He was speechless. Elspeth was full of surprises but now ...

'Well? Who is it, for God's sake, Elspeth? Tell me!'

'Not yet, John. Not yet.'

'Not yet? What do you mean - not yet? Elspeth, this is a multiple murder enquiry, you simply cannot withhold information. Why, I could.....'

'I know you could but John, trust me. Just trust me for a day or so. Then, as in the best detective novels, all will be revealed and you will be able to bask in the reflected glory of my deductive powers.'

16
Friday, 4th May

That Friday evening, while driving back home to his cottage in Dunkeld, Detective Inspector White reflected on the week's events.

The first was Elspeth's remarkable revelation that she thought that she knew who the killer was. She could be utterly infuriating at times but not to tell him whom she suspected was typical of the woman. He was tempted to insist that she inform the police - especially Chief Detective Elliott, let alone himself - but some instinct had told him to hold back. Her record as one of the best Profilers in Europe was such that occasionally she had to be indulged. No doubt, she would reveal all soon enough. The problem was, how much time did any of them actually have before this dangerous killer decided to strike again?

In short, how long could he 'indulge' his talented Profiler?

The appearance of Georgina's left arm on the face of the clock of the Kirk in Portree had shocked everyone - not least the good citizens of Portree still recovering from the possible murder of four people within their small community, including their Assistant Librarian who was widely liked. What was also remarkable was *how* it had appeared. Even if placed there in the middle of the night, any pedestrian walking past the kirk could have seen someone on that tower fastening a severed arm to the clock face - a face that was, moreover, illuminated. It was an act that was both bold and audacious - and exactly as Elspeth Grant had predicted it might be.

It was also clear that his boss was becoming as frustrated as he was, a frustration also shared now by his 'Gang of Five'.

He felt proud of the way his team of young, inexperienced police officers - few of whom had ever had any serious crime exposure - had bonded together. Not only had two of them shown exceptional bravery when boarding McPherson's boat but each one of the team had shown remarkable research skills. What they lacked in practical crime experience they made up for in sharp, lateral thinking and an evident ability to think 'outside the box' - something Elspeth Grant had advised them all to do, including himself.

They clearly belonged to that new generation of police officers - well educated, exceptionally bright and highly computer-literate.

These were skills that were clearly vital when dealing with someone who, from the evidence of the two lap tops that had been 'erased', was also familiar with advanced computer technologies.

He liked also the way they had bonded socially. While all lived in different parts of the country and clearly missed friends and family, none had complained once about the long hours or the weekend duties they had been obliged to take on. While he had tried to stagger the hours, giving alternate weekend passes to members of his little team, circumstances and a rapidly unfolding series of new and at times shocking events meant little rest for anyone. They had coped well with this pressure although he could see that they were now at the ragged edge and badly needed some down time.

The problem, though, was that Elspeth was right - their killer might well strike again soon. If they were dealing with a madman within the community, then it was patently impossible to anticipate his next move. Even if Elspeth had her suspicions, it was one thing to have a theory but quite another to provide sufficient evidence to satisfy the Procurator Fiscal.

No matter how brilliant Elspeth Grant's deductive powers were, without solid evidence they were all buggered.

* * *

When Detective Inspector White got home that evening, Poppy welcomed him with a glass of chilled Chardonnay. They strolled, arm in arm, across the lawn and down to the river Tay that ran past their garden.

It was a warm, tranquil night. The air was filled with the smell of newly-cut grass from their neighbour's even bigger, fastidiously manicured lawn.

'What are our plans this weekend, my darling?'

Poppy could sense that her husband was exhausted and somewhat morose. She would need to handle him gently.

'Nothing much. I promised to meet Tamsin tomorrow morning for coffee in Dunkeld. You are not expected to attend; it's a strictly girlie event. On Sunday, if you feel up to it, we need to clear out the small bedroom. Your sister is travelling north on Tuesday and stopping off here for one night. We need to find her a bed under all that junk we have squirreled away in the spare room.'

'OK. If you insist!'

He made a sulky face then took another sip of his wine.

'Oh yes, Jim and Fiona are coming for supper on Saturday. I have booked a table at Mario's for eight o'clock.'

'Oh God, I had forgotten all about that. He's bound to talk shop. He usually does!'

'Well, Robocop - we will *not* let him! Serial-killers are decidedly off Saturday night's menu. I shall see to that. Now, finish your drink because I have prepared a delicious supper for you, to be washed down with copious amounts of an even better Chardonnay than the one you are currently sipping in such a desultory and, I might add, wholly uncharacteristic, manner!'

* * *

The Ledbetters met them in the car park near the cathedral in Dunkeld at seven-forty-five that Saturday evening.

Fiona Ledbetter - a plain, rather shy woman who said little in company - was five-feet-five-inches tall and slightly on the plump side. That evening she wore an expensive trouser suit in dark, charcoal grey that made her look even shorter. The string of pearls round her throat looked real - or so Poppy thought when she spotted them. Fiona Ledbetter always seemed to enjoy Poppy's company so it was no surprise that Fiona smiled and waved at her as she got out of Jim's car and moved towards the Whites.

That, thought Poppy, boded well.

Jim Ledbetter was tall, dapper, clean shaven but with thinning reddish hair. He was dressed in a rather elegant, pale fawn, linen suit. John noticed that he smelled of Eau-de-Cologne. Jim always had expensive tastes. Mind you, he earned a great deal more that a common-and-garden Detective Inspector so he could afford to indulge them. Since Jim had once owned a beautiful, thirty-foot yacht John had always assumed that he had a private income. Mind you, they had no children and Fiona had once worked, so perhaps that gave them the spare cash to pay for such luxuries.

They greeted each other warmly and strolled from the car park to the entrance of the restaurant in the High Street. It was a lovely, warm evening. John thought Poppy looked ravishing in a long, flowery summer dress. He loved his wife so much and it was a moments like this, when she appeared so relaxed and beautiful in the company of friends, that he knew how lucky he was to be married to such a wonderful creature.

The Whites' favourite restaurant was a small but *chic* Italian establishment near the centre of Dunkeld. Mario himself met them at the door and escorted them to a table in one corner. The Whites were regular customers.

For a third-generation, Scottish restaurateur of Italian extraction, Mario's Scottish accent - with largely incomprehensible Veronese embellishments - always amused John. He was, therefore, not only even more enamoured of his wife Poppy than usual that evening but in a particularly happy frame of mind when, at

Mario's bidding, all four of them sat down, sipped their chosen *aperitifs* and ordered their food from a menu that promised countless gastronomic delights.

Indeed, the meal proved a great success and Jim was in sparkling form throughout the evening - witty, urbane and devastatingly wicked, particularly when telling outrageous stories about his colleagues back in Aberdeen. Even Fiona perked up - probably with a little help from the fine Veronese Bardolino wine that Mario had chosen for them - and actually told a joke or two. That's a first, thought John at the time, surreptitiously winking at his wife across the table. She smiled, knowing exactly what he was thinking.

As predicted, from time to time Jim tried to talk 'shop'. Both Whites knew from previous experience that he loved talking about work, especially if it was *his* 'shop' that was the centre of attention. Poppy, however, kept her promise and every time someone mentioned the investigation she shut them up. After a while even Jim got the message.

After their meal they retired to the comfortable coffee lounge with its deep-seated chintz armchairs. They ordered coffee and one or two of Mario's formidable Nardini grappa.

'How you getting on with Elspeth?', asked Jim over his second grappa. As he asked this question he surreptitiously glanced at Poppy on his right, guessing that she might once more intervene. To his surprise she did not, engrossed as she was in conversation with Fiona.

John, who had drunk rather a lot that evening, was glad Poppy was driving them home. She had had only one glass of wine all evening. Short straw, and all that.

'Elspeth Grant. How are you getting on with your new Profiler, John?'

'Elspeth? Mildly eccentric. Smokes too much and is somewhat unpredictable in her moods. It seems she has an elderly mother back in Edinburgh. That's where she is this weekend. Bright, though. Extremely bright.'

'What's then is her slant on this lunatic? He's not exactly your text-book psychopath, from what I have heard.'

Poppy had now stopped talking to Fiona and appeared to become somewhat agitated at the line of Jim's questioning. She fiddled with her bracelet and gave her husband several stern looks across the coffee table. Fiona simply looked on anxiously, knowing all too well that her friend hated their men bringing their work home. In her case, married to a pathologist, that was something that she dared not contemplate, even as a joke!

'Jim, do we really have to discuss this dreadful man? John really needs a break from this case. Its getting us all down.'

'Sorry, Poppy. Habit, I'm afraid. Besides, I'm curious. We boffins seldom get news from the sharp end. One last question and then I will shut up. Are you any closer to catching him - before he strikes again?'

'Nope.'

And that was the extent of the discussion about the serial-killer that evening, thanks largely to Poppy's enforced embargo on the subject.

When they left the restaurant, John and Jim led the way back to their respective cars. Poppy lingered behind, talking to Mario at the entrance to the restaurant. Fiona stayed with her friend.

It was a beautiful Spring evening with a cool breeze stirring the leaves above their heads. The two men paused within the shadow of the ruined cathedral, enjoying the moment. The river, partly illuminated by a crescent moon, was just visible through the trees that lined the river bank.

Since they were now out of earshot of their wives, Jim seized the opportunity to speak once more about the case - this time, he hoped, without danger of Poppy intervening.

'John, I have now examined both women. I would say that those amputations are the work of a skilled surgeon. Very clean. Very professional. I think you should be looking for someone in the medical profession. I know that it is not my place to make suggestions to an Investigating Officer but these crimes have 'doctor' written all over them. He knows, moreover, how the police work. He's been one step ahead of you all the way. It must be someone from the inside. Your killer, John, is a medic. I would bet my pension on it. That's where you should be looking, if you want my expert advice.'

* * *

Later that night Poppy and John celebrated the evening's success with a large brandy while sitting on the terrace overlooking the river; a beautiful river tinged now with moonlight.

John had always known that his wife was not only very intelligent but hugely supportive. They had first met when he was in training at Hendon. It had been love at first sight. Moreover, she had stuck with him through all the ups and downs of a policeman's tricky early career. Now, with a case on his hands that could make or break him, he saw that she was even more supportive than usual.

He loved her for that. That night they both fell asleep almost the moment they got into bed - but with their arms around each other.

* * *

Dunkeld. Sunday morning. Nine o'clock. John was still fast asleep when the telephone rang. Poppy was in the kitchen - in her dressing gown and making tea. She picked up the receiver. It was Elspeth, calling from her New Town apartment in Edinburgh.

'Well, did he ask about me? Did he actually ask how I was getting on?'

'Elspeth he did exactly as you said he would. It worked brilliantly.

Mind you, I thought I overdid it once or twice but you could sense his frustration all through the meal!'

'Yes!'

Poppy could imagine Elspeth punching the air in triumph.

'What about John?'

'He was fine. Even when *he* tried to talk shop I jumped in. When it came to coffee, Jim could not contain his frustration any longer. That's when he asked how John was getting on with you and if the police in Inverness were any closer to finding the killer.'

'God, men are such fools! What else?'

'It would seem that at the car, when I was out of earshot, Jim even told John that he though the killer might be a medic. Talk about arrogance! John told me about that later. I think he thinks that too. I'm pretty sure that he does not suspect Jim Ledbetter, though.'

'Well, said Elspeth, the sooner we disabuse your lovely husband of that the better, eh Poppy?'

At this point a rather sleepy John appeared in his dressing gown at the kitchen door. He looked rather the worse for wear, having drunk too much fine wine the previous evening.

'Who's that, darling?'

'Its Elspeth.'

'Elspeth? What, our Elspeth?'

'Yes. She would like a word with you.'

17
Monday, 7th May

They met, by arrangement, in Edinburgh. For security reasons, Elspeth had chosen a rather discrete wine bar near the Grass Market in Edinburgh - and partly because she liked their choice of Tuscan wines, particularly their Chianti Colline Pisane, for which she had always been partial.

'More wine, John?'

John placed his hand over the top of his glass and shook his head. He was, it would seem, in an extremely foul mood.

'Elspeth, why did you not let me in on your plan? Its one thing to have your suspicions but quite another to treat the Investigating Officer as if he were some kind of idiot, not to be trusted!'

'Because, dear heart, you might have given the game away completely. It was vital that you acted normally. If you had known that I suspected Jim Ledbetter then it was likely that Ledbetter would have picked up on your inner anxiety or body language. It was essential that he believed *you* of all people had no idea, as yet, that he was the serial-killer.'

'Yes, well - I am not at all happy at the way you have gone about this. Besides, what have you proved with your little experiment? That the Consultant Pathologist assigned to this case is interested in knowing if we have made any progress? Hardly incriminating, I would have thought. And another thing, when exactly was this set up and when did you talk to Poppy?'

'When you told me that Jim and his wife had invited themselves to supper I though it too good an opportunity to miss. I immediately rang Poppy, told her of my suspicions, and asked if she would help. She agreed at once. I had some concern about allowing a suspected killer into your home but Poppy dismissed my fears. 'He's not going to kill John or me', she said. 'He needs us too much to do that'. Brave girl! I'm not sure, John White, that you deserve such a talented wife.'

'Perhaps not. It was a clever plan, Elspeth but I'm still not sure what you have actually achieved. It is one thing to have your suspicions 'confirmed' (I use the word advisedly) but quite another to *prove* that Dr. James Ledbetter, eminent Consultant Pathologist, is our killer. What possible *proof* do you have? Where is your evidence, for God's sake? Or is this merely Profiler's intuition? I am afraid that even your celebrated intuition will not stand up in Court without concrete evidence to support it?'

'I agree. We are not there yet by a long chalk but it's a start.'

She took another sip of her wine and smiled sweetly at John across the table. He looked as if he had just won and lost the pools.

'I must say, Elspeth, that I find it very hard to accept any of this. I have known Jim Ledbetter for years. He does not strike me as a psychopath. In fact, he has a long and distinguished record as a doctor and pathologist. What makes you think him remotely capable of murder, Elspeth?'

'John, if I am right then we are dealing with a very clever man. Ledbetter is extremely clever. I have studied his record.'

'What? You have studied his record? When? How long have you suspected him, Elspeth? Tell me, for God's sake.'

'Since the very beginning.'

'Since the beginning? What do you mean, since the beginning?'

'Well, I said the first time you and I met that you should be looking within the medical profession. Not butchers. Not chefs with big knives. Doctors. Surgeons. Men with *little* knives. Ledbetter fitted the bill from the moment he entered the case. Let's start with his surgical skills. A man like that can amputate an arm in two minutes flat. He also knows the region like the back of his hand, can sail a boat in a storm at night and has climbed more Munros than you and I have even heard of. If he *is* our man then he has run rings around an entire police force since day one and now I suspect, after supper at Mario's, he thinks he can walk on water. However, such arrogance - typical, I might add, of hugely successful killers - may well turn out to be his Achilles heel. Let's hope so. When are we going to tell the boss?'

'I don't know. Not yet, even assuming for one moment you are right. No, not yet. Not immediately, anyway. I need to think about this, Elspeth. We need absolute proof to nail this one. Its one thing to have your suspicions but quite another to prove Ledbetter's guilt. It would be fatal if one of my team inadvertently said or did something to alert Ledbetter that we might be on to him. He's one of us and those upstairs at Police HQ in Inverness, let alone Aberdeen, will not take kindly to wild accusations levelled at their own Consultant Pathologist.'

'Agreed.'

'So, let's take this one step at a time. Let's.....'

'What about his wife, John? Do you think Fiona knows?'

'I doubt it. You can tell from her body language when she's with him in company that he is the dominant partner. If he can fool most of us he can certainly fool her, assuming of course that you are right about Ledbetter. My God, Elspeth! To think that I have been a friend of Jim Ledbetter all these years. Why, we have even sailed together. To believe, as you clearly do, that he has murdered four people in cold blood is too much to take in. No, I will need a lot more convincing than a chance remark or two over supper.'

'OK. Let's take a look at his toxicology report on Alison Rutherford. Its one thing to ensure that a crime scene is clean of anything that might incriminate a murderer but more difficult to conceal drugs within someone's blood stream or urine. Anyone with even a basic knowledge of forensic science can take precautions and clean up after a murder or some other atrocity. If your criminal is one of the best forensic scientists in the country then you have no chance. That's why Forensic have failed to come up with anything, anything at all at any of the crime-scenes in this case. That in itself should give us pause for thought.'

'Yes, but....'

'However, the one thing even a bent pathologist cannot conceal is the presence in a body of drugs. At the SPSA Forensic Science laboratory their toxicologist found traces of Lorazepam in Alison's body, suggesting that at some point she may have been heavily sedated - probably at the time they carried her on to McPherson's boat. But what Ledbetter did in *his* report was cast doubts on that finding. 'The margin of error', he said, 'was too great to be decisive'. In other words, he was trying to dismiss or at least diminish the toxicologist's report within his own, definitive overall report - the one he submitted to the police and the one you and I have read. The moment I spotted that I knew James Ledbetter could be a prime suspect.'

* * *

Driving back to Portree that Monday afternoon, Detective Inspector White considered the enormity of Elspeth's deductions.

There was, he thought, a good chance that her suspicions were correct for it had been pretty obvious to both of them - not-with-standing the false starts involving Portree's young butcher and the pub's errant chef - that someone with surgical skills was involved. The manner in which both women had been mutilated was a clear indication of that. Consultant Pathologist Jim Ledbetter fitted the bill in that regard, at least, for he was recognised as a very skilled surgeon.

Did that make him a torturer and mutilator of young women? Surely not. That was a step too far!

He also fitted the bill with regard to local knowledge and sailing skills. John knew from direct experience how well he could handle a boat in rough seas and that he had the requisite navigational skills and qualifications. He was also quite capable of crossing the Coullins at night and climbing out onto the narrow ledge beneath the clock of the kirk in Portree. John had himself tried this manoeuvre and had found it extremely tricky but anyone with Ledbetter's mountaineering experience would have found it easy. But again, there were hundreds of men on and around Skye capable of such climbing feats.

Then there was the matter of the missing boat and how Alison Rutherford had got on to it during the storm.

When they found Neil's boat with the murdered lad tied to the skipper's chair it proved, if nothing else, that White's theory as to how Alison was got to the lighthouse was also probably true. Namely, that Alison had been drugged and carried onto the boat under cover of night and in the middle of a violent storm when most people were tucked up in their beds.

The mooring lines that McPherson had found also suggested that they had been deliberately cut, thereby allowing three boats (including Neil's) to drift out into the Sound of Raasay. The problem, though, was that Ledbetter had said in his final report to the SPSA in Inverness that the toxicology findings were 'inconclusive' and, at best, 'misleading'. This was the view that, given Ledbetter's professional expertise, the police had wholeheartedly accepted.

Perhaps that had been a mistake.

If there was no convincing evidence that a drug like Lorazepam had been used to sedate Alison then either the murderer had used some other method to get her on board the stolen boat or there was something seriously wrong with the toxicology report.

Perhaps Detective Chief Inspector Elliott could instigate a second toxicology examination of the woman's body fluids? It would have to be done discretely, mind you. If Ledbetter found out he would know that the police were on to him. On the other hand, if a new test revealed the presence of some drug in Alison's body fluids then that could only mean one thing - that the original report that Jim Ledbetter had put his name to was fraudulent or at best deliberately 'misleading'.

That kind of evidence might not convict him of multiple murder but it would suggest that they were on the right track.

Of course, any errors regarding the presence of drugs in Alison's body fluids could have been incompetence on Ledbetter's part. However, John White knew his old friend well enough to know that a control freak like him did not make those kind of mistakes. If anything, Ledbetter was overly scrupulous. If, therefore, the police could *prove* that their Consultant Pathologist had deliberately misled them, then that would be grounds for arresting him and subjecting him to extensive questioning.

Moreover, it was evident, from the conversation in Mario's, that Ledbetter had only wanted to know if Elspeth had anything on him that might expose him. That was his only concern. Since he was possibly responsible for the crimes, he had little need to ask the Investigating Officer himself what progress they had made. No, it was Elspeth Grant he feared. If he knew that *she* was off course, then he was safe. If he knew that he had fooled even her then his self-confidence in his own ability to fool the police was thoroughly reaffirmed. Elspeth had anticipated this brilliantly. Ledbetter's desperate need to know that even the celebrated Dr. Elspeth Grant PhD - with a conviction record as long as her arm - was off track clearly met some kind of inner need.

Elspeth had predicted that too.

Dr. James Ledbetter, prime suspect in the brutal murder and mutilation of at least four people, had therefore walked straight into her trap. That much, at least, was now clear to Detective Inspector John White as he drove to Portree that Monday afternoon.

18
Tuesday, 8th May

The minister of the Kirk in Portree had by now been questioned extensively regarding the break-in and the discovery of Georgina's arm wired to his church clock. On the three occasions that he had been interrogated by the police he had appeared flustered.

No one who knew the man, however, was surprised. The Reverend Cedric McNish was, according to Sergeant McGreggor, a 'garrulous old fool' - and so, unfortunately, he had proved to be.

When John White himself eventually cross-examined him he noticed that the man kept forgetting significant details given to the police in earlier statements. He also kept changing his mind about how he thought someone might have entered his Kirk, ascended the bell tower and edged their way round to the clock face before wiring some poor woman's am to his clock.

One significant new detail did emerge, however.

The Parish Council had met that Friday (27th April) evening in the church. They were there to discuss the possibility of funding some restoration work to the base of the tower. This the police knew about. They had even interviewed some of the Parish Councillors by way of confirmation and to find out who had been there that evening. Jim Ledbetter again fitted the frame. He had been on the Parish Council for several years when he and Fiona had lived in Portree.

Although they now lived and worked in Aberdeen, Ledbetter had retained an active interest in the fundraising work of the Portree Parish Council.

Jim Ledbetter was certainly there that night. Could this, mused White, be his first serious mistake? Was this the breakthrough they, the police, had been looking for?

John White and the police in Portree had always assumed that

Nish had been an integral part of that meeting. However, what he was now saying was that he had sat in on the meeting for half-an-hour or so and had then 'left them to their own devices'. Later, when they had gone, Nish returned, turned off the lights and locked up. This meant that someone could easily have stayed behind and then hidden themselves somewhere within the kirk.

Rather than look for signs of a break-in, the police needed to look for evidence of a break out!

Then there was the matter of the clock itself.

It had always been notoriously unreliable, frequently stopping for no apparent reason. Most folk in Portree, knowing of the clock's erratic behaviour, seldom bothered therefore to look up to consult it. This was only speculation, of course, but it may explain why no one was seen on that church tower that night. However, it was obvious that - for the killer's little set-piece to work - the clock hands would have to be deliberately stopped from moving. This the Forensic examiners had discovered had been achieved by the simple expedient of stuffing a rolled-up magazine into the clock's movement, thereby stopping it all together.

The killer must have done that at exactly three-thirty in the morning. It was then that he climbed out onto the outer ledge and audaciously wired Georgina's arm to the clock face.

The magazine itself proved to be nothing one might normally find in a Kirk but a sex-magazine called *Buck*. The police had assumed that this was another sick joke on the part of the killer. Later, having dismissed the Reverend Nish as a garrulous old fool, Detective Inspector White reopened the files and had another, closer look at that magazine.

It was dated 5th January, 2011. This would appear to have been the last edition because, according to Wikipedia, *Buck* ceased publication in the UK after that date. It was, in other words, a *special* edition. Had the murderer therefore chosen it deliberately? The answer was 'yes'.

When John looked inside he saw why.

Amongst the women strutting their stuff in that magazine was a young girl whom White vaguely recognised. It took a moment or two for the penny to drop. The young girl showing off her curvaceous figure - and a lot more besides - was none other than that of the woman purporting to be 'the author' on the back cover of novels written by Sarah Daniels.

Wednesday, 9th May

Detective Inspector White was summoned into DCI Elliott's office early the next morning. The drive from Portree to Inverness took ninety minutes. He reached Police HQ at about ten-thirty.

Detective Chief Inspector Paul Elliott had in front of him an email.

'I gather from this lengthy email that you sent me last night that Consultant Pathologist James Ledbetter is now your prime suspect? I hope, Detective Inspector, that you have the evidence to make *that* stick!'

'Well, not exactly. He fits Elspeth's profile in many significant aspects but as yet we have nothing to pin him directly to any of the murders. The best we can do so far is place him in the Kirk in Portree the evening before Miss Cousins' arm turned up, wired to the church clock.'

'Indeed, but that could equally apply to any of the other nine people present at that meeting. What also troubles me is that it is going to prove very difficult indeed to accuse Dr. Ledbetter of falsifying the toxicology report on Alison Rutherford. The traces of Lorazepam found by Dr. Netherson when he had a discrete, second look at Rutherford's blood and urine late last night - at my request - were themselves 'marginal'. Its not unusual for results to be marginal. Jim could argue, convincingly, that he might just have missed something. Nothing criminal in that.'

'Indeed, sir. The suit found on 'Gibbons' is also marginal. Its certainly the right size for Ledbetter, as far as we can ascertain at this stage without actually measuring him, but again there is no DNA evidence. Jim did not himself first examine that suit so we cannot accuse him of tampering with it in any way. He does, however have some links with Florida. He and his wife have been there several times on holiday but then anyone can order a 'Three-Thirty' suit online. So far we have been unable to trace recent online purchases in the Aberdeen area for a suit such as this one. However, the 'three-thirty' coincidence does seem too remarkable to ignore but that alone does not link it to Jim Ledbetter.'

'I agree. There's another problem with that suit. We only have McClure's word that 'Charley Gibbons' or whatever he called himself was not wearing it on the day he met his death. Mr McClure is not the most reliable of witnesses, considering that he has already been charged with conspiracy to rob and is currently under investigation for possible murder. No, the suit is not going to take us very far. What also worries me is the lack of sightings. No only has no one anywhere seen a man fitting Murdo's description but not one single person has reported anything suspicious at any of the locations where this killer is thought to have been. That in itself is very unusual - unless he is being protected, as detective Sergeant Watson suggested the other day.'

'I agree, sir. On the other hand, in a city like Inverness its very easy to be anonymous - we are all strangers here. In a small community like Portree, however, the people there *only* notice strangers. If Jim Ledbetter was a familiar figure in Portree once it is unlikely that he would attract much attention today. He would be able to move remarkably freely.'

'By the way, are you sure that your friend is capable of sailing a fishing boat at night in the seas off Skye? Pretty dangerous area, or so I am told.'

'Yes, absolutely. He is an experienced sailor and has the relevant qualifications. When he lived in Portree he owned a thirty-foot *Oceanus*. He sold it when he moved to Aberdeen but he surely knows how to handle a boat. Neil McPherson's fishing boat has quite sophisticated navigational equipment. Jim knows all about that stuff too. He knows both the Inner and Outer Hebrides well. Indeed, I myself have sailed with him in those waters. If that were not enough, he was in his youth a rock-climber. Scaling a sea-cliff at night, then making your way across the Coullins would not be at all difficult for him.'

'Well, that certainly fits the profile of the man you have been searching for but then it could equally apply to hundreds of men living on Skye and beyond. Jim Ledbetter is not the only rock-climbing yachtsman in our region. Neither is he the only surgeon or doctor in the region with the skills required to amputate some poor woman's arm.'

'Indeed, sir. We need to link him definitively with the two murdered women. If we can do that then we have the makings of a case against him. So far we have not managed to make that link.'

'Precisely, Detective Inspector. That is what troubles me.'

Both men paused for a moment, lost in thought. Inspector White reluctantly picked up the thread.

'What is clear is that someone had access to both cottages. I think he took Alison from her own cottage and dragged her, probably sedated, onto McPherson's boat at the height of the storm. It is also pretty clear that whoever tampered with the women's computers was the same person. The 'style' of that interference is too similar to be mere coincidence. That also means that he had access to Georgina's laptop *before* he murdered her. That, for me at least, is very significant although I cannot as yet say how it was achieved. What has also become a characteristic of this killer is the thoroughness in the way he covers his tracks. Ironically, that in itself is helping us as there is a consistency now that we can look for. He may, in short, be too meticulous.'

'Interesting theory, Detective Inspector. What is your next move?'

'We will concentrate on trying to establish links between James Ledbetter and the two murdered women.'

'Very well. I will dig a little into Ledbetter's history and background. I can always authorise some kind of staff review - God knows those upstairs are always looking for cuts! That way it will not seem that we are merely targeting our - or should I say, John - *your* prime suspect?'

'Thank you, sir. By the way, we might have one possible breakthrough in that regard. The photograph of the woman Georgina used to represent her on the back of her books turns out to be a certain Caroline Wear. We checked our records on the off-chance that she was known to us. Not only did she turn out to be a prostitute who worked Edinburgh's Salamander Street but it was there, sometime in 2010, that she was knifed to death.'

'Interesting. Very well, Detective Inspector. I will accept that Ledbetter is a credible suspect but I warn you to tread with extreme caution. Keep this to yourself for a few more days. I will make some discrete enquiries into Ledbetter's background and movements and get back to you. I do not want him to have even the slightest suspicion that we consider him a suspect. That means that you should probably not tell your team anything until I give the go-ahead. Keep it between you and Elspeth. That's an order. Meanwhile, the sooner you can establish even the slightest link between Ledbetter and those poor women, the better - for all our sakes. Good morning.'

* * *

It was Detective Sergeant Tom Watson who had discovered the identity of the young woman used on the back cover of books written by 'Sara Daniels'. He had managed to track down her photographer in London.

He interviewed him by phone.

The man could only remember that particular girl from the hundreds he had photographed over the years because, after she was stabbed to death in the street where she worked, he was questioned by the police. For a while he might even have been their prime suspect - until a witness in Edinburgh claimed that she had been attacked by a gang of youths. However, because of that police enquiry, her name was indelibly printed on his memory.

Caroline Wear.

They had first met in a club in Edinburgh where she worked as a lap-dancer when not working the streets of Edinburgh. He was always on the look-out for young women with a good body and some personality and had come north for that purpose. Caroline had both. In fact, she was rather striking and very unlike many of the women he had used in magazines in the past. This one had a certain charisma, which was unusual among girls who posed nude in the kind of magazines photographers like him serviced. Moreover, she had clearly been educated. She spoke well and seemed widely read, despite the somewhat sordid life she now led.

She first posed for him sometime in 2009. Thereafter, he photographed her several times, usually working out of a rented studio in the Cowgate area of Edinburgh. The third and final session was at his studio, off London's Portobello Road in June, 2010. When he made a pass at her she rebuffed him with a force that had, at the time, alarmed him. He suspected that she had what he called 'problems'.

She was, he had concluded, a 'fucking lezzy' and thereafter had nothing more to do with her. Three weeks later she was dead.

Why she had died and who had killed her remained a mystery, largely because the Edinburgh police never caught any of the young lads who were thought to have attacked her so brutally. Many assumed that it might be some kind of gang killing. Others put it down to the violence of the times.

How she came to appear on the back of books by Georgina Cousins was yet another mystery.

The photographer could shed no light on that subject either. He had never heard of 'Sarah Daniels' and had no idea if Caroline had known either Alison Rutherford or Georgina Cousins. The photograph itself had been destined for a magazine but was deemed unsuitable - probably because the woman was fully-clothed. He could not recall giving it to anyone other than Caroline. She had said she liked it and he had simply handed her a copy. He still had the negative somewhere. He admitted that he was never sufficiently interested in the girl to bother asking about her life, her family or her friends - if she had any.

He found her 'in-yer-face' feminism a turn-off. If she was a lesbian - he added - then let her stick with her own kind, 'the perverse little cow'.

Tom, however, was determined to find out more. Some instinct told him that Caroline Wear might be the key to the spate of murders he and his colleagues had been investigating for the last few weeks. He was not sure why he should feel this but even young policemen have instincts and sometimes it is best to 'go with your gut', as he put it.

Mind you, it took a while to convince his boss that Caroline Wear was that relevant to the case.

John White had acknowledged that discovering her identity was significant but no one was really sure where it might take the investigation. Tom pointed out that Caroline Cousins had left London and moved to Portree the same year in which Caroline died. Was that coincidence or was there a connection that might explain Caroline's subsequent choice of image for the books? DI White was sceptical. It could have been, he argued, an entirely arbitrary choice on Caroline's part, even perhaps selecting that particular photograph from some agency's files. If there was a link, then it was somewhat tenuous. But then....?

Tom won the day.

With Detective Chief Inspector Paul Elliott's formal approval, Detective Sergeant Tom Watson was given the go-ahead -

provided he liaised throughout his investigation with the Metropolitan Police.

Soon after his 'go-ahead', Tom established contact with someone in the Met's Clubs and Vice Unit willing to guide him through the secretive, arcane labyrinth that is lesbian London.

It was known that Caroline Cousins had lived and worked in London until 2010, before moving to Portree. If, as Tom suspected, she had been part of London's lesbian community at that time, then that was the most likely way in which she could perhaps have met Caroline Wear who had, from time to time, stayed in London. It was still only speculation of course but Tom was convinced that Caroline's sexuality and her possible interest in the violent abuse of women as a sexual 'turn on' lay at the heart of this case. If he could establish that then it might just lead them to the murderer.

Tom, like the rest of the team working on the investigation in Portree, did not yet know that Dr. Jim Ledbetter was now their prime suspect. If everyone knew then there was a good chance that Ledbetter himself would soon discover that he was being targeted. That could be fatal, in every sense. Tom, like the others, would be told in good time. That was still John White's plan, such as it was.

Thus it was that DS Tom Watson set off for London to find out as much as he could about the mysterious Caroline Wear, alleged 'author' - or so millions of readers had always assumed - of hugely popular books by Sarah Daniels, late of this parish.

19
Thursday, 10th May

While Detective Inspector John White and 'Profiler Extraordinaire' Elspeth Grant had got on fairly well - even from the start of their professional relationship - it occurred to John that he knew very little about his distinguished colleague. It was, therefore, with some curiosity that he accepted her invitation to visit her one day at her apartment in Edinburgh. The date was Thursday, 10th May - nearly three weeks since they had first met in Portree.

It was Paul Elliott who had recommended her in the first place, although it was John who had made the initial request for a Profiler. It seems that Elliott had worked with Elspeth on a case in Birmingham in which her inspired analysis of the man they were hunting proved a turning point in what had, until then, become an intractable case. John hoped that her deductive skills would help solve his case with equal success. So far, so good. They had Ledbetter firmly in the frame. All they needed now was proof - something even brilliant Profilers are not really required to provide.

Their job is merely to point the police in the right direction. Was Ledbetter the right direction? That still remained to be seen. Moreover, John was still finding it hard to come to terms with the fact that one of his oldest friends was a serial killer. Their respective families had been close for years. Elspeth's 'intuition' may prove right in the end but it was a difficult for those who knew Ledbetter well - like he and Poppy - to readily accept that their charming, urbane friend was, after all, a dangerous psychopath!

Elspeth apparently lived with her elderly mother in Moray Place - a very smart part of 18th Century Edinburgh. While she was well paid as a Consultant Psychologist, Criminologist and Oxford Lecturer John suspected that she had a private income. When he saw how sumptuous her enormous apartment was he was absolutely sure of it.

She met him at the door with open arms and a big smile on her face. Her tiled hallway with its impressive brass chandelier was almost as big as John's sitting room back in Dunkeld.

'John, dear heart! Welcome to my humble abode!'

She was dressed in a long, Persian caftan with baggy Turkish 'harem' trousers underneath. Her hair, which she usually wore in a tight bun when at work, was long and flowing, almost reaching the small of her back. Her feet were bare, each toenail painted a lurid fuchsia. She wore on her fingers more rings than John could ever remember seeing her wear before. What he was seeing today was an Elspeth that he had never imagined existed. She was more like Dame Edith Sitwell than Dr. Elspeth Grant, PhD and bar.

It was quite exciting! If only Poppy were here to share the fun.

She led John into her sitting room. The room itself was enormous but was filled with Turkish and Moroccan furniture, rich wall-hangings, ornate carpets and pendant lamps of an exotic design. John felt that he had been transported - lock, stock and barrel - to the heart of Marrakech.

'Wine or whiskey? I have copious amounts of both.'

'Wine please. Do you have red?'

'My dear John, I have forty-three shades of red and about as many of white, some quite rare. My father, bless him, was rich as Croesus. When he popped his clogs I inherited the larger part of his cellar. I bought this flat largely because it had a cellar big enough to accommodate all his wine and, I might add, that priceless carpet you are currently standing on.'

John looked down. He was indeed standing on a thick Persian carpet with a pattern that was full of intensely dark reds and blues. It looked like it must be worth thousands.

'I bought that carpet from a brilliant economist called Ephraim

Shah. In 1998 he was simultaneously offered a Professorship at both Wadham College, Oxford and Trinity College, Cambridge. He chose Wadham - only because it had a room big enough to house his beloved carpet. When he fell from grace in Oxford - don't ask me, it's a complicated story - I bought his carpet. Do please sit down and I will organise the drinky-poos.'

John did as he was told and selected a large, wicker chair. He had only once seen a chair like this and that had a scantily dressed Sylvia Kristel sat on it. The film was called *Emanuelle*.

That thought alone made John White feel quite warm inside.

It was widely known within the Edinburgh police force and beyond that Dr Elspeth Grant was unmarried and lived with her mother, when not away on some investigation. True, few if any had ever met Mother but everyone assumed that she was quite elderly, if not chair-bound. Many times Elspeth had to interrupt her work on a case and rush back to attend to her ailing mother.

Her mother's dependence on her brilliant daughter was something of a joke within the police force but Elspeth Grant was such an outstanding Profiler that no one ever really complained. Elspeth returned, holding the door open for someone apparently following her into the room.

'John, I would like you to meet my 'Mother'.'

At that point a tall, thin, extremely elegant young man entered, carrying a tray on which there were two glasses and a bottle of red wine. He was incredibly handsome and very black.

He placed the tray on a low, Moroccan table in the centre of the room, crossed to where John was sitting, bowed courteously and shook John's hand but said nothing. The young man then turned on his heels and left the room, gently closing the sitting-room door behind him.

'I know what you are going to say, John. He's far too young for me. I know! I know! I agonise over it constantly. Anyway, it does not seem to worry *him* so why should I blow against the wind?'

* * *

Detective Sergeant Tom Watson checked into The Fielding, his London hotel just off Bow Street. He then unpacked and lay down on the bed.

He had had a first, brief meeting with his colleague from the Metropolitan Police earlier that afternoon - on his way from Euston Station to his hotel.

The Met. had assigned to him a Detective Sergeant who had been with the Vice Squad of old and had survived the many changes since, following accusations of corruption and God knows what else in the unit's ranks.

His name was Mike Baker.

Mike had arranged to pick Tom up at his hotel later that night and show him some of the seamier parts of London. Since this was only the second time that Tom had actually been to London, he was both anxious and - dare he admit it - somewhat excited at the prospect of entering such an unfamiliar world.

Tom had told Baker what they were looking to establish, not least a lesbian network that thrived on sexual violence to women - something which Baker immediately acknowledged narrowed their search. Clubs that provided a focus for such activities were rare. That should make it easier to target such places. Of course, Georgina Cousins had left London some years before. The networks that existed then had probably gone but the online activity of both Cousins and Rutherford were current at the time of their deaths.

What Tom needed was to find was someone willing to provide him with the necessary contacts to enter such a secretive world.

It would not be easy.

Perhaps, he mused, they should have assigned a woman to this task? That might have made access easier. On the other hand, it was not the women themselves who were being targeted, but those who created these online sites. They could be anywhere and were probably not women anyway.

Mike Baker arrived promptly at midnight, finding Tom waiting nervously in the entrance to his Bow Street hotel.

* * *

Elspeth, lounging on her Moroccan sofa, was in expansive mood. She had drunk rather a lot of fine red wine and was now occasionally slurring her words. Mind you, Inspector John White was nor far behind her.

He had become both garrulous and sentimental, in equal measure.

'Fret not, my precious little Plod! Ledbetter is too fucking arrogant to spot that you are on his sordid, psychotic tail. Its ME he fears. The more you can let slip that I am a waste of space (not true, of course, darling, as you well know!) the better! He needs to believe that I, of all people, have lost the plot. A difficult notion I grant you, considering my record, but there you go!'

'I could always sack you.'

'Brilliant! Best idea you have had all evening. Sadly, it wont' be the first time that I have been sacked. Now, what shall I do to warrant such a dastardly action on your part? Trash the Portree Community Centre? Nick your petty cash. Ah! Got it! I could seduce that rather dishy WPC Stephens who works for you. The one with the very tight arse and wide, blue eyes. Would that be sufficient cause for you to sack me?'

'Be my guest but what do I tell her poor mother? Charlotte Stephens is a very proper young lady, or so I am told. No, I suggest we have a public quarrel - in the pub in Portree, for example - in which you disagree, *loudly*, with my approach to this case. Not difficult for you, I know, but sadly credible, never-the-less.'

John paused briefly to pour himself another glass of wine. The bottle was now nearly empty. John noticed that his hand was a little unsteady as he reached across to fill Elspeth's glass.

'The next day' he continued, 'I will let it be known that you are officially off the case. That should throw Ledbetter off the scent. We would have to communicate privately, thereafter. Mind you, 'Mother' would like that - you stuck at home here, secretly solving my case for me and unable to move your learned but shapely bottom from off that sofa.'

'Inspector White, you wicked old thing! I really think that you are finally getting the hang of this dangerous game of ours. As to the sofa bit, I'll drink to that!'

Elspeth staggered to her feet and with a flourish and addressed the door of her sitting room. She was now swaying slightly and making extravagant gestures with her free hand.

'Mother!' she shouted, 'please bring us another bottle of Merlot, my darling!'

She turned back into the room with a flourish, twirling unsteadily and dropped onto a large pile of cushions at the foot of John's wicker chair.

'Now, dear heart. I would like to tell you all about another fiendish little plot that I am hatching. A plot designed to catch a certain screwed up, extremely dangerous and hugely arrogant serial-killer.'

'Plot? What kind of plot, Elspeth?'

'Are you sitting comfortably? Good. Then I will begin?'

20
The Secrets of Soho

It would be fair to say that young Detective Sergeant Tom Watson was shocked by what he saw that Thursday night in London's Soho.

True, Mike Baker rather over-egged the pudding by taking young Tom to some of the roughest clubs in town, painting a lurid picture *en route* of the wicked underbelly of London's gay scene.

He soon realised that his young colleague from Scotland was somewhat innocent and unworldly - who wouldn't be if you had spent the first nineteen years of your life in Wick? It was true that Tom had attended The Scottish Police College at Tulliallan Castle in Kincardine-on-Forth but throughout his training he had lodged with his Presbyterian sister in Stirling. No late-night clubbing in Edinburgh or Glasgow for her wee young brother!

Since then, as he rapidly rose in rank from Constable to Sergeant with the regular constabulary in Mallaig, he had led a blameless and rather dull life. He may be good looking and fit as a butcher's dog but Tom Watson was also rather shy. He certainly liked women and most of the young girls of Mallaig adored him but a regular girl friend? Nope! As for biker leathers, tattoos, body piercing and sado-masochistic paraphernalia in gloomy cellar bars with even seedier rooms 'at the back' - well, they were certainly *not* part of Tom Watson's quintessentially nice Scottish upbringing.

Despite his surprise at some of the more outrageous people and places he saw that night, Tom had to admit, however, to a certain enjoyment in seeing, for the first time, how the more extreme members of the gay community of London conducted themselves. Life with his sister in Stirling had not prepared him for much that he encountered that night, not least having his bottom pinched in The Friendly Society on Wardour Street by a young man dressed remarkably like Lady Gaga, but more butch.

He suspected Mike Baker had set this up but he took it in good spirit.

The problem was that DS Baker was a well-known figure in this part of London. He had been with the Vice Squad, as it was once known, for many years so that the club owners had a certain respect for both him as a person and for his role policing their world. Sometimes they needed police intervention, particularly when fights broke out among their more violent clientele. By and large they preferred to help the police whenever they could, rather than hinder their investigations.

Mike, for his part, was always discreet when approaching a club, particularly if it was for women only - such as the Candy Bar or Drill Hall. Here he would use the back door, remain 'back-stage' as it were or use his extensive list of doormen and bouncers to obtain the information he was seeking. It was one such bouncer at the Candy Club that put him on to Kitty, better known in the gay community she frequented as 'Kitty Cat'. She turned out to be a slim, strikingly beautiful brunette with pale skin, heavy makeup and studs through both cheeks. She wore a short leather skirt, ragged tights and denim top - and not much else.

They met, not in her club full of women similarly dressed, but in a little café round the corner. After the gloomy interior of the Candy Club, the workmen's café with its stark neon lights and shiny plastic tablecloths was very bright. Still, thought Tom, Kitty Cat would look good in any light.

'Well, Mike! Where did you find this gorgeous young man? Not my type, of course but my brother might fancy him!'

'Hands off, Kitty! He's here on business. Police business. He's looking for anyone who might have heard of Georgina Cousins, Alison Rutherford or Caroline Wear. They were all living in London until 2010. The first two were almost certainly gay and both probably into S&M. Caroline was a prostitute who was killed in Edinburgh but may have been here in London at the same time as the other two. Any ideas who might know?'

'SM is not my scene but I know someone who was well into all that stuff. She once tried to strangle me, until I kicked her in the crutch. I swear she had balls! Anyway, we are friends again now but I try never to be left in a room with her by myself, know what I mean?'

She flicked open her iPad and called a number. While the number rang she stared straight at Tom, fluttering her lashes and licking her lips merely to embarrass him. It worked though for Tom coughed, shifted in his seat, broke her gaze and blushed.

Mike simply grinned and discretely kicked Kitty under the table.

'Hello? Is that you, darling? Its Kit Kat. No, I do not want you to tie me to your bed, you outrageous old Queen! Listen, do us a favour. I have a very dishy young plod here who wants to know if you have ever heard of Georgina Cousins, Alison Rutherford or Caroline Wear?. All three left London about 2010. Loved the stuff you are into, know what I mean?'

She looked up at Tom and gave him a cheeky wink. Tom actually blushed.

'Anyways, young Plod here with the glossy black hair and strange accent would very much like to meet all three of them for a little SM orgy. Is that something you could arrange, you extremely wicked old Masochist?'

* * *

It was Friday morning when Detective Inspector White gathered his team in the Portree Community Hall for a special briefing.

He appeared in sombre mood.

The 'Gang of Five' (minus Tom Watson) settled in their seats and waited expectantly.

'Dr. Grant and I have come to the conclusion that our prime suspect is Consultant Pathologist Dr. James Ledbetter of

Aberdeen's Royal Infirmary and the SPSA Forensic Science Laboratory.'

A gasp of astonishment ran round the room.

'We have had this suspicion for a few days now. I have not told you before today because secrecy was, still is, of the utmost importance and because for a few days more, at least, I wanted you all to retain an open mind on this case. Now, however, we are entering a particularly dangerous part of the investigation and it is only right that you should know who we are up against. Detective Sergeant Watson, who is currently in London, will be told later today - that is if he survives a night on the town in London's Soho!'

This remark prompted a round of laughter - although it was noted by some that Janice did not join in.

For the next thirty minutes or so John White told his team everything he knew about Jim Ledbetter and why he and Elspeth considered him their prime suspect. He concluded with a grim warning.

'It is absolutely essential that Dr. Ledbetter knows nothing of our suspicions. If he were to find out then, God knows what he might do! He is very clever, extremely dangerous and if he feels cornered, then capable of anything. For the time being we must keep our suspicions to ourselves until we have sufficient evidence to arrest him.'

Here John paused for a moment and gazed round the room intently at his team of young, relatively inexperienced officers.

'I beg you all to proceed with the utmost secrecy and with extreme caution. If Ledbetter knows that we are on to him then he might well take violent measures against anyone in this community - and that includes us.'

* * *

White had received a phone call earlier that morning from DCI Elliott giving him permission to tell the 'Gang of Five'. It was now necessary for John White to inform Sergeant McGregor and the local Constabulary.

'Fancy a breath of fresh air, George?'

They left McGregor's tiny police station and headed for the harbour. Once there, both men - as was their habit - leant on the harbour rail and stared into the murky waters of the dock. Both lit their pipes in silence.

'Albert, our prime suspect now is a Consultant Pathologist called James Ledbetter. You probably know him. He lived here for a number of years and was on the Parish Council. We have reason to believe he is our murderer. My lot know but its still pretty hush-hush. I am telling you because the information your Debbie has given us is the only description we have of the alleged murderer.'

'How does it compare?'

'Stature - height, build etc, is OK but everything else does not fit, especially the dark beard.'

'Could easily be a false one, John.'

'Sure, but the Scott's accent and tan does not fit Jim Ledbetter either. He is fairly pale and very English. No doubt it is possible to pretend to be Scots - or from Nelson for that matter - but would it fool a real Scot like Murdo MacColl?'

'I doubt it, Inspector. Murdo is no fool, even if he was drunk at the time - which is likely, knowing his record.'

'Really?'

'I have only met the man a couple of times here on Skye. On both occasions he was drunk and disorderly. Besides, why should he have cared who that 'fisherman' really was, as long as he could sell him two jerry cans of fuel at double the going price?'

'Do we know how much he was paid?'

'No but I am pretty sure we can get Debbie to persuade him to tell us. She knows his family. If she threatens to tell them what he *really* gets up to in Glasgow - and it has nothing to do with buying fishing tackle - then I am sure he will spill the beans. If it turns out that he got at least *twice* the real price for diesel fuel then I think we can say with some certainty that the man on that boat was neither a local nor indeed a Scottish fisherman.'

It was some hours later, as Albert was puffing his second pipe that day, that the penny suddenly dropped.

Green anorak over a roll-neck sweater and dark blue jeans!

That, exactly, was what George McClure had said 'Gibbons' was wearing when he took him to the lighthouse that fatal day. The man on Neil's boat that went to Soay to buy fuel for his boat was dressed *exactly* like that. He had, in short, been wearing Trevor Burns' clothes!

21
Friday, 11th May

Tom Watson, accompanied still by Detective Sergeant Mike Baker, emerged from the lurid labyrinth of London's Soho into St. Martin's Lane and strolled towards Covent Garden.

It was now dawn. Dark rain clouds hung over London but to the east, across the river, a pink sky was slowly emerging. The air was fresh and sweet after a night spent largely in smoky interiors, dark and sometimes menacing.

They reached Covent Garden and found a small café where they ordered large mugs of strong tea and an enormous egg-and-bacon buttie each. For a while they sat and munched in silence.

* * *

The night had ended rather unexpectedly - not in some sleazy nightclub but in a little apartment off Regent Street. It was very 1950's in décor but on every wall, on every shelf or table top there was the largest collection of Princess Diana memorabilia that Tom Watson had ever seen.

This remarkable collection consisted of commemorative mugs, egg-cups and plates, glossy photographs, posters and prints, statuettes and dolls - including a 'bride' figurine - and countless books, albums and magazines. In pride of place, above an ornate Victorian gas fire, was a framed portrait of Princess Diana in glittering white dress and tiara.

This proved to be the home of the woman who had once been London's Queen of SM. One would have expected some enormous dyke, perhaps, with tattoos and studs but she turned out to be a little old lady who might have been Tom's grandmother from Wick. Indeed, when she shook his hand and invited them both to sit down Tom was in mild shock. This, surely, is not the woman Mike Baker had described as once ruling with an iron fist a world of extreme violence, whips, chains, flagellation, bondage and self-mutilation?

'Tea dear, or would you like a whiskey? I'm drinking whisky. Mike, I know what you like dear, so please make yourselves comfortable and I will fetch us all a 'wee dram'. Is that not what you lads up north call it, Sergeant Watson?'

She tottered out of the room, re-emerging almost immediately with a tray, three glasses and a bottle of Glenmorangie. Mike helped her pour three large slugs of whiskey then all three settled into her comfortable arm chairs. Tom noticed that he was sitting on a cushion with Diana's face embroidered on it. Rather than sit on HRH's face he quickly put it to one side, hoping that their host had not noticed.

'So dear, how can I help you?'

'We are trying to trace three women', said Tom, carefully placing his untouched whisky on a small table at his side.'

'They are Georgina Cousins, sometimes called 'Sarah Daniels', Alison Rutherford and a young prostitute called Caroline Wear. They were all here in London until about 2010. The first two were almost certainly gay and probably into SM. We think, moreover, that they 'got off' on violence done to women by others, rather than inflicting it themselves. Caroline was a prostitute who also got into glamour modelling. She was murdered in 2010 in Edinburgh, possible victim of gang violence. I, we, need to know as much as we can about any of these women and if any of them knew each other or were linked in some way. Can you help, Miss Butterworth?'

Miss Butterworth smiled sweetly and helped herself to another large slug of Whiskey. Tom noticed that she did not offer her guests the bottle this time.

'Well, dear. Let's start with 'Sarah Daniels'. I never heard her called Georgina Cousins but everybody knew our Sarah.'

Tom got out his notebook and pencil began to make notes in

shorthand.

'Sly creature, was our Sarah', continued Miss Butterworth. 'I first met her when she came to my club off Bond Street. Nice figure, almost voluptuous by today's anorexic standards. Very blue eyes, I remember. She had long, blond hair which she wore scraped back from her forehead in a tight ponytail. She was certainly lesbian and into SM but only as a lone *voyeur*. We all knew she wrote books and most of us suspected that she only came to my 'salon' to gather ideas and information. I read one or two of her novels. Trash, if you ask me. Very second hand. She had a vicious streak in her, though. Got quite excited once when one of my girls got injured by some stupid big dyke. Even started taking photographs on the tiny camera she always carried with her. I threw her out when she started doing that. Never came back. Not one of us, really. Something cold and distant about her. Not one of us at all.'

'What about the photograph on the back of her books. This is Caroline Wear pretending to be author 'Sarah Daniels'. Did you ever see them together? Were they an item perhaps?'

Miss Butterworth took out her spectacles from some dark recess deep within her cardigan and gazed at the photograph Tom showed her.

'No, never seen this girl. Is this the one that was murdered in Edinburgh? Poor young thing. Quite pretty really but certainly nothing like Sarah Daniels, or whatever she called herself. No. Can't help you there.'

'OK. That leaves Alison Rutherford. This is her photograph, taken in about 2008. We found it in her cottage in Portree.'

Miss Butterworth stared at the photograph.

'Is she is dead too?', she asked. Her voice was very quiet. Her hand holding the photograph was visibly trembling.

'I'm afraid so. This is a murder enquiry. Both Georgina and Alison have been murdered. Both lived in Portree in Scotland and both died within days of each other. So you see, we need all the help you can give us.'

Miss Butterworth took out a rather grubby handkerchief from another pocket in her cardigan, dabbed her eyes then blew her nose loudly. She then reached for the bottle of Whiskey and poured herself a generous tot. Tom noticed that both her hands were now shaking badly.

'So, Miss Butterworth. Do you recognise Alison? Do you know who she is or anything about her? Have you ever seen her with Sarah, perhaps? Perhaps she visited your salon or was one of your regular clients? Perhaps....'

'This girl's real name is Emma Butterworth. She was my daughter, Sergeant Watson. Emma Butterworth was my only daughter.'

* * *

Back in Portree the team was coming to terms with the news that they were now trying to convict a very senior police pathologist.

Detective Inspector White had asked them all to go back over their notes, witness statements and other data and look for any possible links with Dr. James Ledbetter that they might have missed, not knowing at the time that he was a suspect.

DC Nick Fellows was the first to come up with an interesting observation.

'When I went back over the statements I got from those members of the Portree Parish Council I looked first, naturally, at Dr. Ledbetter's statement.'

'Go on Nick.'

'He claimed to have left with the others. What was curious, though, was that he never asked *me* about that arm.'
'Why should that be significant?'

'He had examined the arm itself, of course, at his Forensic laboratory in Aberdeen but not to ask me about *how* it came to be attached to the clock face seemed very odd, even at the time. He was, after all, 'one of us' and involved in the case from the start. You would have thought that the kind of background information even I had would have interested him. The fact that he did not ask me any of those kind of questions now strikes me as extremely odd. What do you think, sir?'

'Can any of the other counsellors', asked Detective Inspector White, 'corroborate his claim that he left with them?'

'Not really, sir, Not with any certainty, anyway. One thing, though that might interest us is that one of the Councillors there that night is a retired doctor. His name is Rory MacBeth. Memorable name, by the way.'

'Yes, thank you Constable. Stick to the point, please.'

'Yes sir. Sorry. Anyway, Dr. MacBeth had been a orthopaedic surgeon at the Royal Infirmary in Aberdeen before he retired. He may even have been there when Dr. Ledbetter transferred from the hospital near Dunkeld where he was Senior Pathologist before joining SPSA in Aberdeen. Dr. MacBeth and Dr. Ledbetter must surely have known each other, if not at the Royal Infirmary in Aberdeen then here on Portree. Both lived here at roughly the same time. Both were active on the Parish Council. In his statement, however, Dr. MacBeth says that Dr. Ledbetter never spoke to him once all evening. Rather strange, do you not think, sir?'

* * *

After their breakfast in Covent Garden Tom left Mike Baker and staggered back to his hotel and crawled into bed. It had been a long night. At noon he got up, showered, shaved, dressed and then went out for a walk.

It was a bright Spring day and London was looking its best. He ended up on the Thames embankment and on impulse caught a boat for a trip to Tower Bridge and back. There was a stiff breeze on the river and the flags on the South Bank near Tate Modern were fluttering wildly.

Tom leant on the ship's rail and pondered the nights events.

He and Mike had left Freda Butterworth fast asleep in her chair. It was about four in the morning when they tip-toed out of her apartment, closing the door quietly behind them.

It would seem that Freda Butterworth had not seen her daughter for fifteen years.

The news that Emma was now dead confirmed her worst fears. It was hard to take but the possibility that she was dead had always been there. London can be a violent place, she knew that. She had kept her daughter away from the business and had brought her up at her large country house near Hemel Hempstead. By the time Emma was a teenager she knew more or less what her mother did for a living but she never came to the 'salon' nor showed much interest in what went on there.

She had vanished when she was seventeen.

The police were informed but were not that interested. Each year thousands of teenage girls left home for one reason or another. Emma was nearly eighteen. She could do what she wanted. For some years Freda searched for her missing daughter but then eventually gave up, assuming that she was gone for ever. Besides, her 'salon' now occupied the larger part of her time. Finally, Emma became a memory of the past. A daughter lost and virtually forgotten.

Tom had now reached Tower Bridge. It was as the boat was turning mid-stream for its journey back that Tom's mobile rang. It was Detective Inspector White.

He told Tom about Jim Ledbetter and the need for extreme secrecy and caution. When Tom told him of his progress and the identification of 'Alison Rutherford', White said that he should stay on in London for a few more days and see what else he could find. Now that they had Alison's real name they might be able to trace her back through the missing years prior to her arrival in Portree. Then there was Caroline Wear. How did she fit into this story?

'Tom', he said, 'we need to know how these three women are connected and if any of them have links with Ledbetter. All we have on Jim Ledbetter is some circumstantial evidence and a pile of suspicion. Not good enough for the Procurator Fiscal, let alone a Scottish Court.'

Tom spent the rest of that Friday as a tourist, wandering about London in something of a daze. He started in Trafalgar Square and Piccadilly and then explored the book shops on Charing Cross Road, eventually finding his way to the Stanley Gibbons shop on The Strand.

Tom had collected stamps since he was a little boy. It had begun with stamps which he laboriously steamed off the letters sent to his parents from relatives in New Zealand. Now he had a stamp collection that ran to several large albums. He spent, therefore, a very happy two hours in Stanley Gibbons store before returning to his hotel off Bow Street and a pizza that evening in Covent Garden. He did not revisit Soho but went instead to bed where he read for an hour or two before dropping off to sleep.

He spent Saturday and Sunday exploring parts of London that he had only ever read about - Westminster Abbey, Buckingham Palace and the House of Commons.

He walked everywhere, thoroughly enjoying the break. Not once did he think of the case or Freda Butterworth or the sad death of her daughter. On Sunday he took a boat to Greenwich and on the way back stopped off at The Globe Theatre on the South Bank. That evening he treated himself to a meal in a small Italian restaurant on Henrietta Street, near Covent Garden It cost far more than he had budgeted for but he enjoyed every mouthful. He had never been much of a wine drinker but he managed to consume a small carafe of red Valpolicella all by himself that evening. That was a first!

Tom checked into New Scotland Yard early on Monday morning and was given a tiny office on the third floor. It was little more than a broom cupboard but it suited him fine. It had a table and chair and a telephone. With his laptop plugged in, Tom was as cosy as a bug in a rug. If that were not enough, the Clerical Assistant from the Met. typing pool DI White had booked to help him type up his notes and statements turned out to be a very pretty girl called Penelope Jones.

22
Tuesday, 15th May

Detective Chief Inspector Paul Elliott was in his office in Inverness when his phone rang. It was an officer from the Obscene Publications Unit in London with a message that made the small hairs on the back of his neck rise.

'Good morning, sir. This is Detective Inspector Mills of the OPU. I think you should know that another of your photographs has surfaced on the net. It shows a naked woman hanging by her ankles in what appears to be the interior of a lighthouse. She has only one arm.'

There was a long pause.

'Are you there sir? Well, this image is now in wide circulation. We have managed to trace it to a source in Dubai but beyond that we have no further information. It would appear that there is a new dealer on the block, someone we have not come across before. He clearly has material of an extreme nature and there is talk in certain chat rooms of more in the pipeline. We have no direct contacts in Dubai but I have two officers now assigned to this case. We will do our best to find out who is selling this material. So far, he or she appears to be only 'trailing' their wares.'

'Trailing? What do you mean?'

'Well sir, trailing means that you tease the market with a 'hot' image with the promise of more - if the price is right. If the photograph of that poor woman finds 'favour' with the sick individuals who get off on this stuff, then the seller can name his price. What this seller is doing is preparing the market for even more graphic material, probably on video. This needs to be stopped now if we are to prevent an extremely nasty situation.'

* * *

Dr. Elspeth Grant had been fairly quite for the last few days. She had been 'plotting' - that at least is what John White assumed she was still doing for he had heard nothing from her since their last, informal meeting at her apartment in Edinburgh.

But plotting what? She had refused to say what she had in mind. 'Secrecy', she said 'was essential!'

They met at Police HQ in Inverness that Tuesday afternoon and were confronted by a somewhat shaken DCI Paul Elliott. He was in a foul mood. He told them of the news about the photograph of 'Alison' now in circulation on the internet.
True, it was only available on a handful of extreme, hard-core sites but from there it could soon go 'viral'.

They clearly had the makings of yet another major disaster on their hands; a disaster that might prove very difficult to contain.

Elliott stared at them across his desk. He looked pale and drawn. With one hand he repeatedly struck his desk with a pencil. It was a nervous twitch White had seen him display before, but only occasionally. Normally, Detective Chief Inspector Elliott was a calm individual who seldom raised his voice. Today, although he still spoke quietly, it had a deadly edge to it.

'This investigation has taken a very serious turn. I have no idea how we can contain the situation. For the moment we must just hope and pray that the press do not get hold of this photograph. I need you both to redouble your efforts. If Ledbetter is your man then bloody-well prove it, and fast - before the Chief Constable falls on us all from a very great height or before some other poor woman ends up plastered all over the internet!'

From Paul Elliott's demeanour that morning it was clear to both Elspeth and John that news of the photograph had profoundly disturbed their boss, although he must surely have been anticipating something like this for some time now. He concluded that meeting with a clear exhortation to 'pull their fingers out and get some results before it gets even worse' - hinting darkly that it was now not only his job that was on the line but theirs too.

'Upstairs' needed results. And fast!

John and Elspeth retired to the police canteen for a restorative coffee. Elspeth was not her usual ebullient self, nor indeed was John White much better. The news had shocked him too. He felt helpless.

'I suppose we knew that this would happen sometime. I simply cannot imagine the kind of mentality that finds the image of a mutilated girl hanging by her ankles and bleeding to death exciting!'

'John, we are not dealing with sane people here. The people who collect this stuff are sick. They all need treatment. It's the purveyors of hard-core that are the ones to concentrate on. There is little we can do about human nature - not, at least, those extreme forms of it who enjoy these images. No, we must concentrate on how this stuff gets there in the first place.'

'But is that what this whole case is about - selling porn? I though we were dealing with a lunatic, a serial-killer not some grotesque photographer!'

'Jim Ledbetter, if he is our man, is some sick individual. He may or may not be a serial-killer in the conventional sense but there is something about him that really puzzles me.'

'What is that, Elspeth? For God's sake, talk to me!'

'Well, this matter of the 'three-thirty' obsession. I have said already that it was, in a sense, his 'signature'. Maybe it is not some deep, psychological trauma that prompts this obsession but something simpler. Maybe he stumbled by sheer chance upon that damaged watch of Jenny Chancellor's and the severed arm and ran with it. Maybe his 'signature', initially prompted by that watch, is simply being used to label his products. To *brand* them.'

'Brand them? Are you crazy, Elspeth?'

'Maybe but if you are selling product in a highly competitive market you need to ensure that it not only has what advertisers call a USP or Unique Selling Proposition but an identity that is also uniquely yours. I think Ledbetter is simply marking his territory and showing those internet dealers he is selling to that he has product that is uniquely his and in volume. He might be a serial-killer but he is also a brilliant salesman!'

* * *

Tom Watson went back to interview Freda Butterworth twice more before he left London. On both occasions he went alone.

She had, by now, recovered somewhat from the shock of her daughter's death. She was not told, of course, of the circumstances of Emma's murder, nor was she told that the grotesque photograph of her daughter's mutilated body was even then in circulation on the internet.

'Freda, who was Emma's father?'

'Wish I could tell you, sunshine! Could have been any one of four or five men I was seeing at that time. Mind you, I hate to think that she was fathered by some sick fuck in a rubber suit and mask with his cock hanging out. I was nearly forty when I got pregnant so it was something of a surprise all round!'

'Where was Emma brought up. Not in Soho, surely?'

'No, I had a large house in the country, near Hemel Hempstead. I was rich then so finding nannies and nurses was no problem. She was a very happy little girl, even though I did not see that much of her when she was growing up. Bright as a button. Loved books and music. Said once, when she was only ten, that she wanted to be a librarian.'

'Well, it might please you to know that that is what she was in Portree. She helped run the local library. She was very popular with the locals, I gather.'

Freda leant back in her chair and gave a big smile. That information clearly pleased her. She took another sip of tea.

'She was also into computers. I bought her one of those early Amstrads, remember them? She was very quick and could do all kinds of things with that little computer. Later I bought her a bigger and better PC. When she was old enough she went to Watford Grammar. In the Sixth Form she studied French and Computing and one other subject which I forget. She did well but I never knew if she went on to University because she was still at school when she disappeared out of my life.'

Freda began to cry. She groped around in her cardigan for a handkerchief. Tom gave her his. She blew her nose loudly and pocketed the handkerchief.

'What about boyfriends, Freda?. Did Emma have any regular boyfriends?'

'None that I can recall. I'm not even sure if she liked boys. I think she was more into books than boys.'

Tom took another sip of his tea, made a note in his notebook and waited for Freda to continue.

'When she was old enough she would take the train into London and spend hours in Foyles book shop, you know, that big place on Charing Cross Road. She told me once that it was there that she met famous authors at book signings and the like. She though that quite glamorous, being a writer that is. She said that she would like to be a writer. That and a librarian, of course.'

* * *

John had had a tacit agreement with Elspeth that at some point soon they would have a flaming argument in public and he would announce to all concerned that Dr Elspeth Grant, had, in fact, been sacked. News of this row would probably filter back to Ledbetter in Aberdeen. Knowing that the one person he probably most feared was off the case he might drop his guard and give the police the break they badly needed. That, at least, was their theory.

In the light of Detective Chief Inspector Elliott's recent exhortation, this no longer seemed such a good idea.

'I think', she said, chewing on an unlit cigarette, 'that it is time we took the initiative. Do you remember telling me that one of your bright young things back in Portree had said that the way to trace a pornographic image, provided it was digital, was to secretly 'tag' it ?'

'Yes, but that would mean releasing....'

'Since the CEO squad uses this trick on a regular basis, I propose that we release a new, secretly tagged image and see who picks it up. That might just lead us to a distributor, which in turn might reveal our seller. It also has the advantage of seriously pissing off our killer.'

'And if it doesn't work? What then, Elspeth?'

'Why, then Detective Inspector White, you could sack me!'

23
Thursday, 17th May

Detective Sergeant Tom Watson finally reached Portree at about five o'clock on Thursday afternoon.

It had been a long journey all the way up from London - although the train had given him time to collect his thoughts, get his copious notes in order and draft his report. He was, by-and-large, pleased with his work in London. It had been something of an eye-opener but he had also acquired some good, solid evidence. True, it was mostly background information but he had established credible links between the two murdered women and had miraculously found Alison Rutherford's real identity - Emma Butterworth.

On reaching Kyle of Lochalsh Tom picked up his car from the railway station car- park and drove across the Skye Bridge, then north to Portree. On arrival at the Community Centre he immediately reported to his boss, John White.

'Good to see you back, Tom. I trust you found London productive? My spies tell me you rather hit it off with the ladies in New Scotland Yard. A certain Penelope Jones in particular was mentioned.'

Tom actually blushed.

'I don't know who has be telling you stuff like that, sir but Miss Jones proved to be a most attentive clerical assistant.'

This was entirely true but Tom thought it best not mention that the delectable Penny Jones had seen him off at Euston station with a very ardent kiss full on the mouth. Another first for DS Watson.

'Well, Tom. What have you discovered, other than the wicked pleasures of London?'

Tom opened his brief case and placed a large sheaf of typewritten statements on the table in front of them.

'Tom, I think you should tell me in your own words. I will read your report later. Just give me the gist of it for now, please.'

'Very well, sir. Alison Rutherford's real name is Emma Butterworth. She is, or rather was, the illegitimate daughter of Freda Butterworth - former 'Madam' of a brothel in London's Bond Street. This establishment was hugely successful but was closed by the police three years ago. This 'salon', as Freda insists on calling it, catered primarily for clients of both sexes interested in SM and it was there that Georgina Cousins, known only as 'Sarah Daniels', often hung out.'

'Good work, Tom. What else?'

'According to Freda, Georgina was more of a voyeur than a participant in the SM activities of the 'salon'. She was clearly lesbian and drawn to violence but only if she was not herself directly involved. She took photographs whenever she could, and on one occasion took snaps of a young girl who had been badly hurt by another lesbian. It was at that point that Freda threw her out. Freda says that she never saw her again after that.'

'What about Emma Butterworth. Do you think she knew Georgina?'

'Yes I do but not in the context of her mother's brothel. When she was sixteen or seventeen Emma was very much into books. She attended a number of book events at Foyles' book shop on London's Charing Cross Road. I think it was there that she probably first met Sarah Daniels. I checked with the Promotions Manager of Foyles. He had no idea when but Sarah Daniels had certainly promoted her books in their bookshop on a number of occasions, particularly round about 2006 when her books were selling particularly well.'

'But Tom, I though that Georgina Cousins had always fought shy of publicity and never showed her face in public?'

'Yes sir, so did I - until Foyles told me otherwise. These book signings is the first instance we have of the famously reclusive Georgina Cousins appearing in public. What is also interesting is that her first books, starting in 2004, did not have a photograph of anybody on the back. The photograph purporting to be that of the author - the one of Caroline Wear - did not appear regularly on Georgina's covers until 2010, the year Caroline was killed and the year when Georgina retreated to Portree.'

'What then - other than that of a literary fan - is Emma's connection with Georgina Cousins?'

'I suspect that Emma met Georgina at Foyles and was smitten. Or perhaps Georgina seduced her. Either way, I think they were lovers in London for a year or so. That would explain her abrupt disappearance in 2006. When Georgina retreated to Portree in 2010, Emma went with her. Georgina got on with her writing and Emma, having changed her name to 'Alison Rutherford', became Portree's Assistant Librarian. We always assumed that they did not know each other but I think we were wrong. They were always lovers, very discreet lovers mind you, but they certainly knew each other intimately.'

'Tom, what about the computers? I see from your notes here that Emma was highly computer-literate. Do you think she had anything to do with the way in which both women's computers were tampered with?'

'Yes sir. We have always assumed that it was our serial-killer who wiped those computers to remove his name but I now think it was the other way round. I think Emma and Georgina were trying to protect *themselves* but from what or from whom I cannot say. Emma certainly had the computing skills. We know that from her work at the library. Even her mother told me that she had these skills from an early age. If I am right, then that removes the problem of Georgina's computer being interfered with by our killer *before* he murdered her. I had always though that unlikely or at least difficult to explain satisfactorily. That does not mean that our killer did not have access to Alison's cottage before abducting her but it does probably mean that he had nothing to do with either computer.'

'Great work Tom but it still raises more questions than it answers. What part, for example, does Caroline Wear play in all this? And what, more importantly, does either woman have to do with our prime suspect? So far, none of us have linked him directly with any of the victims. Without that we are never going to be in a position to charge him with anything.'

John White stood up, crossed to the window and stared out into the street, lost in thought. It was getting dark and the lights around the harbour had just come on. He turned back and looked at Tom. Tom had stood up and was gathering his notes together and stuffing them back into his brief-case.

'Sergeant, you have done really well and I am grateful for all your hard work but without that link to Ledbetter we are - legally speaking, that is - completely stuffed!'

* * *

That Thursday evening the team gathered for their usual 'get together' in the 'snug' attached to the saloon bar of the Royal Hotel.

John White's team had been assembled from several far flung corners of Scotland to assist the investigation but over the weeks of working together they had bonded well. WPC Debbie Saunders was the only 'outsider'. She was technically with the local constabulary in Portree but she had been unofficially 'adopted' by the team and welcomed into their social, after-work activities. With nothing much else to do in Portree on a Thursday evening, they had decided to welcome Tom back with a pint or two of Scotland's finest ale.

It was also a great opportunity to talk 'shop'.

'The dates don't tie up,' said Janice.

Janice Ward was the eldest of the 'Gang of Five'. She was an attractive brunette with an incredible figure - lean and highly toned. She was very sporty and something of a fitness fanatic. She was also very intuitive and highly intelligent. Whenever the others came up with new data, it was she who scrutinised it, applying her very logical brain to any new theories or speculations - often with devastating effect.

'Emma Butterfield disappeared in 2006, when she was just seventeen. That means that she and Georgina got it together at about the same time, having first met each other at Foyles - if Tom's theory is correct. That also means that they were probably living together somewhere in London for the next four years. Correct, Tom?'

'Er, whatever you say Janice. I know that I out rank you but I wont let that spoil a good theory, if that's what you are leading up to.'

General laughter. Since the other girls knew that Janice rather fancied Tom, they were not surprised when she blushed at this gentle repost.

'Well, its not so much a theory as an objection. If both women left London together in 2010, Emma would have been just twenty or twenty-one when she arrived in Portree. Not only did she have a cottage to move into but she was now called 'Alison Rutherford' and had the right qualifications and references to walk into a job at our local library. Very impressive, I would say. What do you say, Detective Sergeant?'

'You are right, Janice. Very impressive. My only explanation is that Emma changed her name by Deed Poll. Once she was eighteen she could do that legally. I think she then fabricated her qualifications, references and age. Not difficult if you are a computer wiz. She knew enough about library work to fool the Local Authorities who interviewed her for the job. She probably forged her own references or got Georgina to write them for her. Her computer skills were a bonus. That may have blinded her employers to her lack of experience elsewhere. Either way, it worked. She got the job as Portree's new, young Assistant Librarian. I suspect that Georgina's name is somewhere on the deeds for Alison's cottage. She bought it for her. This is not as crazy as it sounds. Writers like privacy. To put her lover in a cottage nearby not only prevented gossip but gave her the daytime quiet she needed to write her trashy but highly profitable novels.'

Round of applause. Tom grinned. He knew - they knew - that he was making this stuff up as he went along. Still, it felt credible. Someone soon would need to prove it. He hoped that it was not him who was given that task.

'Tom, you have not mentioned the dodgy websites both women were probably into. Did you find anything in Emma's background to indicate that she was into violence to women?'

'No. But Georgina was and with Emma's computing skills she could access the kind of stuff she drew upon for her books and, ultimately, her sexual kicks. Georgina was the dominant partner. I suspect Emma would do anything Georgina asked of her, including accessing vulnerable women on the internet. Nothing Emma's mother told me, however, indicated that her daughter had SM tendencies. On the contrary, to me she seemed absolutely normal - as lesbians go, that is!'

There was a gasp at this.

Political correctness was not exactly a police characteristic. However, most of the young police officers in the snug that evening - especially the women - were aware of the need to tread carefully on the subject of sexuality. In a police force that was still very much a male preserve and, in some areas, still dominated by old-school, male misogynists, the subject of homosexuality was still a very touchy subject. There were now many gay officers of both sexes in the police but that did not make life easy for them. Tread carefully was the golden rule.

'And what, Tom Watson, makes a 'normal' lesbian?', asked Charlotte. 'Would you know one - even if she came up to you and smacked you across the face?'

'Charlotte, that's surely not likely to happen here, is it?'

'That's what you think, Tom Watson!'

With that Charlotte got up from her chair, crossed the room and gave Tom a none-too-gentle slap across the face.

'I'm a lesbian and I do not like to hear misogynistic generalisations about what is sexually 'normal' or not from a stamp-collecting, male virgin from Wick!'

Loud laughter and applause.

Charlotte resumed her seat, grinning broadly from ear to ear. This time it was Tom's turn to blush. Since this was the first time any of them within the team had realised that Charlotte was a card-carrying lesbian, they all agreed there and then that the day was truly hers.

Game, set and match to WPC Charlotte Stephens!

Detective Sergeant Tom Watson apologised to Charlotte, gave her an awkward hug and bought the next round of drinks.

24
Friday, 18th May

Friday morning. Inverness. Dull, grey skies. Spring had definitely not yet sprung in Inverness. Anyway, that's what Chief Inspector Paul Elliott thought as he stared gloomily out of his office window on the seventh floor of Police HQ.

He was on the phone to Detective Inspector Mills of the Obscene Publications Unit in London.

'What news, then, of the Dubai connection?'

'Not much sir, I'm afraid. Each time we dig deep, we have to dig even deeper. It's a bit like those Russian dolls. You uncover one, only to discover another one inside. And another. Web-sites have web-sites hidden within them. So, no luck so far. There is one other thing, although you are not going to like it!'

'Tell me anyway.'

'Our labs have been taking a close look at the two photographs that have emerged thus far. In the old days porn was shot on 35mm standard cameras. Today, though, most porn is shot on sophisticated camcorders. This means that the producers of this material start with a ten-minute video they can sell. From this they subsequently pull of, say, fifty or so stills which they can also sell. It's called economy of scale, I'm told.'

'Where is this leading to, Detective Inspector?'

'Well sir, the images of both the McCallister lad and Alison Rutherford began on a camcorder. The labs can prove this quite easily. Normally images recorded from a camcorder on a tripod, for example, only reveal traces of movement *within* the frame. Your images reveal both that and digital traces of actual camera movement.'

'Which means....?'

'Which means, sir, that we think that there were probably two people involved, one dealing with the victims, the other holding the camera. In both the lighthouse and on board that fishing boat, it is very likely that there were *two* people present at the time of the murders.'

* * *

Poppy White had not seen her husband for some time, what with pressure of work and all that is a policeman's lot. It was, therefore, with some surprise that she saw him turn into their drive Friday afternoon, some hours earlier than expected.

He got out of his car and crossed the lawn to where she was cutting spring flowers from the border adjacent to the river bank.

'Darling, what a lovely surprise! You are home early. Or is this just another of those flying visits policemen sometimes spring on their wives before vanishing for weeks on end?'

He kissed her.

'No. I just thought I would grab and extra hour or so of prime-time with my lovely wife, to recharge my batteries as it were.'

With that he slumped into a garden chair.

'Right. I will make you a cup of tea. That will soon perk you up.'

When she came back ten minutes later with the tea-tray Detective Inspector White was fast asleep.

* * *

Over supper that evening John raised the matter of engaging Poppy in another of Elspeth's stratagems.

'Really? That sounds interesting. I enjoyed the last one. What now?'

She laid her knife and fork neatly on either side of her empty plate and leant forward attentively across the dining room table.

'Well, that's partly the problem. She wont tell me exactly what she has in mind but she needs an accomplice with theatrical skills - and that means you.'

'Theatrical kills? You mean costume and makeup? I have never acted in my life, except when I was courting you, my darling.'

'Quite. Makeup, primarily. We need, not to put too fine a point on it, to simulate a murder, photograph it and shove it on the net with a secret 'tag' attached to it. That way we can trace its progress and maybe find out who is behind its distribution.'

'Goody! Who are we going to murder?'

'Elspeth'.

* * *

It was decided to murder Elspeth in the comfort of her own home. Mother was reluctant at first and showed a squeamish side to his character that surprised even his lover.

However, with Poppy's gentle encouragement, he soon warmed to the task and in so doing revealed that he could sew - a skill that assumed some importance as the project progressed. Indeed, he began to show such enthusiasm for popping Elspeth's clogs that she began to worry, not for Mother's sanity but for her actual safety.

The entire crew - John, Poppy and a middle-aged police-cameraman from Birmingham - decamped to Elspeth's apartment that Friday evening. The flat contained five bedrooms so accommodation was no problem. After a sumptuous supper, cooked by Mother and washed down with copious amounts of fine red wine, they moved to the sitting-room to plan in detail how to despatch one of Britain's most talented Profilers.

It was not going to be easy, not least because if she was going to go, Elspeth - like Elsie from the musical *Cabaret* - was determined to go out with a bang.

The plan had been approved, after some tense discussion, by Detective Chief Inspector Elliot on Thursday.

Elliott had been at first extremely reluctant to even consider such an unorthodox stratagem but the phrase 'desperate means requires desperate measures' somehow resonated with him. He knew from working with Elspeth in the past that lateral thinking was her *mètier* and that her daft plans often produced spectacular results. And results, as the Chief Constable of the Northern Constabulary had earlier that day reminded him, are what this case badly needed.

After detailed consultation with Detective Inspector Mills at the Obscene Publications Unit in London as to the feasibility of such a project, a cameraman with the requisite equipment was assigned (he travelled up from Birmingham that evening with a van-load of cameras and lighting equipment) and the plan given the official green light. The photograph of the late Elspeth Grant would then be secretly tagged and offered to the highest bidder on the internet. That part of the operation would be accomplished by the OPS team under DI Mills. It was then a matter of waiting and watching to see who took up the 'offer' and if it were possible to trace it back to a specific source in Dubai.

It would also be interesting to see how Dr. James Ledbetter reacted to what amounted to a copy-cat murder.

He would not like that, even if it showed that Elspeth had finally met her Maker, something that he probably wished would happen anyway. It was Elspeth's contention that he would realise that someone was moving into his territory and effectively devaluing the product he was preparing to launch onto an expectant public of deviants and perverts, avid for hard-core images of murder and mutilation.

There was also the matter of whether he believed that the

photograph was a fake or not - which he surely would if it was obviously Elspeth Grant.

Indeed, Elspeth rather hoped that he would quickly recognise it as a fake. Her image was not credible, at least to him. Yet to Ledbetter's punters she was just another old biddy who had been murdered - on film. But for James Ledbetter it would signal, loud and clear, that they knew the murderer's methods. His methods! That did not necessarily mean that they had identified him as their serial-killer but it did mean that they were on track. Perhaps now it was now only a matter of time before he was arrested. It was at best a sign, a threat perhaps, from the police. Either way James Ledbetter would have to take it seriously.

For once - or so Elspeth argued - the pressure would be on him and not on the police. What he did then would define how the case went thereafter.

If he fled the country, then he would be seen to be guilty. If he did nothing then all his hard work would go down the pan and dealers would assume that everything he had released thus far were also fakes. His hard-core porn stock would devalue overnight and everything he had done, everything he had risked thus far, would have been wasted.

Well, that at least was Elspeth's plan.

Meanwhile, there was the little matter of how to despatch Dr. Elspeth Grant with the maximum visual impact.

Over whiskey, in Elspeth's 'Moroccan' sitting room, they discussed how best to murder her - scheduled for Saturday morning.

Elspeth herself favoured multiple amputation - arms and legs - but that was ruled out as too complicated and somewhat 'over the top'. Besides, while Poppy's makeup box contained plenty of blood she had no prosthetics to make even the most basic amputation look convincing in lurid Technicolor.

John favoured a slit throat. This was readily faked and would call for plenty of blood. Even as he said it he saw in his mind's eye the real cut throat of Gabriel McCallister on board Neil McPherson's boat. For the next twenty minutes or so he said nothing further.

Poppy favoured a stabbing. She had a fake dagger in her theatrical box. Her idea was to show a man's arm administering the blow in real time then select a still frame to release on the internet. This would replicate the method already used by the killer and therefore appear more authentic. If the recorded blow was one of several, then there would be plenty of blood.

This idea prompted a murmur of approval.

The quiet, middle-aged cameraman called Nigel was next to speak. His idea was to string Elspeth up by her ankles from the chandelier and then cut her throat, causing a pool of blood to gather on the carpet beneath her head.

This was considered very photogenic but for John it was too close to the dreadful image he constantly had in his head of Emma Butterworth hanging in the stairwell of the lighthouse off Skye.

Elspeth also ruled this idea out for entirely different reasons. She considered hanging by her ankles un-ladylike. Besides, she did not want any blood - even Poppy's fake blood, on her Persian carpet. It was far too valuable for that and she could see problems with the insurance if she subsequently put in a claim against damage caused by her own 'murder'.

In the end, after much heated discussion and far too much Napoleon brandy, it was agreed that Elspeth would be the victim of a multiple stabbing, to take place at ten o'clock Saturday morning - to allow the very nice cameraman to get back to Birmingham for his grand-daughter's Christening later that afternoon.

While the men washed up the dishes, Poppy and Elspeth enjoyed a nightcap together in the sitting room. Elspeth gleefully lit her thirty-ninth cigarette of the day and puffed away contentedly.

'Mother is absolutely gorgeous. Where did you find him?'

'Oxford. He attended a lecture I gave then he followed me back to Arseholes (she meant All Souls). They wouldn't let him up to my rooms so we arranged to meet later. After supper at The Elizabeth we checked into the Randolf Hotel and bonked for two days.'

'Wow! And I thought romance was dead! He doesn't say much. What does he do?'

'He's rather shy, actually. But very bright. He's got an MA from The University of Mogadishu in Somalia, and two PhD's, the last one from Oxford.'

'But what's his subject?'

'Not entirely sure. Once I got over the shock of discovering that he was better qualified than me I actually asked him to explain his work. Something to do with 'dark matter', whatever that is. He's a Cosmologist.'

'Right. See what you mean.'

And so they all went to bed.

* * *

'Is this crazy plot of Elspeth's going to work, darling?' asked Poppy as she slipped into bed. John was already tucked up under the Egyptian cotton sheets. It was a four-poster bed with tasselled canopy and quite dramatic. Very Elspeth.

'God knows! We need some kind of break. Perhaps this will do the trick. I for one find the whole thing distinctly tacky, not to say distasteful.'

'I agree, but if it will flush out a dangerous criminal and stop other murders then surely the means justify the ends?'

'Funny you should say that. That's what Paul Elliott said.

Goodnight Poppy. Sleep well. We have a busy day ahead of us I fear.'

'Goodnight, darling Detective Inspector Plod. By the way, Mother has got four degrees.'

'Yes, I know. I checked him out with MI5. Can't have just anyone shagging our Elspeth, can we? Goodnight.'

25
Saturday, 19th May

Elspeth entered the kitchen early next morning dressed like a movie star. She wore dark glasses and a black shawl draped across her head, looking like Melina Mecouri's Phaedra. From the neck down she looked like Elizabeth Taylor as Helen of Troy in the Oxford stage production of *Dr. Faustus*, swathed in a long white robe. All that was missing was the dry ice. Mind you, she was slightly stouter than Elizabeth Taylor and not quite as beautiful as Melina Mecouri but the overall impression was astonishing.

This dramatic entrance was met with a polite round of applause from those cooking breakfast and laying the table - which was everyone apart from Elspeth. Mother then hovered about her like some anxious Paris couturier, darting in now and then to adjust a sleeve or hem or replace an errant hair from her head. It would appear that he had run up this concoction the night before, which for a Cosmologist was mightily impressive.

'Since I am the condemned woman I demand something special for my last breakfast on this earth.'

'Scrambled eggs on toast, American bacon cooked to a crisp, orange juice followed by French coffee', said Poppy.

'Perfect! Bring it on!'

With that Elspeth sat down on at the kitchen table and tucked in.

'You are also entitled to a last wish', said Poppy.

Elspeth stopped eating for a moment, then took Mother's hand - he was standing beside her.

'I would like, as my last wish', she said sweetly, 'another hour in bed with my darling Mother. That is my last wish.'

This was rejected unanimously, not least because the mild-mannered photographer from Birmingham had to get back home for his grand-daughter's Christening later that afternoon.

With breakfast over, they all retired to the sitting room. Lights, cables and camera tripods were everywhere.

The little man from Birmingham had been busy, transforming Elspeth's 'Moroccan' sitting room into a scene from dark horror movie, set in down-town Casablanca.

Elspeth herself was placed stage centre, sprawling in a large armchair. A rope was passed round her throat and fastened behind, forcing her head back. Another rope bound her arms, accentuating the swell of her bosom beneath her dazzling white gown. After close examination from several angles it was decided to untied her hair and let it fall naturally. The transformation was dramatic. She now looked like someone from *Thriller* although none present dared volunteer that information at the time.

Then came the blood.

This was applied to her chest and throat with a large brush and allowed to run down her arms and legs. The effect was quite startling and Poppy had to be stopped from applying too much, so excited had she become.

The dagger itself was one of those stage daggers where the blade - made of plastic - disappears into the handle. Applied with swift stabs it looked very convincing. Mother had had the foresight to line the front of Elspeth's dress with cardboard, thereby protecting her ample bosom.

It was decided that Mother would be the assassin. To cover his black arm and hand, he wore an anorak with long sleeves and rubber gloves. After several ferocious attacks by way of rehearsal it was decided that they were ready to shoot.

The house lights were turned off and the room plunged into semi-darkness. A white light cut a sharply-defined swathe across Elspeth's corpse-like body, with the rest of the room plunged into eerie darkness. There were hints of gold and brass as ambient light glanced off Elspeth's Moroccan artefacts, especially the hanging lamps. It was clear that the mild-mannered photographer from Birmingham really knew what he was doing.

'Stand by. Action!'

On cue, Mother leapt into frame and savagely attacked the helpless victim. What no one had expected were the blood-curdling screams that Elspeth let out when attacked and the struggle she put up to try and escape this ferocious assault. Everyone was aghast at the noise and were relieved when it was over thirty seconds later. It seemed longer.

A profound silence then fell over everyone - except Elspeth, who was now grinning wickedly from ear to ear.

'How was that, chaps? Did I scare the shit out of you? Mother, you are a brutal swine and I'm not sure I love you anymore.'
Mother looked genuinely shocked and tears welled up in his eyes. He immediately cast the bloody dagger aside and threw his arms round his lover, hugging her passionately.

Sometime later, after Nigel had downloaded his disc onto his laptop and fiddled around with selected images, he showed the results to the others.

The chosen still was fantastic and caused an intake of breath when they saw it for the first time.

Elspeth was revealed slumped in the chair and bleeding profusely. Her face was drained of all colour but the great splotches of blood on her white dress were ghastly to behold. It was very convincing and, in the half-light that Nigel had created, truly shocking.

One of Elspeth's blood-stained arms hung down the side of her chair, inadvertently pointing (or so it seemed) at an old gramophone at her feet.

On the turntable was a black, shellac disc with a bright yellow label. It was a record by Duane Eddy. It was called 'Three-thirty Blues'.

* * *

Detective Inspector White arrived back in Portree early on Monday morning to address the troops. He had had a faxed report from his boss whose staff had been looking into Dr. James Ledbetter's career. It made interesting reading. He stood in front of his team and read the document out loud.

Those present noted that his voice seemed tired, strained.

'James Ledbetter was born in 1969 in Alderley Edge, Cheshire. His parents were comfortable, middle-class. His father was a solicitor. He was an only child, very bright and in 1980 won a scholarship to Manchester Grammar School. He ended up with four science 'A' Levels, all distinctions.

In 1987 he went up to Manchester University to study medicine, graduating in 1992. He did his Foundation Year at Wythenshawe Hospital, Manchester working first in general medicine then, for the remaining six months, in surgery. It was during this time that he expressed an interest in trauma and was able to acquire some of his surgical skills in the A&E Unit at that hospital. In 1993 he moved to the Manchester Royal Infirmary where he studied for his MRCP Part 1 examination in Histopathology. Two years later, in 1995, he was employed as a pathologist at Ninewells Hospital, Dundee where he studied Forensic Pathology for three years. He obtained his CCT (Certificate of Completion of Training) in 1998. He then became Consultant Pathologist, first at Raigmore Hospital in Inverness (at this time he owned a cottage in Portree) and then Aberdeen where he is to this day. He become a Consultant Pathologist to the SPSA Forensic Science Laboratory in January, 2000. He has Home Office accreditation and has attended the Expert Witness training Course required of police surgeons. He is, in short, a very experienced, highly regarded Consultant Pathologist.'

He paused for a moment, placed the fax on his desk and polished his glasses. The small team waited patiently. Everyone of them saw that their boss was looking tired. It was clear that the enormous strain of this case was getting to him.

'I should add at this point that I have myself known Jim Ledbetter for some years. I have always considered him my friend. These latest developments have, therefore, come as something of a shock. However, I have made some notes for your use, copies of which I will distribute afterwards. Let me read what I have written about Dr. Ledbetter.'

At this point John White put his glasses back on and read from a typed sheet of paper. His hand shook a little as he read from it.

'I first met Jim Ledbetter when he moved to Dundee in 1995. He never seemed short of money, buying a holiday cottage in Dunkeld soon after starting at Ninewells. We were, therefore, neighbours for at least part of the year. He was married by then, to Fiona (née Pawley). Miss Pawley was at that time an NHS Administrator, also in Dundee. They had met in 1995 and were married the same year. Fiona appears reticent in public, somewhat shy but it is said that she is a formidable negotiator and administrator. They have no children. When we first knew them Jim Ledbetter was a keen sailor and kept a yacht at Onich, on Loch Linnhe. He sailed most weekends and on several occasions I sailed with him, exploring the Inner and Outer Hebrides. In terms of sailing and navigational skills he certainly fits what little we know about our killer. That applies equally, of course, to his surgical skills.'

He paused and looked around the room. His face was an ashen grey. Some of the team exchanged looks of concern with each other.

'I will distribute copies of DCI Elliot's notes plus my own. Please study them carefully, particularly with regard as to where this career outline places James Ledbetter from year to year. Those dates may become significant in this enquiry. Paul, you have something else to add?'

'Yes sir. I went back to re-interview the barman at the pub Georgina visited, prior to her death on the beach. He's changed his tune somewhat regarding when he thought she left the pub. He originally said two-thirty. He now thinks it might have been nearer two o'clock because he was already watching a football match on the TV in the bar when she paid her bill and left. That mach started at 1.55. It takes twenty minutes to reach that part of the beach where the body was found. That would place Georgina at the scene of the crime nearer two-thirty.'

'Meaning?'

'Meaning, sir, that the murderer had plenty of time to strangle her and amputate one arm before calling the police. Georgina was wearing a tweed skirt, blouse and long-sleeved, Fair Isle sweater. Forensic noted that the murderer had first cut her jumper and blouse at the shoulder before amputating her arm. To cut clothing that way is common practice in A&E when surgeons are working under pressure with living patients.'

'Maybe old habits die hard. Carry on, Paul.'

'The difference here of course is that Georgina was already dead. However, I am told a skilled surgeon can amputate an arm in under two minutes. It also means that he could have affected his escape well before he called the police in Portree. We always assumed somehow that he called from the beach but that need not have been the case at all.'

'Thank you, Paul. Charlotte?'

'I have been looking into the missing manuscript of Georgina's new novel. Georgina's agent was definitely expecting a first draft more or less now but then we found nothing at Georgina's cottage, not even a memory stick. Since at that time we did not know that the two women knew each other, perhaps we have been looking in the wrong place. If 'Alison Rutherford' was her amanuensis it is possible that she handled Georgina's work. She was the computer expert and it is likely that she prepared manuscripts before forwarding them to Georgina's agent. Perhaps the missing book is in Alison's cottage?'

'Good point, Charlotte. Tom, you seem to have got on well with Freda Butterworth. See if you can get her permission to have another look at that cottage. Forensic have done with it and I suspect it now belongs, technically, to Emma Butterworth's only living relative - her mother. Use your celebrated charm to get inside that cottage and have a really good search.'

'Yes, sir.'

'OK, any one else have anything to add? Right. I am going to give us all a few more days before we haul Ledbetter in for questioning. We only have circumstantial evidence as yet and absolutely nothing that links him directly with any of the three known murders. There are other cases from the past that Detective Chief Inspector Elliott is looking at. We suspect there may have been other, earlier killings but there is still much to do to prove that there is a link here also with our prime suspect. I beg you, watch your backs! You all have new tasks and lines of enquiry to pursue. Please get on with it. We are now seriously running out of time.'

26
Unsolved Murders

That evening Detective Inspector White checked into the Royal Hotel as usual. Had he known that this case was going to take so long he might have rented a local holiday cottage. On the other hand, he liked his creature comforts and the idea that he could order room-service at any ungodly hour of the night suited his current life style.

Once in his room he rang Elspeth.

'Did you know, John, that last year there were seventy-nine murders in Scotland?'

'Yes, as a matter off fact. It actually represents a drop from previous years, I'm pleased to say.'

'That's as maybe. What interest me is that there are still three *unsolved* murders, between 1997 to 2001. One of these involved some poor man being tortured to death with a blow-lamp.'

'Yes. I read about the 'Blow Lamp' murder. The theory at the time was that it was gang-related. Some kind of punishment. Somewhere in Perth, I think. Do you think it might be connected?'

'Quite possibly. What I have done is match the location of each of these *unsolved* murders with the career movements of our friend, as outlined by DCI Elliott. They match pretty well.'

'Go on, Elspeth.'

'There was, for starters, a stabbing in Pitlochry in 1997. This was thought to be the result of a drunken brawl. The assailant was never found but the man's body turned up in a dark alleyway off the high street. Both his ears had been cut off!'

'Wow! What else?'

'Then there was the infamous 'blow-torch' murder in Perth in 1998. This was widely covered by the press at the time, scenting a gag-land killing. That was never proved - nor indeed was the man who tortured Ken Sutton to death ever found. Both Pitlochry and Perth are not that far from Dundee where Ledbetter was then studying Forensic Pathology at Ninewells Hospital.'

John White added this information to his notebook. He was rapidly creating a kind of time line, matching Ledbetter's movements to the murders Elspeth was now adumbrating so eloquently.

'In 2001 there was yet another unsolved stabbing, this time in a forest near Aviemore, about twenty miles from Inverness. Here there was no mutilation but the man had been tied to a tree before his throat was cut. He was found days later by a hill-walker. So you see, each of these unsolved murders took place within a forty mile radius of where Ledbetter was living or working at the time. This may of course be coincidence but perhaps here we have a pattern of killings that began much earlier than those we know of on Skye. It would be interesting to see if the Obscene Publications Unit knows if any photographs from these three killings ever surfaced on the internet. If they did, then I think we probably have a distinct pattern we can link to Jim Ledbetter.'

'That's fantastic, Elspeth. But what about the ten-year gap, between 2002 when he started work in Aberdeen and now. Had he simply stopped killing or are we missing something?'

'Once started these people never stop, John. No, I think either we have not been looking hard enough here in Scotland or he worked abroad, on his frequent vacations in Florida, for example. Maybe they too have a number of unexplained, unsolved killings. It would be interesting to find out - if we had the time!'

So, shall we call him in for questioning? We are surely going to have to do it sometime soon.'

'Not yet. You will need more to justify an arrest at this stage. Besides, it would show that he is our prime suspect and we do not want that yet. No, if you can hold off for another week or so then I think there is more to come crawling out of the woodwork. For example, most serial-killers I have studied work in pairs. Take, for example, Fred West. Without his ghastly wife Rosemary it is unlikely that he would have been so successful. Which brings me to my next question. What do you really know about Fiona Ledbetter?'

* * *

After a lonely supper of cheese sandwiches, crisps and a bottle of beer, John phoned his wife back in Dunkeld.

She sensed at once that he was tired and depressed and for the first few minutes of their conversation she chatted on about inconsequential matters, village gossip and the like. He seemed to cheer up. Eventually he came round to what he really wanted to talk about.

'Poppy, what do we really know about Fiona? She has never talked much to me but you two seem to get on reasonably well. How do you find her?'

Poppy at once realised the darker implications of her husband's question. If Jim Ledbetter was their prime suspect, then so too must be his wife. She paused for a moment, choosing her words carefully.

'We do get on, that is true but only within limits. Fiona does not seem to have much of a social life but she occasionally likes to talk to me about her work. She was once a successful NHS Administrator. In those days she was called Fiona Pawley. She has had a series of high-powered jobs, largely in major hospitals in Lancashire and later Scotland. I think it was in that capacity that she and Jim first met. When he got the Consultant Pathologist's job at the Royal infirmary in Aberdeen she retired from the NHS. I think she now keeps her hand in with consultancy work.'

'Like what, for example?'

'Well, she often advises senior managers within the NHS on industrial employment issues arising in Tribunals or UCAS mediations. She also teaches part-time, especially at universities where there are post-graduate Hospital Administration courses - such as Nottingham, Sheffield, Stirling, Edinburgh, Manchester and.....'

'Did you say Stirling?'

Yes. Why?'

'My darling wife, you have just earned yourself another slap-up dinner at Mario's.'

'Oh goody! Mind you, I am still waiting for my diamond. Anyway, what have I done to deserve a Mario treat this time?'

* * *

The following morning Detective Inspector White drove all the way to Stirling University to meet, by arrangement, Dr. Eleanor Sutherland.

'I hope, Detective Inspector, that you have not come to ask for Jennifer's arm back. If you have, I'm afraid you are too late. It was incinerated ten days ago.'

They were seated in the staff canteen - a barren space of plastic tables and chairs, neon lights and highly suspicious 'plants'. The coffee was almost as bad as the futuristic décor.

'Not exactly. I wanted to ask you if you had ever met Fiona Pawley?'

'Yes, as it happens. She teaches here quite regularly. Hospital Administration, I think. Not my subject area but I have a chum who regularly attends her lectures. She's very good, I'm told. Why do you ask?'

'Because she may have had something to do with the theft of Jennifer's arm.'

Deborah let out a long, low whistle and leant forward across the table in what can only be described as a conspiratorial manner.

'Wow! What makes you think that?' she whispered.

John looked around nervously, as if this intimate conversation were being observed by the Stirling University Thought Police.

'Well, I don't actually have any proof as yet so please keep this under your medical bonnet but is it possible that Fiona Pawley could have accessed your office?'

'Not really. She would need to know the lock combination to begin with. On the other hand, its just possible I suppose. She is frequently in this part of the University because the staff that teach her subject have offices in this block. I will have to think this through. Can I call you back sometime soon?'

'Yes please but 'mums' the word, right?'

'Of course, of course, Inspector. Mums the word. What larks, eh?!'

John stood up, shook hands and returned to his car. Eleanor Sutherland was a very attractive young woman but he was not entirely sure anymore that he was dealing with a truly responsible adult.

* * *

The funerals of all three victims took place during the next few days. The first was that of Gabriel McCallister at Ullapool.

His funeral was well attended for Gabriel had been a popular student at the West Highland College where he had been studying Adventure Tourism Management. He was also well known and liked within the local walking and climbing community, of which he was an active member.

There were many young men and women therefore at the graveside that chilly Spring morning.

Detective Inspector White attended, in dress uniform. He spoke briefly to Gabriel's parents. They did not ask him how the case was progressing nor did they seem particularly interested in the fate of the other two victims. DCI Elliott had eventually released information to journalists about the circumstances leading to young Gabriel McCallister's death but it appeared as if the press had become jaded. One more death? What they wanted was the murderer. No sign of that yet so a number of tabloids had moved on - to more current scandals. That was a relief all round for the police in both Inverness and on the Isle of Skye were still struggling with one of the most complex cases that Scotland had ever experienced.

As for the McCallisters, they had enough to contend with in dealing with the loss of their only child, a young man of nineteen years and barely at the start of his career.

The second funeral for Georgina and 'Alison' took place the following day in Portree. It was now Wednesday, 23rd May. Either by chance or design, the two women were buried simultaneously, side by side in adjacent graves. This may have been the Reverend Nish's inspired idea but to those few present who knew of the secret relationship between the two murdered women it seemed absolutely right.

The funeral attracted a large crowd.

Few there really knew Georgina Cousins but 'Alison Rutherford' - as she was known in the village - had been a popular Assistant Librarian and a well-known figure about the place. These villagers, out of communal respect, hung back from those clustered around the new graves, standing quietly under the trees to one side of the graveyard.

It was a sunny morning with only a slight breeze stirring the leaves. The Reverend Nish had opted for a joint funeral for a number of good reasons, not least that he soon discovered, when making arrangements, that neither woman was likely to have many official mourners. He also reasoned that a joint service would more quickly absolve the village of additional and extended distress.

Notwithstanding these somewhat pragmatic considerations, the Reverend Nish conducted the joint service with eloquent professionalism, expressing heartfelt grief at the circumstances of the deaths of two local women. While he knew little detail of either women - or indeed anything about a possible relationship between them - he found sufficient generalisations about 'relatively young women being tragically cut off in their prime' to both justify and serve the needs of a joint funeral. His words served also to voice the anxiety and concern of an entire village, fervently wishing in their collective hearts that such a horrible disaster had never, ever struck their community.

The idea also that a serial-killer was patently on the loose, perhaps even still on the island, was also never far from their minds although the Reverend Nish, for once, was silent on that subject.

There was considerable surprise amongst the villagers present when 'Alison's' real name - Emma Butterworth - was revealed on the simple gravestone her mother had commissioned. Freda Butterworth was also there, a rather sad figure with a black shawl over her head and wearing a long, black coat. No one there knew of course that she had once been the 'Madam' of a notorious brothel in London nor that she was known there as the 'Queen of SM'.

It is likely, had they known that, that the good people of Portree would have driven her off the island. Not that long ago she might have been burnt to death or drowned in the loch.

Detective Sergeant Tom Watson had met Freda off the train at Kyle of Lochalsh and then driven her to Portree. He had then escorted her in private to the Funeral Parlour where she was able, for the first time, to identify the body in person as that of her daughter, Emma. Tom was not sure if she knew any of the circumstances leading to her daughter's death. Perhaps she had read the lurid and largely inaccurate accounts in the tabloids. If she had, she said absolutely nothing to Tom. At the funeral itself she looked pathetically frail. Tom had to steady her several times with his arm.

Afterwards, he took her back to 'Alison's' cottage to gather together some personal effects and to make her last farewell to the daughter she never really knew for a large part of her life.

Georgina's funeral arrangements had been made by her London agent. Once the Coroner had given notice that the bodies could be released, she had liaised directly with the local police. The gravestone had been commissioned by her and carved by a stone-mason from Sligachan.

Her gravestone simply said 'Georgina Cousins, Portree, 1980-2012' thereby retaining her anonymity until the very end. No one there, other than those involved in her investigation and her agent who had never actually met her, knew that she was author of a dozen or so hugely successful novels published under the name of 'Sarah Daniels'.

Her secret went with her, literally, to the grave.

It was as the women were being lowered into the earth that Detective Inspector White realised that James Ledbetter was amongst the crowd that had gathered. He sensed him at first and felt the hairs on the back of his neck rise. When he turned round, there he was, at the edge of the crowd, standing alone under a tree to one side of the small graveyard.

Ledbetter, seeing that he had been spotted, simply waved one hand.

John White was astonished that the man had the nerve to attend the funerals of the two women he had most probably mutilated and then murdered. What arrogance! What audacity! He felt a sudden, overwhelming urge to go over and arrest him there and then but luckily thought better of it.

'Not yet', he said to himself. 'Not yet, you bastard!'

Afterwards, Ledbetter joined him as he was heading back to the Community Hall. He seemed relaxed; almost too relaxed, thought John.

'Hi John. Sad day.'

'Yes. By the way, Jim, what are you doing here? Not official, surely?'

'No. There's another Parish Meeting this evening. I'm on the restoration fund-raising committee. I was just passing when I saw you and your team here in the churchyard.'

'Well, thanks for stopping by.'

John managed to swallow an violent urge to strike the man hard in the face with his fist. Or worse.

'How's the investigation going? Any arrests imminent?'

'No, sadly not. We have one lead though. A third photograph of a murdered victim has surfaced on the internet.'

'Third? Third photograph?'

'Yes. Some poor woman. Looks like she was stabbed to death. It would appear that our man has struck again. It has his signature on it.'

'Signature? What signature?'

'Three-thirty. In the photograph there was, in one corner, a gramophone player and on it an old disc by Dwayne Eddy. It was called 'Three-thirty Blues'. Clever, eh?'

27
The Ghost of Rebus

The chance encounter with Jim Ledbetter that afternoon in Portree had unnerved DI White, even if he had subsequently taken advantage of it.

He sensed, however, that Ledbetter had been thrown by the news of a third photograph, one for which he - the killer - was *not* responsible. On the surface, the man had remained his usual urbane self but a slight tightening of the mouth had given the game away - as far as John White was concerned.

If he had any doubts as to this man's guilt, then they vanished in that churchyard that afternoon.

Perhaps it was just a policeman's instinct at work or perhaps Ledbetter's body language could not readily conceal what his outward demeanour tried so hard to hide. Either way, the man was guilty. That, anyway, was what John White now believed.

All that remained was to prove it!

After work, John wandered round to see his old chum, Sergeant McGregor who happened to be on duty that evening in the local police station. He had called him earlier, after the funeral to tell him that Ledbetter was in town.

'I checked that Parish Council meeting, John. It did not start until five. That means that your man was in Portree far too early. He came to that funeral deliberately because he was curious and needed to find out how you were doing. Cool customer, I must say. Its as if he is starting to taunt us, coupled with his need to really know how we are doing. Still, he has a bloody nerve, I must say!'

'I agree, Albert. The arrogance of the man is astonishing!'

'Yes. That is partly what makes his so dangerous. Are you and your boys and girls any nearer to arresting him?'

'Yes. We are going to have to pull him in soon. There is the matter of alibis. Where was he on the day of the murder, and so forth? The only way we can get that kind of information is by questioning him. However, once we call him in he will obviously know that he is our primary target.'

'I suspect that he has already sorted out alibis so we are going to need something solid to nail him. Between you and I, that is something that we do not have as yet.'

* * *

The next morning began with a telephone call from Dr. Eleanor Sutherland from the University of Stirling. She sounded excited.

'Calm down Eleanor. Tell me what you have found, please.'

'I checked with HR. They have a contract for Fiona Pawley which is dated Wednesday, 18th April. She was here to give a lecture to Third Year students in Hospital Administration. That was the day my arm went missing!'

'Are you absolutely sure?'

'Yes, I double checked with my colleagues. It was there when we left work that evening. Pawley's lecture did not finish until about six, after which she took questions. That means she was still in the building at about six-thirty, *after* we had left my office.'

'How would she know the combination to your office.'

'Don't know.'

'OK. That's fantastic news, Eleanor. Please keep this to yourself for now. I do *not* want anyone to know as yet that Fiona Pawley is in the frame for the theft of Jennifer's arm.'

'Anything else I can do, Inspector?'

'No thank you, Doctor Sutherland. You have already done a great deal to help us. Remember, 'mums' the word!'

* * *

After the funeral service on Wednesday afternoon Sergeant Tom Watson spent nearly two hours with Freda Butterworth at her daughter's cottage outside Portree.

It had been a harrowing experience because Freda broke down a number of times when going through her daughter's effects. She had aged visibly since Tom had first met her in London - the cocky former 'Madam' of a hugely successful brothel. Now she seemed a frail old lady, much older than her sixty-five years. The funeral had also been a tough experience for her, not least withstanding the stares the locals had given her.

Who was this women, they seemed to be asking? What has she to do with our lovely young librarian?

This visit also gave Tom a chance to look for the missing manuscript of Georgina's last, unpublished novel.

Each one of the team had read at least two of her previous novels. Between them they had now poured over almost everything she had published over the last twelve years. At work they had pooled this information.

The book called 'The Lighthouse' had first prompted the team to look for 'clues' in her work, not least snippets of biographical detail that might flesh her out as a woman. It was Elspeth who had put them onto this particular novel. The violence of Georgina's books had shocked most of them - as had the blatant lesbianism and anti-male agendas within each text. As to 'clues', well they had not been particularly forthcoming. While Georgina may have drawn on the desperate tales of women who had been subject to male violence she had gleamed off the internet, the 'autobiographical' element of her work was well disguised.

It was Freda who actually found the missing novel - more or less.

In 'Alison's' bedroom she had come across a soft, rather threadbare teddy-bear. It was something she herself had given her daughter years ago, long before she vanished from her life. The bear had a zip down its middle. It was used to keep pyjamas or a nightdress in.

When she found this, under Emma's pillow, Freda broke down and cried.

This gave Tom the chance to feel inside the teddy-bear where, to his astonishment, he found a small, blue memory stick which, without Freda seeing, he promptly pocketed.

Later that afternoon, he took Freda in a police car to the railway station at Kyle of Lochalsh and saw her off on the long rail journey back to London.

Although 'Alison's' cottage would eventually be shown to be part of Georgina's estate it was unlikely that Freda Butterworth would ever contest ownership.

It was also unlikely that Freda Butterworth would ever come back to Portree, even to visit her daughter's grave. That's what Tom thought, any way.

* * *

After her melodramatic 'demise' Elspeth had been strangely quiet. It was known that she was working on other cases - normal practice for a Profiler of her experience and quality - but John White was starting now to panic. The investigation seemed to have ground to a halt. The 'Gang of Five' were still digging up interesting background information and a picture of the relationship of the two murdered women was beginning to emerge. However, they had found nothing yet to definitively link Ledbetter with either of them.

Detective John White was never the most confident of investigators. He had a number of successful cases to his credit but in between there had been one or two failures, including one botched case that collapsed due to an informant that was subsequently discredited. Although not his actual fault, White had taken responsibility for losing a conviction that was otherwise thought to be rock solid. The Police Prosecution Service had not been best pleased at that. Thoughts now of resignation had again surfaced in his troubled mind. He was tired and depressed and his health had deteriorated noticeably in the last week or so. Poppy had seen this and had expressed her concern.

Perhaps he should resign, after all.

He was relieved, therefore, to receive a 'summons' later that afternoon from a buoyant Elspeth to a meeting in Edinburgh the next day - not at their usual restaurant near the Grass Market, but in a small pub on Young Street.

Since White had a desperate need for any help or support he could get, he accepted her invitation and early the following morning got in his car drove all the way to Edinburgh.

'Elspeth, why are we here?'

'For inspiration!'

'Well, you can say that again. I am feeling particularly uninspired.'

'And because this is Ian Rankin's favourite watering hole. The ghost of 'Inspector Rebus' haunts these very walls. That, surely, should be inspiration enough. Pint or mega-tot?'

John opted for a pint of Stone Ruination. When in Rome....

'Now', said Elspeth, propping herself up against the bar in one corner of the room, 'I have a theory.'

'Good, because I am bereft of theories. Mind you, I would rather have facts but beggars cannot be choosers at this stage of the game.'

'Quite. My theory is that Jim Ledbetter is not a serial-killer in the conventional sense. His greed, his interest in snuff-movies and the like, is only a *secondary* motivation. This may partly explain his rather elegant life-style but it is also to do with control. What greater control can one man have than the death, or not, of another human being?'

'That still makes him a crazed killer?'

'Sure, but a *special* kind of killer. Deep down he may be psychotic. You have to be slightly odd to go for pathology as a career anyway but it is still the *death* of his victims that matters most to him. *That's* his primary interest. Killing, not torture or mutilation, is what turns him on. The amputations, death by blow-torch, hanging from lighthouse pulleys, throats cut - these are all melodramatic *settings* for his murders. True, he can sell these images but beyond the money there is the ultimate power of life and death. Every day of his working life he is dealing with dead bodies. Unlike God, he cannot breath life into those sad corpses on his examination table. However, like God he *can* dispatch others at will. That gives him the ultimate control he needs. He chooses whom to kill and when. That way he is both judge and executor. That must surely be the ultimate power trip.'

''So where does Fiona fit into all this?'

'Up to her neck. However, she is more the little wife who will do anything for her brilliant, charismatic husband than a serial-killer herself. She's the fixer. I would not be surprised if she is not the one arranging the sale of her husband's hard-core images and videos. I'm sure she stole that arm but only at Ledbetter's bidding. I'm pretty sure too that she is the camera operator behind his mutilations and killings. She is more than an accessory, she is an active participant and that makes her dangerous but she will only crack if he cracks.'

'How are we going to do that?'

'I said once that his Achilles heel is probably his arrogance. I might need to adjust that notion. I think his weak spot is his desperate *need* to kill. Deny him that, then he is nothing. Deny him the freedom to select victims and execute them at will then he has no purpose to his life.'

'Meaning?'

'Arrest him at once. Any pretext will do but lock him up in solitary for as long as you can within the laws pertaining to an investigation. He's far too clever to ever give us the evidence we need to nail him absolutely. We are wasting our time - as the last five weeks have shown. But lock him up now and I guarantee we will watch him fall to pieces.'

28
Friday, 25th May

Doctor James Ledbetter, Consultant Pathologist at Aberdeen's Royal Infirmary, was arrested at eight o'clock the following morning.

As he parked his XJ Jaguar in his numbered parking space in the staff car-park he was approached by three uniformed officers. They told him that he was wanted for questioning in connection with at least four murders in the Portree area. He was not handcuffed but escorted on foot round to the front of the building to a waiting, police car and immediately driven to police HQ in the centre of Aberdeen for questioning.

This whole operation took place in full view of the Hospital and the many staff who were also arriving for work that morning.

Detective Inspector John White would have no further direct involvement with this part of the investigation, although he was still in charge on the Isle of Skye. The cross-examination of Ledbetter would be conducted by specialist officers working under Detective Chief Inspector Paul Elliott at Police HQ, Aberdeen.

Elliot had agreed to DI White's proposal the previous night - a proposal fully endorsed by Elspeth Grant. Elliott immediately assigned a Detective Inspector Scott Thompson to conduct the initial interviews. Elspeth drove from Edinburgh to Aberdeen early that morning and briefed Thompson thoroughly as to the best way to handle Ledbetter. Thompson was an experienced investigator. He knew what was at risk. He knew also that hovering in the wings, as it were, was one of the best Criminologists in the country. Elspeth would be there at every stage of the series of interviews planned over the next few days. She would watch on video monitors each interview and, where necessary, feed comments or questions into Scott's earpiece.

It was hoped that Ledbetter would realise that Scott was not alone with him in that room; that there was a *second* interviewer prompting him. This was deliberate, as was the very visible arrest earlier that morning. These were 'mind games' with someone whom Elspeth knew was himself a master 'player'. She knew too that he had a reputation in Court for his medical erudition and communication skills. He had even taken a course in how to deal with difficult questions from aggressive barristers - for either party.

He was going to be a very difficult person to cross-examine successfully. The question was, how long would it take to break him?

In Scottish law the police have thirty-six hours before having either to charge him or release him. The most they could hold him for would be a total of ninety-six hours, but only if that extension were granted by the Crown Court in Aberdeen.

The question Elliot and his team (including Elspeth) was asking themselves as they prepared to interview Jim Ledbetter for the first time, was would just four days be long enough?

* * *

Detective Sergeant Tom Watson had taken the memory stick 'stolen' from 'Alison Rutherford's' flat and opened it up that same day on his laptop at the Portree Community Centre.

This was the cause of some excitement by his colleagues. They crowded round his desk in anticipation.

It was indeed the 'missing' manuscript.

It was called 'Murder on the beach'. That alone sent a communal shiver down the backs of the young police officers hovering round Tom's computer. He ran off a hard copy which Janice then photocopied. For the next few hours, each member of John White's team read the manuscript from cover to cover.

It made for shocking reading.

* * *

On arrival at Police HQ, Aberdeen James Ledbetter gave his name and address and handed over all his personal possessions - wallet, car keys, mobile phone, pager etc. - to the Duty Officer. All this was conducted in a polite and respectful manner. Ledbetter himself seemed calm and self-assured.

He was then conducted to a police cell to await his first interview. The door was left open but he was asked not to leave the cell.

The Arresting Office, accompanied by a Forensic Examiner, then took Ledbetter's car keys and returned to the hospital car park.

Ledbetter's car was immaculate and contained nothing untoward. In the boot they found a snow shovel and snow chains, both apparently new. There was also his doctor's case, the sort most doctors carry for emergencies. It contained surgical pads, bandages and tape, together with three scalpels still in their protective wrappers. There was also a number of syringes and several small plastic bottles containing various drugs. The Forensic Examiner consulted a list he had with him then removed several bottles, placing them in an evidence bag. He then pulled a number of fingerprints off parts of the car interior and made a preliminary examination with a magnifying glass of the floor and sides of the boot He bagged a few hairs from the head rest on the driver's side. Both officers wore surgical gloves throughout. Afterwards they returned Ledbetter's car keys to the Duty Office back at Police HQ. The entire operation had taken only forty-five minutes.

* * *

Dr. James Ledbetter was taken from his cell to a small but comfortable interview room in the basement .

The room contained a large wooden table, four chairs and a smaller side table on which sat a recording device. There was a video camera pointed at Ledbetter and a microphone on the table in front of him.

He appeared very relaxed. Detective Inspector Scott Thompson introduced himself and shook hands. The PC, who had accompanied Ledbetter from his cell, went away to fetch coffee and biscuits for both of them. He returned with a flask and several cups. He then left the room. Scott then poured coffee for them both. They then sat, facing each other.

'I'm afraid, Dr. Ledbetter, that you are not allowed to smoke in here but if at any time you need a comfort break then please say so.'

'Thank you. I have never smoked.'

'I have to inform you that it is your right to be accompanied at any point by your lawyer if you think that appropriate or necessary.'

'Am I being charged?'

'No sir. We merely want to ask you a number of questions in connection with four murders that took place on the Isle of Skye. I know that you are familiar with those cases and, in your role as Consultant Pathologist, have been directly involved yourself with this investigation from time to time.'

'Then in that case I waive my right for legal representation - for the moment, anyway!'

This was said with another bland smile. The man, as Scott now realised, was as cool as a cucumber - considering the serious crimes that he could well be charged with. Elspeth had anticipated as much. Scott, however, was already less confident that his mentor's plan was going to work.

It was going to be difficult to 'break' this particular individual.

'You should know, Dr. Ledbetter, that this interview will be videotaped for later use. We also have a back-up audio system, the one on that table over there. As you can see, I am wearing an ear piece in order that I might take instruction from others watching this interview next door. This is normal practice in interviews of this kind. There is nothing sinister in it, I assure you.'

'Thank you for that assurance, Detective Inspector. I am not entirely sure I believe you, however!'

This was said with another slight smile. If Elspeth had hoped to phase Jim Ledbetter from the start then it had not worked. So far, at least.

'I want to start with a few basic questions concerning your whereabouts at the time of the four murders in question. Are you comfortable with than, Dr. Ledbetter?'

'Absolutely. Fire away, Inspector Thompson.'

* * *

It had taken DI John White three hours to read Georgina's manuscript. Like his young colleagues, he was shocked by its contents. But also strangely encouraged.

They all reconvened in the Community Hall later that morning. John laid on sandwiches, tea and coffee and sticky cakes from the Royal Hotel. The idea was to pool ideas as to the relevance of this manuscript. There was a palpable buzz of excitement in the room because every one there realised that they had at last stumbled on something that might give a clue perhaps as to *why* Georgina and 'Alison' in particular had been singled out and murdered.

It was DS Tom Watson who opened proceedings.

'The most obvious connection between Georgina Cousins and James Ledbetter is her inclusion of a blow-torch to torture the man at the centre of this new novel. We know, from what Detective Chief Inspector Elliott told us, that this real murder took place in Perth in 1998, only a few miles from where Ledbetter was then living. That is, for me at least, a coincidence too far -

even if, as yet, there is no actual evidence to link Ledbetter with this earlier, unsolved murder. Moreover, this episode of torture by blow-lamp is pivotal in Georgina's novel. The entire action leads up to her version of that horrific scene.'

'Agreed, but it could still have been lifted from any newspaper at the time. That too is how writers sometimes work, surely?'

'Yes sir, you are right but knowing now what we know about Georgina's creative methods, that scene has to be more than mere co-incidence - just as the murder in the lighthouse was somehow anticipated by this author. That has never been satisfactorily explained. How could she *know* that that was what was going to happen to 'Alison Rutherford'? She even hints at her own death in that novel when she describes the rape on the cliff tops in chapter nineteen. She may be a smart writer but she is no clairvoyant!'

'I agree, that is difficult to explain. As to the blow-torch episode, I still think its possible she simply took that story from the tabloid press. There was plenty of coverage - some of it quite lurid - in both the national and local press at that time Anyone else have a view on this?'

WPC Debbie Saunders was the next to speak.

'Yes sir, I accept that it is possible that Georgina simply lifted her story from the press but I think I also agree with Tom. There are details in that episode that were *not* in the press. Details that may well be present in police reports but which never surfaced in the papers.'

'Such as?'

'Well, for example, the press widely assumed that it had been a gang murder, some kind of punishment for an errant drug dealer. However, according to DCI Elliott the man had no connections with drugs of any kind and yet that information was simply not acknowledged by the press. They *wanted* a gang-land killing and that's what they published. It simply made for better copy.'

'What though, has this to do with Georgina?'

'What is significant for me is that in this new novel Georgina goes for the more plausible explanation - that this was a man, picked at random and simply tortured to death for pleasure - or commercial gain. That is what she reconstructs in her novel. That is what our killer does. Somehow she has stumbled on his exact *modus operandi.* The whole novel is geared to expose that while at the same time celebrating, as only Georgina knows how, the pleasure women like her get from such violence. This time, rather than vulnerable women, it is a man who suffers. That alone is a new departure for her and, in the light of previous work, sticks out like a sore thumb.'

'So, what are you saying, Debbie?'

'What I am saying, sir, is that not only had Georgina stumbled on the methodology and ghastly motivation of the person who tortured that poor man to death in Perth in 1998 but that she probably knew *who* the murderer was. I am not sure I can prove this yet but I think that if we all read this new manuscript again we would find other clues or hints to support my supposition. I believe that not only did Georgina *know* who the murderer was but that she intended to *expose* him in this new book. Somehow he found out and murdered both Georgina and her lover to save his own skin.'

'Very interesting theory, Debbie. Do please go on.'

'Georgina herself did not in any way 'anticipate' the way she and Emma would eventually die. That's nonsense. What happened was that the murderer, when he found out that she knew about him, immediately targeted both women. He simply killed them both to protect himself. He killed them using methods and circumstances that Georgina had previously devised for her story. That was his 'revenge' for nearly exposing him. Sick but effective.'

'What then about the computers. Can you explain why they were wiped in the way they were?'

It was DC Nick Fellows who spoke up next.

'I think I can, sir. Like Debbie says, I believe both women knew that they were under threat and that the killer was coming after them. It was essential to hide the evidence they had on him. Hence the scramble to wipe both computers. This Emma did, as she was the computer expert. She then hid Georgina's memory stick in her teddy-bear which Freda Butterworth subsequently found hidden under her late daughter's pillow. Thanks to Tom's nimble fingers, we found the memory stick and the 'missing' novel.'

'But Nick, none of this explains *how* the killer found out about the threat to him contained in the new book nor indeed even where Georgina and Alison lived. No one, as far as we know, knew that Georgina Cousins was indeed 'Sarah Daniels'. Nobody, as far as we can ascertain, even knew that Georgina and Emma were lovers, living under assumed names in Portree. Why should our killer?'

'My only explanation, sir, is that he stumbled on the information online. We know that both Georgina and Alison surfed the net for hard-core. That is the world in which our killer also moves. Maybe he just stumbled across them and put two and two together. Maybe he came across Georgina's actual online research into the blow-torch murder. That would have rung a few alarm bells for him. She would also have checked newspaper sources if she was adapting that story for her novel. Alison might even have hacked into police files. Nothing new there, I'm afraid to say.'

'Yes Nick, but....'

'Once you spot something like that, then it is relatively easy to trace it back to its source. It is even possible that the killer knew one of the two women, most probably 'Alison'. We need to check this but both Alison and Ledbetter were into fund-raising for local projects. They may well have come across each other here in Portree. Either way, he found out that Georgina had stumbled on his methods, motivations and probable involvement in the blow-torch murder. That alone would be sufficient motivation for him to track them down and kill them both. He may never have seen the manuscript for the new novel but he had acquired enough information online to show that it posed a real threat - a threat that could only be met with murder.'

Detective Inspector John White left the meeting feeling that something significant had been achieved. He immediately phoned Elspeth In Aberdeen to bring her up to speed.

29
Tell-Tales

Elspeth had spent most of her lunch-break watching back the video-tape of their first interview with James Ledbetter.

As she had predicted, Ledbetter was flawless and handled DI Scott Thompson's preliminary questions with an adroitness and fluency that was fascinating to watch. He gave clear, logical and utterly convincing answers to questions concerning his whereabouts on dates relevant to the murder enquiry. While someone would still need to check these out, Elspeth knew already that he would have covered his tracks in his usual, meticulous way. What was fascinating, however, was his body language and for some of the time when watching the playback she turned off the sound and simply observed his expressions, postures and body movements.

James Ledbetter was tall, slim and dapper. He was forty-five. Although his hair was thinning now he was still an elegant man. He reminded her somewhat of a younger version of Dennis Potter, the celebrated TV dramatist. He had a thin mouth and perfect teeth. His hands were his best feature with long, tapering fingers - rather like those of a concert pianist. Although he no longer had a yacht or climbed mountains, he was obviously fit. His skin, since he had sandy hair, was pale. His eyes, Elspeth noticed, were dark grey.

When seated opposite his interviewer Ledbetter looked relaxed and in control of his emotions. He leant back slightly in his chair, crossed his long legs somewhat languidly and held his hands together, one on top of the other in his lap, in a relaxed pose. She also noticed that when he first sat down, he pulled his chair slightly away from the table, as if wanting to distance himself from his interlocutor. When handed a cup of coffee, he placed it precisely on the table and at one point even adjusted the position of the spoon on the saucer. When he drank, he only took small sips, never taking his eyes off Thompson.

Occasionally, as if to verify something, Elspeth would run the tape back and freeze frame. She made frequent notes in her notebook.

His eyes, she observed, were steady and his blink rate appeared relatively normal. However, closer observation showed that if anything, his blinks were slightly fewer that what behavioural psychologists would consider normal. The only thing that revealed any kind of nervousness was his right foot which, hidden under the table, Scott Thompson would not have seen. It twitched slightly, as if beating time to an imaginary beat. It was only slight but the camera had caught it. Elspeth made a mental note to ensure that the camera angle was changed slightly at the first opportunity so that Ledbetter's feet were visible at all times. She knew from her studies in unconscious body movements that the feet were clear indicators of inner anxiety or tension. Someone uncomfortable in an interview situation would subconsciously seek the nearest exit and it would be that person's feet that would, quite literally, point the way. Two women in conversation, for example, standing facing each other, will turn their entire bodies to welcome a third person into their conversational group. If they did not want that third person to join them, they would only turn the upper part of their bodies - leaving their feet literally facing each other.

In short, Dr. James Ledbetter was disguising his nervousness extremely skilfully. Too skilfully, perhaps.

She also noticed that when Thompson later removed his cup and poured Ledbetter a fresh coffee, his head did not turn nor did his eyes follow the officer across the room. Instead he stared ahead to where the man had been sitting moments before. When Scott returned to the table and placed the fresh cup in front of him, Ledbetter leaned back, again trying to distance himself. This in itself was a slight reaction but, for Elspeth at least, a significant 'tell'. It was these unconscious reactions that the body made that were often the most revealing. It was the FBI who had first recognised the importance of 'tells' and had used them in numerous criminal investigations involving interviews with suspects. They had proved more effective than so-called lie detectors or polygraphs. Elspeth Grant had read everything that had been written about this aspect of behavioural science. She rather hoped that Ledbetter had not.

She examined this video tape in the company of DI Thompson who sat beside her throughout her analysis, also making notes. For the short time left before Thompson was due to resume his interrogation, they went into what Elspeth called 'huddle mode' and plotted their next moves.

Meanwhile, James Ledbetter had been allowed to eat his lunch (tuna sandwiches and a bottle of still water) in an office belonging to an Inspector, rather than back in his cell. He had also been offered the use of the Inspector's landline should he want to make any calls. Although Ledbetter probably guessed that his calls would be recorded (common practice in most police offices nowadays) he still chose to make three calls while eating his lunch.

He was observed throughout this by police officers in the large, open-plan office beyond where he sat, clearly visible through the glass partition that divided this 'private' office space from the much larger, general office.

His first call was to his wife, saying that he was 'helping police with their enquiries' on the Skye murders. When Elspeth was shown the transcript of this call she read it as a coded message to his partner-in-crime that he had been arrested and that she had better tread carefully.

His second call was to a colleague back at the Royal Infirmary, explaining that he would not be back that day and arranging for any necessary cover. This call was made in a tone of voice designed to calm and assuage his colleague at the other end. It was, as Elspeth divined, the call of someone anxious to 'explain' or diminish the humiliation of being arrested in a public place by uniformed officers and then put into a police car in front of hundreds of people. It served no other purpose - other than to tell her that here was a man anxious only to maintain control of the situation he now found himself in. He was, she knew, a control freak. What control freaks do *not* like is to lose control. Ever. His body language had told her that and now this phone call confirmed it.

The third call that lunchtime was much more interesting and when Elspeth read the transcript she almost fell off her chair with hysterics.

This third call was not to Ledbetter's solicitor, as one might have expected of a man possibly facing multiple murder charges, but to his bookie in Aberdeen with instructions to place a £10 bet on the three-thirty race at Cheltenham that Saturday afternoon.

The horse in question was called 'Fearless'.

* * *

The significance of the part Caroline Wear had taken in the life of Georgina Cousins in particular was still troubling Detective Inspector White and his team back in Portree.

Some weeks ago now White had obtained copies from Edinburgh of the police files relating to her murder. White had decided to revisit these files in the light of what they now knew about their two victims. He had, therefore, spent most of the afternoon that Friday reading through them carefully. As had his team.

What struck them all was that Caroline's presence in Georgina's life seemed almost an irrelevance. Perhaps she never did know this troubled young woman? Perhaps her choice of Caroline's photograph to put on the back of her books was entirely gratuitous; a random choice from some agent's portfolio?

It was WPC Janice Ward who thoroughly scotched that idea.

'Have you noticed sir, how few references there are in these files to Caroline's parents. We know she was probably illegitimate, which may explain why her father never appears, but why not her mother? Its often the case with young girls that go off the rails in the way Caroline did for the mother to feature somewhere in a known prostitute's juvenile criminal-record, in some case even going back to that girl's time at school. But here, in Caroline's file, there is hardly anything of that nature. Now, either the Edinburgh police did a sloppy job or such information has been suppressed or overlooked for some reason.'

'Did anyone else spot this? Charlotte?'

'Yes, sir. I think Janice is right. But there are one or two clues that might explain this anomaly. For example, the earliest known address given for Wear is not Edinburgh or London - both places she later knew well, 'professionally' - but Cheadle Hulme, in Lancashire. This address dates from 1992 and can only be the address of her mother. After this brief appearance it never features again, which probably means Caroline's mother moved soon thereafter.'

'Go on, Charlotte.'

'The next address we have in the police files for 'Wear' - almost certainly Caroline's mother - is East Pilton, a rough housing-estate in the Muirhouse district of Edinburgh. If Caroline was eighteen when she died in 2010 and her birthday is recorded as October, 1992 then Caroline's mother must have become pregnant whilst living in Cheadle Hulme, moving soon thereafter to Edinburgh where her daughter was born.'

'Do we know anything about Mrs Wear?'

'Yes sir.'

It was Paul who spoke this time.

'With Charlotte's help I tracked this Cheadle Hulme address on Google map. It was then, as now, a hostel for nurses.'

A murmur of excitement went round the room at this news. John White, however, tried to stay calm. Was this the break-through they had been waiting for, he wondered?

'Go on Paul. I think we can all see where this might be leading.

Please continue.'

'What this means, sir, is that Caroline Wear's mother was a nurse, living and working in the Greater Manchester area in 1992. That puts her close to Dr. James Ledbetter in his first year in a hospital in Wythenshawe, between 1992 and 1993. He would have been twenty-three at the time.'

'Yes, but...'

'I would go even further, sir, and take a wild guess that James Ledbetter might even be Caroline Wear's father! Only a DNA check can *prove* that but I think Caroline's involvement in this case has less to do with Georgina Cousins and everything to do with our killer.'

30
Catchee, Catchee Monkey

The second and longest interview with James Ledbetter took place that afternoon. If they were going to shatter his defensive armour then it was now or never. While they could keep him in over night and squeeze one more interrogation out of him before they needed to apply to the Court for the full ninety-six-hour extension, they would need to have something to convince the Judge that such an extension was even worth applying for. Such applications were not always granted, as DCI Elliott knew from bitter experience.

Without some compelling evidence with which to charge James Ledbetter, they faced the imminent prospect - within the next twenty-four hours - of releasing him without charge.

It was clear to Elspeth and the other observers in the room next door - following the second interview on video monitors - that James Ledbetter's manner had not changed. If anything, he seemed more confident and self-assured than he had been in the morning. He sat in his chair, crossed his legs and smiled wanly at DI Thompson, fussily sorting his notes before sitting down opposite. This time it was Thompson who appeared nervous. After the formal, predominantly polite exchanges of the morning session, Thompson's manner of interrogation now seemed hurried and sometimes even flustered. It was in marked contrast to the assured, confident manner of the interview he had conducted earlier that morning.

'Dr. Ledbetter, I would like to start with your relationship with Alison Rutherford.'

'What relationship?' replied Ledbetter.

'Well, I understood you had met her on a number of occasions, in connection with fund-raising activities in Portree. Is that not true?'

'Yes, but I hardly knew her, least of all socially.'

'I didn't ask her if you knew her socially. I asked you if you had simply met her.'

There was a momentary pause before Ledbetter replied. To Elspeth, closely observing Ledbetter's behaviour from the room next door, he looked slightly surprised at the aggressive turn Thompson's questioning had suddenly taken. In the morning session, Thompson had matched Ledbetter's body postures exactly. This was what experts call isopraxism. If, for example, Ledbetter crossed his leg but placed one hand on the table, palm facing down then Johnson mirrored it exactly. This was taken in, at an unconscious level, and gave the person being mirrored - in this case, Ledbetter - a sense of well-being. At some deep, unconscious level, Ledbetter's brain was telling him that Johnson clearly liked him and was not hostile or any kind of threat. Exact imitation - being the best form of flattery - was subconsciously persuading Ledbetter's brain and body to relax and not feel threatened.

Now, this afternoon, it was different.

Scott not only failed to copy Ledbetter's pose or position but often assumed an opposite or diametrical posture. From flattering mimicry, Scott now did the opposite. When Ledbetter leaned back with his long legs crossed casually, Scott leaned forward, his legs splayed. This had the affect, as Elspeth was quick to observe, of unsettling Ledbetter. At first it was only slight but as the interview continued in this vein, the more Ledbetter began to shift uncomfortably in his chair. She could not tell if Ledbetter was aware of this at a conscious level but it was increasingly obvious to all those watching that his self-assurance was being slowly, ineluctably undermined - for the first time.

Could this be the psychological break-through that Elspeth had hoped for? If Ledbetter was unsettled in any way, then he became more vulnerable and more susceptible to tough, aggressive questioning. His defence mechanisms - largely conscious actions controlled by the neo-cortex - would become 'compromised' by the 'honest', mammalian or limbic brain. His involuntary body movements would expose what his conscious mind was seeking to conceal. This Elspeth and Scott had fervently prayed might happen. Would it really work though? That was the million-dollar-question!

'Had you met her? Yes or no, Dr. Ledbetter?'

'Well, yes. She came to one or two meetings of the Parish Council but made little real contribution. I hardly noticed her, to be frank.'

'Then why did you not volunteer that information when the police began their enquiries into her murder?'

At this point Ledbetter uncrossed his legs, shifted position, then crossed his arms, leaning back slightly in his chair. Elspeth could swear that his blink rate had slowed down but without a tight shot on his face it was difficult to be sure. He was now clearly on the defensive but still sufficiently in control of himself not to give too much away. If he played poker then he would surely be a formidable match for anyone, thought Elspeth.

'Because it did not seem relevant. There were people on that Parish Council who knew her a lot better than I. Why don't you ask them?'

Thus far Elspeth had not spoken directly to Scott Thompson on his earpiece but now she spoke - quickly and quietly.

'Scott, fiddle with your papers' said Elspeth.

Scott immediately starting shuffling his papers, as if looking for the next line of questioning. This was watched closely by Ledbetter who clearly found his method of interrogation curious, to say the least. Was he rattled by it? Impossible to say as yet but it was a start.

Elspeth again spoke into Scott's earpiece.

'Great start, Scott. Coffee. Get into his personal space then go back to charm mode.'

Thompson stopped shuffling his papers. He started to put a question to Ledbetter but then unexpectedly interrupted himself. Ledbetter looked puzzled, if nothing else. This was proving to be a very different interrogation from the urbane exchanges of the morning. He must have sensed that things were different. For a man who liked everything to be exact, precise, even 'scientific' the alternating mannerisms of his interrogator were curiously disturbing. Doctors, scientists - especially pathologists - are often creatures of habit. They have tidy desks and logical, tidy brains. The work of a forensic pathologist is painstaking and exact. They do not like discontinuity or random, illogical action.

Ledbetter was, Elspeth noted with some satisfaction, now extremely alert and focused - his mind anxiously seeking to cope with Scott's irrational and inconsistent behaviour.

'I'm so sorry, Dr Ledbetter. I completely forgot to offer you a coffee. Please, let me pour you one. Biscuits?'

Thompson at this point got up, shambled across to the table and poured a coffee from the flask on the side table. This time, as Elspeth was quick to observe, Ledbetter's head turned to follow his movement across the room.

'No, its fine, thank you. I will have one later', said Ledbetter, still staring at the man's back stooped over the refreshment table.

Ledbetter's interjection was completely ignored by Thompson. It was as if he had not even heard him speak. He filled a coffee cup to the brim, turned (smiling apologetically) and slowly brought it to Ledbetter's side of the table. He then placed the cup in front of him, spilling some coffee into Ledbetter's saucer in the process. Instead of returning to his chair Scott remained standing close to Ledbetter. Thompson was over six feet tall and now loomed impressively over the seated man.

Elspeth was pleased to note that for the first time, with his personal space thus invaded, James Ledbetter look *distinctly* uncomfortable. He adjusted his chair slightly, pushing it away from the table. Thompson countered by placing both his hands on the table and leaning forward. Proxemics is the study of the 'space' we as individuals require. The closer someone else stands to you, the more you feel your 'personal space' is being invaded and the more uncomfortable you become. It is one of our most basic instincts and one which Elspeth had advised Scott to exploit whenever the opportunity presented itself.

'Did you know where she lived, this Alison Rutherford?'

'No. Not at all. Why should I?'

Ledbetter did not look at Thompson. His gaze was fixed on the saucer. He seemed in two minds what to do. In the end, he pushed it away to one side. Out of his direct line of vision. To a tidy mind, a saucer into which coffee had been slopped, was an irritant. Even in the midst of a serious interview, Elspeth was quick to note, Ledbetter could not bear to gaze at that saucer. His only solution was to push it out of sight as best he could, thereby making the problem 'disappear'. Simple but effective. Scott was playing his part to perfection. But would it, in the long term, have the desired effect?

'Well', said Thompson, looming ever taller over his victim, 'you were seen entering her cottage only three days before she died in that lighthouse. Can you explain that, Dr Ledbetter?'

* * *

It was one thing for John White's bright young things to make wild guesses but quite another to prove that James Ledbetter was Caroline Wear's father. However, it soon became clear, when the team started digging deeper, that her mother, Stephanie Wear, never completed her training as a nurse and did indeed leave Cheadle Hulme somewhat abruptly.

From Social Security information they ascertained that she lived on Benefit during Caroline's formative years in Edinburgh. When Caroline turned fifteen, all mention of Stephanie Wear ceased. Either she had died, moved away or simply changed her name.

From what little was known of Caroline's childhood and education, it is possible that this was when she dropped out, in every sense. For a few years she disappears completely, only popping up again in police records sometime in 2008. She is now sixteen and, according to police records, on the streets in Edinburgh earning a precarious living as a young prostitute.

As to James Ledbetter's part in all this, they could do nothing without a DNA comparison.

To that end, Detective Inspector White formally requested a sample of Caroline's DNA from the police in Edinburgh, to be forwarded to CDI Elliott in Aberdeen with an explanatory note, copied also to Elspeth Grant. It was at this stage a complete shot in the dark but White felt it was one worth taking. Quite how all this linked to Georgina Cousins was another matter but first things first. If young Dr. Ledbetter had had a sexual relationship with Caroline's mother which had resulted in a pregnancy then that at least partly explained Caroline Wear's appearance in this narrative. What it did *not* explain is what, if any, was Caroline's exact relationship with the women her father subsequently killed.

That evening John White rang Elspeth at Police HQ in Aberdeen to bring her up to date with the 'Gang of Five's' remarkable discoveries.

'Darling Inspector Plod, you are so clever that I could kiss you. I may just do that next time we meet!'

She was over the moon that John and his team had found a possible link between Ledbetter and the sad, until now, marginal figure of Caroline Wear.

'Mind you', she added, 'I'm not sure yet how we can use this information to crack this bastard. He's a very tough nut. We are not there yet although our second interview clearly rattled him. There's another long session with him tomorrow. I will let you know how we get on.'

'Elspeth, if anyone can break him I'm sure you can. I'll press on with the Caroline Wear angle. We are also making some progress on 'Alison's' fund-raising activities. I think it pretty safe to say that Ledbetter had indeed met Alison Rutherford, at least once or twice. Your 'shot in the dark' about him being seen by someone entering Alison's cottage will not stand up in Court I'm afraid but I bet it has got him really worried.'

'You can say that again!'

'Anyway, we now have definitive proof from both the Reverend Nish and three Parish Councillors that Ledbetter and Alison Rutherford knew each other. Whether Ledbetter actually knew at this stage that Alison was part of Caroline's world is very difficult to say. It is the first and only connection between Ledbetter and at least one of his victims that we have so far established so I need to make the most of it. By the way, Poppy sends her love and asks if you have recovered yet from your recent murder?'

* * *

Naturally, James Ledbetter denied ever having known where Alison Rutherford lived, let alone having entered her cottage.

This, thought Elspeth, was just as well as they had no witnesses who could have established that as verifiable fact. It had indeed been a 'shot in the dark' but it had worked. Ledbetter was now becoming increasingly unsure about what the police really knew or what they were merely guessing at or pretending to know. Police work is often speculative and cannot always display the same degree of rigour naturally expected of a scientist in a laboratory. Truth is slippery and guess-work, instinct and luck walk hand-in-had with deduction. It ought not to be this vague but in the real world of criminal investigation, with all its human complexities, it often was.

For a Consultant Pathologist whose entire professional life has been spent in the pursuit of factual evidence of a definable, *scientific* nature, this experiential world half-way between fact and fantasy was an uncomfortable place for him to be. That much Elspeth had anticipated.

For Ledbetter himself, it felt as if the carpet beneath his feet had begun to shift. It was not something he was used to or remotely liked.

He also denied, with increasing vehemence, that he had ever met Georgina Cousins or that he knew who she really was. He also claimed that he had been nowhere near Portree at the time both women were murdered. He had, he said, witnesses who could place him on the other side of the country. As to the nature of their murders, he found - as a doctor - the mutilation and murder of women utterly abhorrent. If they thought that he, a Consultant Pathologist of vast experience and some reputation, were capable of such atrocities, then they must be mad, utterly mad!

'Methinks he doth protest too much', thought Elspeth at the time.

That afternoon, at the conclusion of their second interview with the region's most senior Consultant Pathologist, two uniformed police officers entered the interview room and escorted James Ledbetter back to his cell for the night.

This time the door his cell door was securely locked.

31
Saturday, 26th May

It is claimed in 'High Places' that the 'Wheels of Justice' grind slow but true. It is also said that a little oil in the works can expedite matters. That's what the Chief Constable, Northern Constabulary had in mind when he invited the Procurator Fiscal, Aberdeen to his club that Saturday morning for a glass of claret.

'So George, do your chaps think they can make this one stick? I would hate to think what we would do if they failed. James Ledbetter is one of us, after all. He would probably sue. Could cost millions. Most of my budget, probably. If I even have a budget next year, that is!'

'Difficult to say, sir. We have a great deal of circumstantial evidence and are able to place him near the scene of at least three murders. In order to nail him we need to establish links with the two women on Skye that he allegedly murdered. If we can do that, then I am confident that the rest will follow.'

'I gather Elspeth Grant is working for you?'

'Yes, sir. She is making a significant contribution to our investigation.'

'Mad as a hatter, mind you! She once did cartwheels on my lawn, just to amuse my grandchildren. Very unladylike. I gather she is now shacked up with some black fellow half her age. What's that all about?'

'Not sure I know, sir.'

'So, you want me to have a word in old Duggie's shell-like and remind him which day of the year it is? You know that I cannot tell judges what they can or cannot do but I am sure that we can get you your extension. By the way, this is a very elegant claret you have found.'

'Thank you, sir.'

'Fancy sharing a bottle of it over lunch? My treat. Cannot have you or anyone else thinking that the Procurator Fiscal can be bribed that easily.'

'Certainly not. Perish the thought.'

* * *

The Golf Club at Nairn, seventeen miles from Inverness, is a traditional links course, commanding splendid views of the Moray Firth.

While the club has as yet to outlaw mobile phones, it actively discourages their use whilst playing. It was, therefore, with some annoyance that Brigadier Knowles, about to drive off on the fourth hole, was interrupted in mid-stroke by his playing partner's jaunty ring-tone.

'What? For God's sake, Paul, turn that bloody thing off!'

'Sorry! It's the Chief Constable. Must speak. Wont be a minute. Urgent business, I'm afraid.'

'Yes. Very well. Business, on a Saturday?' What's the world coming to?'

Detective Chief Inspector Paul Elliott moved away from his disgruntled partner and answered his phone.'

'Morning Paul. Not disturbing you, I hope?'

'Certainly not, sir.'

'Where are you? I tried your landline. No reply.'

'I'm playing golf, sir.'

'Ah. Very well. Anyway, I spoke to the Procurator Fiscal this morning. He's going to have a quiet word with Duggie McIver. You know what judges are like - unpredictable, at the best of times. Anyway, he is confident you will get your extension. Rum business this Ledbetter affair. Don't fuck up, Paul. Could be messy, what!'

'Indeed. We will do our best. Thank you, sir.'

'What do you think about Detective Inspector White? Not too close to Ledbetter, is he? I gather they are old friends. Know what I mean?'

'I know exactly what you mean, sir. John White is a good man. He has coped exceptionally well with a difficult investigation. Very professional, considering the lack of resources he had to contend with in the first week or so. I am more worried about his health than his loyalty, sir.'

'Very well. You know your man, Paul. But investigating someone your socialise with can lead to problems.'

'Well sir, you could say that of many of us. We have all socialised with James Ledbetter over the years. Why, only a few months ago you and I played a round of golf with him on these very links. You and your partner lost fifty quid, I seem to recall.'

'Yes. Yes, fair point. Very well, I wont disturb you any longer. Tell your team to tread carefully, though. Jim Ledbetter can be an awkward bastard at times. If we get this wrong he will sue, that's for sure. Who are you playing with today?'

'Reggie. Brigadier Reggie Knowles?'

'Oh my God! I had better let you get on with it! Good bye, Paul.'

* * *

The decision to delay the start of the next interrogation an hour or so on Saturday not only left Ledbetter kicking his heels in his cell but gave Elspeth and DCI Thompson time to review their strategy and plan for the big (and possibly, final) interview later that morning.

The first couple of interviews had been deemed a success for they had at least established that Ledbetter knew 'Alison Rutherford' personally. It remained now to try and get him to admit - or reveal somehow - that he also knew Georgina. It had always been DCI Elliott's plan to concentrate on this specific aspect of the case. The other murders on Skye - that of Gabriel McCallister and Trevor Burns - would follow once that link with the two murdered women had been established. As to Ledbetter's possible involvement with other, unsolved murders in the region - well, that too would follow in due course. It was important, at this stage, not to reveal what else they were preparing to throw at James Ledbetter.

Moreover, they still did not have enough evidence to begin to charge Ledbetter with the trafficking of hard-core video or still images on the internet. That could be better established once he was on remand, awaiting trial and they had a bit more time to pursue their investigation.

It was now very much the view at Police HQ that Ledbetter was responsible for other crimes than just those on the Isle of Skye. How many was impossible to say at this stage but Elspeth's work and that of Elliot's own team in Inverness had caused several old files to be re-opened in the light of events in Portree.

What *was* regrettable was DI White's blunder in the Portree churchyard when he told Ledbetter that a 'third' image had surfaced on the internet.

Up until then Ledbetter probably had no idea that the police knew of his possible activities in that murky world. The moment White rashly showed their hand, Ledbetter probably went straight back to his home on the outskirts of Aberdeen and destroyed any incriminating evidence. That was partly why the police had not yet bothered to arrest Fiona Ledbetter - it was probably too late to find anything that could incriminate either of the Ledbetters.

This error of judgement on John White's part had been the subject of a heated debate only a few days before at Police HQ,

Inverness in which Paul Elliott was obliged to defend White against fierce criticism from his superiors. That day Detective Inspector White came very close to being taken off the case. Questions of his loyalty were raised since Jim Ledbetter was known to be a personal family friend of the Whites. Could that friendship, dating back some ten years, compromise White's integrity as Investigating Officer? Was it possible that the lack of any kind of charge or arrest was caused by a personal conflict of interests?

Elliott rejected all these suggestions vigorously. He had known John White longer than White had known Ledbetter. There had been mistakes in the past, errors of judgement perhaps but never once had John White's integrity as a policeman been questioned. No, White was solid and reliable. There should, argued Elliott, be no question of taking him off the case at this crucial stage.

Meanwhile, it was clear to Scott Thompson and his team that they also needed to establish somehow that Fiona and her husband were responsible for the theft of Jennifer Chancellor's severed arm. Evidence here was still rather thin on the ground - thin enough for a good solicitor to tear it to shreds. That was to be avoided, at all costs. The investigation was at a delicate stage. Mistakes now could be disastrous. Although DCI Elliott was not at Police HQ that morning he had given Thompson strict instructions to keep him fully informed of events. This also meant that if they had to release Ledbetter without charge and he decided to sue, for say defamation, then at least Elliot could more readily distance himself when the shit actually hit the proverbial fan.

It had been decided, therefore, to let Fiona sweat it out alone while her husband was in custody for questioning. It was Elspeth's contention that without Jim, Fiona was nothing. Perhaps, left alone, she might crack more readily when they eventually brought her in for questioning. That way they could effectively keep them apart *and* play one off against the other.

The revelation from the team in Portree that Caroline Wear was probably Ledbetter's illegitimate daughter had gone some way to mitigating the damage done by White's blunder. Only a DNA comparison could prove paternity. They were still waiting for a sample of Caroline's DNA to come from Edinburgh. That piece of evidence was now crucial. They already had DNA samples from Ledbetter himself. These consisted of hairs from his car and spittle on the rim of the glass he had been given to use with his bottled-water at lunchtime on Friday. Both that glass and the bottle had been whisked away to the Forensic laboratory the moment Ledbetter left that office and returned to the interview room for the afternoon session.

If it proved true that Caroline Wear was his illegitimate daughter, then this might provide some kind of link between Georgina and Ledbetter. The significance of Caroline's photograph on 'Sarah Daniels'' later books and how it bore on a possible relationship between father, daughter and Georgina Cousins herself was hugely problematical.

If White's theory was true that Georgina knew that Ledbetter was a serial-killer, that her latest, unpublished novel was written expressly to expose him and that his daughter's photograph on the back of her books was there to taunt him (highly speculative, but possible) then they had finally established a possible motive for the killings.

Georgina's research, as revealed in her novel, could also provide valuable confirmation - now widely suspected by the police in Aberdeen - that Ledbetter had killed at least three times before he started his 'work' on Skye.

These same thoughts were being mulled over by Detective Chief Inspector Paul Elliot that Saturday morning as he sat with an extremely grumpy Brigadier Freddy Knowles in the bar after their round of golf. Perhaps Freddy had been put off by Elliott's mobile phone but that was no real excuse for ending up in no less than three bunkers - at the fourth, ninth and tenth and then deep in the rough on the eighteenth.

No, Freddy may have been some hot shot in the Malaysian jungle but he was a poor shot on the links at Nairn.

* * *

The Portree team gathered early that same morning in the Community Centre over coffee and biscuits. Although it was Saturday, every one of John White's 'bright young things' had volunteered to work on what should have been their day off. Even WPC Debbie Saunders of the Portree local Constabulary (honorary, co-opted member of the 'Gang of Five') turned up.

It was going to be a busy day for they knew that the success of the Ledbetter interviews depended partly on what they came up with in the next few hours or so. Moreover, Saturday was not the most suitable day of the week on which to do the kind of telephone research they had all used so successfully in recent weeks. Still, what must be, must be.

But then there was always the internet and the 'Gang of Five + 1' were now highly accomplished 'surfers'.

Their boss had divided them up into three, two-man teams with himself as roving reporter, as it were.

Detective Sergeant Tom Watson and WPC Janice Ward (she had volunteered for this coupling, much to the secret amusement of the others) had been assigned the task of obtaining information about Ledbetter's time as a young doctor in Manchester, between 1992 and 1995, after which he moved to Dundee. Their main task was to establish a possible connection between Dr. James Ledbetter and Caroline Wear's mother, at that time a nurse in training at Cheadle Hulme Hospital in the Greater Manchester area.

PC Paul Miles and WPC Charlotte Stephens had been given the task of looking into Caroline Wear's teenage years in Edinburgh from 2006, when she would have been fourteen, to 2010 when she was killed by youths unknown. They also needed to establish, if possible, a connection between Caroline and Georgina Cousins at that time.

Finally, PC Nick Fellows and WPC Debbie Saunders were asked to revisit 'Sarah Daniels' new, unpublished novel to examine closely the 'evidence' she might have gathered against Ledbetter in the horrific murder in which a man had been tortured to death with a blow-torch near Perth in 1998.

Since this murder was at the core of Georgina's new manuscript and seemingly contained new information that not even the police had, then clearly that text was a significant part of their ongoing investigation. Was 'evidence' contained within a novel admissible in Court? Probably not but at this stage the team were snatching at straws. If the fictional 'reconstruction' within a novel of a real murder could advance their investigation, then why not at least consider it.

Meanwhile, John White moved from table to table, monitoring progress. Each time anything significant emerged during the course of the day he would add it to their communal white-board. That way new information could be shared immediately and acted upon by anyone if it was thought relevant to each teams' specific area of enquiry.

He, like the rest of his talented young team, knew that there was much at stake. What they came up with today could transform the case and help bring Consultant Pathologist James Ledbetter to justice. No pressure then!

32
The Gilded Cage

John White and his 'Gang of Five + One' had been hard at work for several hours in the Portree Community Centre when Sergeant McGregor dropped by to see how they were getting on.

It was strange to see him in his anorak and climbing boots and not his usual police uniform. He looked rather dapper, thought John.

'Fancy a breath of fresh air, Albert?' said Detective Inspector White. This was code for 'fancy a smoke, Albert because I do'!

'Don't mind if I do, thank you John.'

They stepped outside the Community Centre, sat on a bench and lit their pipes. For a while they both puffed contentedly, in silence.

'Been for a walk, Albert?'

'As it happens, I have - up yonder, on that wee hill above the village. I have been up there every Saturday without fail since my missus passed away. She loved that spot. We scattered her ashes up there. Mind you, once a week is about as much as I can manage these days. How are your young Turks getting on?'

'Very well, for the moment. However, we are up against it, Albert. Ledbetter is being interviewed again this morning. At the end of that we have to stick some charges on him or he could walk.'

'Well, John, if its any consolation, I said a prayer for you this morning. I find that usually works.'

'Well thank you, Albert. Much appreciated. I think its fair to say that we need all the help we can get!

* * *.

By three o'clock that afternoon everyone was utterly exhausted. It was clearly time for John White to call a halt to the proceedings.

'Ladies and gentlemen, gather round please.'

The team got themselves another coffee each and pulled their chairs closer to the large white-board at the far end of the room; a board now virtually covered with notes, lines, arrows and what educationalists call 'mind maps'.

Sergeant Tom Watson and Janice Ward were the first to speak. They stood to one side of the board, consulting it or their own hand-written notes as and when required. Tom began.

'We think we can just about prove that Ledbetter and Stephanie Wear met in Cheadle Hulme, sometime in 1992.'

This announcement was met with a spontaneous round of applause and a few shouts or approval from some rowdier members of the team.

'We base this assumption on the testimony of a Dr. Mark Wilson, who knew James Ledbetter at that time, together with staff files at Cheadle Royal Hospital, where Stephanie Wear was in her first year of training as a psychiatric nurse. Cheadle Hulme is part of Greater Manchester. Ledbetter had been living and working in Manchester most of his life. In 1992 he was undertaking his probationary year as a newly-qualified doctor at Wythenshawe Hospital, on Southmoor Road, Wythenshawe.'

At this point Janice took over the narrative.

'We found Mark Wilson through the Wythenshawe Hospital medical alumni web-site. He described Ledbetter as something of a 'lady's man' until he met a young Scottish nurse then in training at Cheadle Royal when he seemed to settle into a steadier, single relationship. Unfortunately Wilson was unable to remember the name of this nurse but according to the Registrar's records at the hospital, one Stephanie Wear abandoned her training abruptly in February of that year and moved back to Scotland. No explanation was given at the time.'

Tom now picked up the thread of their argument once more.

'Wear is a Scottish name. We were unable to find anyone who knew her at that time but it was not uncommon for young nurses to fall for dashing young doctors. In the marriage market, a young doctor is regarded as something of a 'catch'. If Stephanie had a sexual relationship with James Ledbetter and later discovered that she was pregnant by him, then that might explain her abrupt departure. Perhaps he abandoned her? Marriage, or simply a scandal, at that stage of his own training, would have ruined what was likely to be a brilliant career - as it subsequently proved to be. To complicate matters, Stephanie was - according to her birth certificate - a Catholic. That probably meant that abortion was out of the question. She did the only thing open to her and that was to go back home to Scotland. It was there that Caroline was born on 11th October, 1992.'

Janice was the last to speak.

'I'm afraid that is as definitive as we can be at this stage - without DNA confirmation.

What is interesting, however, is that after the sobering experience of fatherhood at the age of twenty-three, James Ledbetter - according to his friend Wilson - abruptly ceased to be 'the lady's man' of old and buckled down to his studies for the next few years.'

Tom and Janice resumed their seats.

'Well done', said White. 'Excellent work. Whose next? Paul. Charlotte. Thank you.'

Paul and Charlotte took their places by the white board. Charlotte was the first to speak.

'We were tasked with finding out something about Caroline Wear's teenage years in Edinburgh. This proved more difficult than we had imagined, not least because her police records are very patchy. If that were not enough, Social Security records also proved woefully inadequate. We *can* show that Stephanie herself was on benefit for the first few years of her life as a single parent but then she starts to drop in and out of the records with alarming frequency. We think she might have had a drug or alcohol dependency at this time.'

At this point Paul took over their presentation.

'To make matters worse, we have been unable as yet to find a single relative who might tell us more about Caroline's mother or indeed about Caroline herself. We may of course be looking in the wrong place. If Caroline was ashamed of her single-parent status she might not have returned to her home town. She was perhaps 'hiding' in the nearest large city she knew - Edinburgh.'

Charlotte:

'The records improve by the time Caroline is of school age. We have traced her to a number of schools in the Greendykes and Niddrie areas of Edinburgh. She was by all accounts a disruptive pupil and was cautioned a number of times by the local police for anti-social behaviour. As was pointed out earlier, her mother hardly features at this time; a time when Caroline was clearly without any parental control. Which brings us to the so-called 'missing years' - from 2008, when she was sixteen, to her death in 2010. Paul.'

'For two years the official records are a complete blank. There is nothing on record about Stephanie nor her wayward daughter. Births and Deaths cannot help, nor was Caroline in trouble with the police. Not once - and that after a number of years of very disorderly behaviour. She has simply fallen off the radar. Completely. We were at a loss to know where to start looking until Debbie here reminded us of parts of a book by 'Sarah Daniels' she had read. Debbie, do you want to explain your theory?'

Debbie stood up. She looked somewhat shy, not being used to presentations of this kind. They were not often needed in Portree!

'Debbie, tell us your theory please.'

'Thank you sir. I should say from the start that its not so much a theory, more a salutary tale of seduction and exploitation by predatory lesbians in the dark and sordid streets of Rome's soft underbelly!'

Laughter and round of applause.

'Blimey! Do go on.'

'In June, 2011 'Sarah Daniels' published a particularly trashy novel set in contemporary Rome. It was called *In a Gilded Cage*. The two central characters are wealthy, predatory lesbians who stalk the streets each night looking for female sex. One night they find a young girl whom they 'rescue'. She is a wayward child of sixteen called 'Carlotta'. This, you will not be surprised to learn, is Italian for Caroline.'

A murmur of delight went round the room at this revelation.

'For the next two years the two wealthy lesbians unofficially 'adopt' their wild girl and slowly 'tame' her. From what started out as their 'bit of female rough' for the night turns into a cosy *mènage-á-trios* that lasts two years. Then, inevitably, the two women begin to squabble over their protégé. 'Carlotta' is now a beautiful, cultured seventeen-year-old. When tempers flare and fights ensue, 'Carlotta' flies the 'gilded cage'. She goes back onto the streets of Rome and becomes a prostitute once more. Months later she is murdered by her pimp with a cutthroat razor. It outline, at least, this is very close to Caroline's own desperately sad story. Like her fictional doppelganger 'Carlotta', she too was knifed to death - but in Edinburgh, not Rome. This book was published with the *real* Caroline's photo on the back cover. We have no idea how Georgina obtained this photograph because it was taken *after* Caroline had run away but there it is, bold as brass and purporting to be the real 'Sarah Daniels'.'

'What do you conclude from that?'

'Publishing Caroline's photograph there was a gauntlet thrown down to Ledbetter, Caroline's father. It was saying: I know who you are, you bastard. I know what you did to your own daughter through neglect and indifference. This is *her* story. *Your* story - one of mutilation and murder - is next!'

As Debbie concludes this summary there is a spontaneous round of applause. John White calms them down with a stern look.
'I see what you mean by 'trashy' but can we really tie this to Caroline Wear's unhappy life in Edinburgh?'

It was Paul who spoke next.

'Yes sir, I think we can. Georgina Cousins' last known address in London was Frognal Lane, Hampstead Heath. When her agent appeared at the funeral in Portree I took the opportunity afterwards to ask her if she had ever had another address for Georgina. Yes, she said. Edinburgh. There were two addresses, in fact. One was The Royal Bank of Scotland, 75 George Street where Georgina (under the name 'Sara Daniels') had an account. It was into this account that her agent and publisher deposited her royalties. The second address was a private apartment in Randolph Crescent - a *very* smart part of Edinburgh.'

Another appreciative murmur went round the room. The others were now sitting on the edge of their seats, clearly enthralled by these revelations.

'Then we had another breakthrough. We had always assumed that wherever Georgina moved, 'Alison' (or rather Emma) moved too. This proved not to be the case. When Georgina moved to Edinburgh in 2008 it would seem that Emma stayed on at their flat in London. How do we know this? Because, according to Open University records for one 'Alison Rutherford' of Frognal Lane, Hampstead she was studying for a Foundation Degree in Computing and IT Practice. This was a two-year, full-time course with some residency requirements. The pathway she had chosen was Software Development.'

Another round of applause. Charlotte then took up the story.

'We have no idea why Georgina chose to move from London but it may have everything to do with the death of her father in 2008. The Edinburgh flat was his so Georgina may simply have occupied it in his absence. Perhaps too she was arranging to move to Portree even then. We simply do not know. The reason Emma did not accompany her was that she was probably too wrapped up in her OU course back in London.'

'Where does Caroline come into all this?'

'Since the dates all match up and because the story she subsequently wrote closely parallels Caroline's own tragic history at that time, I think that they became lovers in Edinburgh sometime in 2008. This is exactly when Caroline disappears under the police radar. Georgina may well have 'saved' her from a life of prostitution but we are pretty sure that she also exploited her wealth to take control of that vulnerable young woman for sexual purposes of her own - just as she had done with Emma Butterworth in 2006. No doubt she went back 'home' to Emma in London most weekends but the disputes described in the novel may have taken place in reality, especially if Emma knew of her lover's new relationship with young Caroline. Perhaps theirs was an open relationship and Emma knew of Georgina's young lover in Edinburgh. Either way, everything changed in 2010.'

Paul then took up the narrative.

'That year Georgina sold her late father's house and left Edinburgh. Emma had now completed her OU course. The two of them moved to Portree where Georgina installed Emma - now officially called 'Alison Rutherford' - in a cottage not far from her own. This took place in May, 2010.'

Charlotte:

'According to police records at this time Caroline is now back on the streets of Edinburgh, earning a precarious living as a prostitute. We can only guess why this happened but in the novel it is 'Carlotta' who deliberately runs away, abandoning her wealthy protectors. No one tries to rescue 'Carlotta' and she dies at the hand of a particularly vicious pimp under whose 'protection' she has fallen. Perhaps, in reality, Georgina did try to rescue *her* wayward protége but by August, 2010 it is too late - Caroline is dead, stabbed to death by 'person or persons unknown' - as the Edinburgh police files coldly put it.'

33
Murder most Foul

The 'Blow-Torch' murder, as it became known as in the press at the time, was one of the most savage acts of violence John White and his young team had ever come across.

The murder took place on the 21st September, 1998 about twenty miles from Perth. A man's badly burned body was found by a tramp in a derelict cottage off the A822, just outside the village of Crief.

The dead man had been tortured to death with an acetylene torch. His injuries were terrible and it was only from his dental records that Forensic were able to firmly establish identity - Ken Sutton, a used-car dealer from Glasgow. Ken's car was found parked at the back of the cottage. It was that which had attracted the tramp to the cottage in the first place.

The torch and gas cylinder had been left on the floor. According to the tramp, the torch itself was still warm so it had been a close-run thing. Any earlier, then the tramp might have himself faced this merciless killer.

Since Ken Sutton had a police record for minor drug-dealing in the past, it was assumed early on that this was a drug-related killing. That is what the press picked up on and ran with. The police, however, later established that Sutton had no known association with any drug dealers in Glasgow or elsewhere. He was what his wallet proclaimed - a used-car dealer from the Cumberland Street district of Glasgow. No one could explain what he was doing in an abandoned cottage near Perth nor how he might have been lured there.

And there the case came to a sickening halt. No arrest. No known suspects, let alone a possible motive for such an horrendous crime.

* * *

When the feedback session at the Portree Community Centre resumed after a short 'comfort' break, it was the turn of PC Nick Fellows and WPC Deborah Saunders to make their presentation.

Nick spoke first.

'I think all of us here recognise that what we may gleam from a novel does not constitute evidence, certainly not in the way a Court might define that word. However, this case has at its centre a successful author of popular fiction who - as has been shown already this afternoon - invariably draws on her own, biographical experience when inventing plot and character. The new novel is no exception. If anything, this...'

At this point Nick lifted a bulky manuscript from the desk and waved it at his rapt audience.

'This is the closest Georgina Cousins has ever came - will ever come - to writing non-fiction. It is a powerful and disturbing account of a murder in which a man is tortured to death with a blow lamp. It is also the story of an unknown serial-killer who, recognising that it is he who is being described in a work of fiction, stalks its author and eventually kills her. It is as close to what actually happened to Georgina Cousins as can be imagined.'

Deborah:

'We realised from the start that Georgina could easily have acquired the basic facts of this story from the largely erroneous press coverage this murder attracted. But this has proved not the case. Not once, for example, does she consider Sutton's murder to be drug-related - something widely reported in the press at the time. Instead, she builds her novel round a killer who seeks out lone victims and delights in mutilation and torture. Ring a bell?'

Nick:

'We began by first comparing information contained within the police file for this case and press statements or transcripts the

Grampian police released during their initial investigation. This gave us a short but accurate list of information that the police have always *with-held* from the press - such as the fact that Ken Sutton suffered from epilepsy, that his son had recently died in a car accident and that his ex-wife was expecting her first child with her new partner.'

Deborah:

'When we cross-checked this information with Georgina's manuscript, every one of the examples Nick has just given you turned up in one form or another. There were many other examples too, leading us to assume that she either had a police informant feeding her this stuff or that somehow she or Emma had hacked into police computers. Either way, she has *inside* information on this murder that gives her fictional account alarming credibility.'

'OK but how does James Ledbetter fit into this, Nick?'

'Well sir, we compiled a broad list of the basic information we currently have on Ledbetter - age, height, colouring, shoe size, occupation, education, wife, hobbies (sailing, rock-climbing, for example), vacation preferences - anything, in fact, that we could reduce to little more than a word or phrase that a search engine could handle. We ended up with 120 bits of specific information about him. We then ran this list through the manuscript, using a simple 'search-and-find' software. The results were staggering. Eighty-seven percent of this information was present in Georgina's text. That is much higher than one would normally expect - so my mate Rory at Microsoft tells me.'

Deborah:

'If you think that this is impossible, then think what advertisers at Facebook or Amazon are doing everyday with the bits of information they have about each of us. Their demographic profile of you or me is modified every time we log on and add some 'useless' snippet of domestic gossip to our homepage or purchase something online. In short, sir, when you take these tiny bits of fragmented information in their totality, Georgina's new novel contains as detailed a portrait of James Ledbetter as one could imagine - without actually naming him.'

A murmur of astonishment ran round the room. It was Tom Watson at the back who asked the next question.

'Nick, how could Ledbetter have possibly known that he was the subject of a new 'Sarah Daniels' novel? In other words, what makes you think that Ledbetter *knew* he was being targeted? We are not even sure if he had read the *Gilded Cage*, let alone something as yet unpublished!'

'With regard to the new, unpublished novel we think that he first clocked Georgina's online research. She probably started with press cuttings. From such simple enquiries its easy to track further, more detailed searches. You may not know exactly who is searching but you can certainly follow their progress. For example, word clusters such as - 'murder, blow-torch, Crief, Ken, tramp' - are always easy to spot, with the right software. If clusters like this show up regularly, then you can bet your pension that someone somewhere is looking at something very specific.'

At this point Deborah intervened:

'For Ledbetter, alarm bells must have rung in his head the moment he discovered someone was revisiting that old case. I'm not saying he immediately identified this mysterious researcher but he *was* able to monitor her progress. From then on it was a case of the hunted turning hunter.'

Nick:

'For us the clincher is that Georgina is the first person - other than Dr. Grant perhaps - to link the other murders at Pitlochry and Aviemore specifically to the one near Crief. Of course the police thought at the time that they might be connected but not in the way Georgina discovered. Somehow, by some miracle of feminine logic or creative deduction, she spotted the one thing that linked all three murders.'

'Which was...?'

'Well sir, we went back and looked at the police files for the other two unsolved crimes. In the brutal stabbing at Pitlochry, the body was found in a disused railway carriage that had been somehow abandoned in a field. The man's ears had been cut off with a knife and left on the floor at his feet. Forensic also found a can of petrol and some screwed up rags. The murderer was clearly intending to set fire to the carriage to cover his tracks but was clearly interrupted or disturbed by something before he could do it.'

'In the Aviemore murder, in which a youth was tied to a tree before his throat was cut, they discovered that the contents of his rucksack had been emptied onto the ground. This made them think that robbery might have been the initial motive but that something had then gone horribly wrong.'

Deborah:

'Among the scattered contents of his rucksack was a postcard from America showing a New York skyline. The lad's parents claimed that he knew no one in New York, even though it had a genuine postmark and a brief, hand-written message wishing the boy luck with his exams. It was signed by someone called 'Sam'. Forensic and other experts spent a great deal of time looking at the handwriting, possible DNA beneath the stamp and the rest. What they didn't really spot was that the stamp itself depicted the Statue of Liberty holding, wait for it, her torch!'

Applause and laughter rattled round the room.

Nick:

'In other words, all three murders had been 'signed' with a 'torch' - petrol soaked rags (Pitlochry), acetylene torch (Crief) and Olympic-style torch held by Liberty herself (Aviemore). This not only links them but shows that, as with Ledbetter's 'three-thirty' signature with which we are now all too familiar, these murders were also for commercial gain. We have had neither the means nor the time to check if the Obscene Publications Unit in London have come across any photographs of these three murders but it is my guess that horrific images were out there pretty soon after each murder was committed. This is so much like Ledbetter's *modus operandi* that we have little doubt now that he is the serial-killer involved in all three unsolved murders - in addition to those four we are investigating here on the Isle of Skye.'

Loud and prolonged applause.
Deborah:

'The remarkable thing is that Georgina discovered all this by herself. Moreover, in her new, unpublished novel she cleverly anticipates every move Ledbetter makes thereafter, in his desperate attempt to hunt down and kill the person who is planning to expose him in such a daring manner. It was as if she was challenging him, drawing him into her trap.'

Nick:

'In the unpublished story, the serial-killer is finally lured to his death on a remote Greek beach. That's about the only bit she got wrong. As it turned out, it was *she* who was lured onto a Scottish beach and murdered. The mutilation and death of Emma followed as night follows day. These murders were not only a further way to make money but vicious and entirely deliberate acts of revenge - the most extreme form of 'damage limitation' one could imagine. We are fairy confident that Ledbetter never found Georgina's manuscript or digital text - thanks to Emma's teddy-bear - but he had at least silenced its author and her partner. Now perhaps, he thought he was safe.'

'But Nick, this whole, brilliant hypothesis is predicated on Georgina knowing all about Ledbetter. How could she know anything about him or even where to begin to start looking?'

'Georgina knew where to start looking probably as far back as 2008. It was Ledbetter's embittered daughter who told her. In other words, it was Caroline Wear who shopped her own father!'

'That's a very bold statement, Nick. Can we prove that?'

'Not really, sir. I can only speculate how Georgina made the connection between the unknown serial-killer she was hunting and Dr. James Ledbetter. Unless Ledbetter himself tells us under cross-examination, we may never know.'

'Indeed. Meanwhile, all we have is speculation, qualified by tried-and-trusted deduction. Please carry on, Nick.'

'Very well, sir. My guess is that Caroline knew who her father was. She would have learned that from her mother. Maybe, like many fatherless teenagers, she now wanted to establish contact with him. If she was in need of money, particularly in those desperate years before she was 'rescued' by Georgina, then he would have been the most obvious person to ask. It would be very easy to trace a doctor with the unusual name of 'Ledbetter'. Maybe she started blackmailing him, threatening to expose him to the press as the 'father of a teenage prostitute'.

'Even if he denied paternity, the scandal alone would seriously damage his reputation as an eminent Pathologist.'

'That's all very well Nick, but it still does not explain how Georgina realised that her lover's own father was the man she was hunting! That might be acceptable in a work of fiction but this is the real world, after all!'

'I agree, sir. It is all extremely speculative. However, my theory is that Caroline told Georgina about her earlier attempts to contact her father. Ledbetter's rejection of her, in every sense, must have hurt her deeply. She was, by all accounts, a very angry young woman when Georgina took her under her protective wing. Perhaps Georgina then offered to help her, even though there was no need now to blackmail him for money. Since Georgina already knew that her serial-killer had medical expertise and operated in the Perth area, it would not have taken much to see a possible link with Ledbetter. It was the final piece in her jigsaw puzzle and the one that would lead to her writing her next (and final) novel. It's called *The Hunter*. That is the title of the new, unpublished novel we have been analysing.'

34
Saturday, 26th May

On Friday night Elspeth had requested a second video camera that would give her close-ups of Ledbetter's face during his next interrogation, together with a better angle showing his legs and feet under the table. This had been readily agreed. Indeed, even as Ledbetter was led by two uniformed officers into the interview room at 11 o'clock on Saturday morning, he found one white-coated technician actually sitting in his chair while another, on a pair of steps, positioned and focussed the camera itself.

Both hastily finished their work and left, allowing Ledbetter to finally take his usual seat.

In the gallery next door Elspeth nearly wet her knickers with laughter at this little charade. She watched gleefully as Ledbetter - waiting for DI Scott Thompson to arrive - kept glancing nervously at the new camera obviously pointing straight at him. Although he had been allowed to wash and brush his teeth, Ledbetter had not been given any opportunity to shave. From the once suave Consultant Pathologist who first entered this room on Saturday, the mirror in the corridor they had passed by moments ago now showed a dishevelled, somewhat sullen individual.

It should be noted that that mirror had not been there on Friday. That too was Elspeth's idea.

DI Scott Thompson eventually entered with a noisy, apologetic flourish. He was carrying his usual bundle of papers, over-filled briefcase and a Tesco plastic carrier bag in which were three large folders. For a senior Interrogator it was a shambolic entrance. He apologised for being late, spread his papers over their table and eventually sat down. Ledbetter watched all this with incredulity. Elspeth noticed that some of his self-assurance had quickly returned - following Scott's pathetic apology for being late and the disorderly state of his notes.

The interview began with a very simple question delivered in a quite, almost apologetic manner.

'Am I right, Dr. Ledbetter, in thinking that you knew that 'Sarah Daniels' - whom we both now know to be really called Georgina Cousins - was about to publish a new book exposing you as a serial-killer?'

'What? What on earth are you talking about? I know of no such novel. This is nonsense? What *are* you talking about?'

'Novel? Who said anything about novel. I said 'book'.'

'Well, she's a novelist, is she not? I naturally assumed that you were referring to a work of fiction...'

'So you deny that you knew that you had been identified as a serial-killer by Georgina Cousins?'

'Of course. I am not a serial-killer, Detective Inspector.'

'Can I also assume, therefore, that when you discovered that she was about to identify you as the killer of a man found dead near Pitlochry in 1997 (he's the one, by the way, whose ears had been cut off) and also of another young man whose throat had been cut in a wood near Aviemore in 2001, that you did *absolutely* nothing about suppressing such information?'

'What? This is lunacy! I know nothing about any of this.'

'Can I also assume, therefore, that you did absolutely nothing about information Georgina had concerning the murder in 1998 of Ken Sutton? You must remember Ken? He's the one who was tortured to death with a blow lamp. I'm told Georgina had specific information which implicated you? That must have rung a few alarm bells, surely Dr. Ledbetter?'

'I have absolutely no idea what you are talking about, Inspector.'

'Quite. Despite knowing that Georgina was about to expose you as the killer of at least three murders, all committed within forty miles of where you were living at the time, I assume that you did not try to trace her whereabouts, destroy that (as yet) unpublished manuscript, and murder its author? Yes or no will suffice, Dr. Ledbetter.'

'This is preposterous. Have you lost your mind, Thompson?'

'I hope not. My friends do sometimes think otherwise, I'm afraid. Oh, would you like some coffee? I think I would.'

Scott got up, crossed to the table and slowly poured himself a coffee. He then returned to his seat, laboriously added sugar from a paper container, stirred it and began to sip - all the time smiling benignly at Ledbetter across the table. It was as if the exchange that had just taken place had never even happened.

Elspeth had watched all this with bated breath.

She and Scott had decided that they should definitely show Ledbetter now that he was in the frame for far more than the Skye murders. It had taken them a while to persuade DCI Elliott to give his permission to show their hand in this way but in the end he had agreed. Elspeth's argument was that Ledbetter was not, perhaps expecting such charges - not this soon, at least. Well, it had worked. Ledbetter now knew that there were other charges he had to contend with - over and above those connected with the killings on the Isle Of Skye.

The next question was: how he would respond?

They had also successfully established in this opening exchange that they had discovered a motive for the killings. It had also been shown, fairly convincingly, that Georgina probably knew far more about him than even Ledbetter dared imagine. This was predicated on the guess - little more than that - that Ledbetter had not found Georgina's manuscript in either cottage - thanks to Emma's skilful work on their laptops and the secret tummy that her teddy-bear possessed.

Back in the interview room, Ledbetter had momentarily recovered some of his composure. Elspeth noted though that his breathing was now shallower than before. His feet had turned slightly towards the door. He was probably unaware of these slight alterations of position but to the initiated they showed that he wanted to 'flee' the room - clear indicators of deep anxiety.

As he watched Scott casually finish his coffee and place the cup back in its saucer, Elspeth also noticed (on her close-up camera) that Ledbetter's nostrils had dilated slightly, several times in succession. This meant that Ledbetter was unconsciously taking in more oxygen, ready for some atavistic encounter - an ancient, non-verbal indicator that had its origins in our psyche millions of years ago. Hard-wired into our brain was the need for more oxygen should it be necessary to flee or stand and fight. What would Ledbetter do, wondered Elspeth?

It was also a sign that Ledbetter knew there was worse to come.

Scott now looked at his adversary across the table. He then leant forward and virtually whispered the next exchange, all the while watching Ledbetter like a hawk.

'Dr Ledbetter, how do you think Georgina Cousin's *knew* that you were responsible for Ken Sutton's death by torture. How do you think she actually knew it was you?'

'I did not kill Sutton. Or anyone else for that matter.'

'That was not the question. I asked you how she knew that it was you. She had never met you - except anonymously on the internet perhaps. We are pretty sure that you had been following her online research into that particular case - and others that interested her. You knew, in short, that she was on to you - that she had finally identified a serial-killer responsible for a number of unsolved murders. But how do you think Georgina Cousins actually *knew* that the man she had been hunting all these years was you - none other than Consultant Pathologist James Ledbetter?'

'I have absolutely no idea what you are talking about. This is a complete mystery to me. You are talking in stupid riddles.'

'Then let me show you something.'

At this point Scott rummaged in his Tesco carrier bag and brought out a large sheaf of papers loosely held together by string.

'Do you know what this is, Dr. Ledbetter? No? Well, I will tell you. This is the final draft of Georgina's new novel that proves, conclusively, that you are Ken Sutton's murderer.'

Scott was now standing facing Ledbetter, whereupon he abruptly lifted the manuscript in one hand and shoved it, almost literally, into Ledbetter's face. Ledbetter immediately flinched, the colour visibly draining from his face. Even though he had now instinctively leant back in his chair he continued to stare at the sheaf of papers still held in Thompson's outstretch arm - like a frightened animal trapped in the lethal gaze of a dangerous snake.

'This is the manuscript you could not find when you broke into Georgina's cottage. It is the sole reason why you murdered those two women, exerting your revenge for their impunity by mutilating their bodies. In Alison's case she was probably still alive when you amputated her arm - all because you could not find this document. You knew that if it was ever published your entire world would come crashing down about you. You could not let that happen, could you? And that's why you killed those two women.'

'This is rubbish! Absolute rubbish! Its fiction. Its nothing more than a story, invented by a woman who knows nothing. Trash! Fiction, pure fiction. Absolutely worthless!'

Ledbetter had now leapt to his feet and was moving back and forth like a caged animal and waving his arms about angrily. His eyes blazed and he was shaking with anger and utter contempt for his interrogator.

Elspeth could hardly believe her eyes at such an abrupt transformation. She had not predicted such behaviour. Had he lost the plot? Was he mad, to lose control in such an alarming manner? Others watching with her felt that the situation was possibly turning dangerous. The uniformed officers in the corridor outside the interview room were immediately informed and told to be prepared to intervene should Ledbetter need restraining.

'Is this your evidence, Thompson? Well, it will not stand up in court. Not at all. This is not evidence. Its, its….trash! Is that really the best you can do? Is that why you have dragged me here, to show me this, this….travesty of a novel! This…..'

During this outburst Ledbetter had moved back to the table and had placed both hands firmly on its surface. He was now leaning towards Johnson in a very aggressive manner - at which point Thompson calmly sat down, throwing the manuscript contemptuously on to the table in front of him. Ledbetter immediately paused in mid-sentence and stared down at the papers. For a split second it actually looked as if he was going to pick them up but then, at the last moment, he stood up straight, backed away slightly from the table and shook his finger angrily at Thompson.

'Besides which', he shouted, 'I did not break into that woman's cottage nor did I murder her or the Rutherford woman. I am not a serial-killer. I want this nonsense to stop right here and now and I want my lawyer!'

35
The Mouse Trap

It took about an hour for James Ledbetter's Aberdeen lawyer to arrive at Police HQ. He and Ledbetter met in a private room that the police provided and remained in deep conversation for about twenty minutes - after which the lawyer informed DI Thompson that his client was prepared to resume - provided that he had full legal representation throughout the interview and that he reserved the right to remain silent if he felt that that was appropriate.

This was agreed and both lawyer and client were taken to the interview room once more by two uniformed officers.

* * *

Elspeth and DI Scott Thompson, together with DCI Elliott and other senior officer, had spent the last hour or so discussing Ledbetter's extraordinary outburst. First thought was that it was an act or some kind of theatrical display to throw them off track.

This was Scott's view.

Elspeth was less sure. She sensed that Ledbetter was profoundly disturbed by the turn of events. If he had mentally prepared himself to deal with the Skye murders it was unlikely that he had been expecting Scott to accuse him of the murder of Ken Sutton. That meant that the police knew what Georgina had been up to because that was exactly what she had been threatening in her emails to Ledbetter. Elspeth did not of course know that but she rightly assumed that Ledbetter had a clear indication of her area of research and perhaps even some notion of what Georgina's new novel contained. Why else would he need to silence its author? That the police now knew that she had linked him to Sutton's murder must have been very worrying for Ledbetter.

What else, he was probably asking himself, did the police know?

Then, when Georgina's actual manuscript turned up - the one thing he had thought he had prevented from ever happening by killing both its author and her lover - well, that was his worst nightmare come true. He had killed twice (excluding the climber and the equally unfortunate 'Charley Gibbons') to stop that novel appearing and now here it was, being waved in his face.

For someone who had tracked his hunters down and eliminated them so ruthlessly, the material manifestation of something he believed could really destroy him - Georgina's actual text - had profoundly shocked him.

When Scott waved the actual text in his face - a provocative action in itself, regardless of the document's actual contents - it had prompted totally unexpected and irrational behaviour; behaviour that could well be Ledbetter's undoing. It was a indicator too of the impotence Ledbetter clearly felt at a situation that was unravelling in front of him.

More importantly, he probably felt that it was a situation over which he had absolutely no control - something which for a control 'freak' like him was complete anathema.

That at least was Elspeth's view.

However, the questions both she and Scott were now asking themselves were: What next? How, if at all, could they exploit the situation in the next interview session?

The presence this time of his lawyer cast an entirely new complexion on the proceedings. Ledbetter might say nothing. Their chance to catch him out or pressure him into some kind of confession - always something of a long-shot in these kind of preliminary interviews - might have vanished.

It was then that Fate intervened.

Just as Scott was about to go next door into the interview room and recommence battle, a messenger arrived with a letter. It was from the Forensic Science laboratory. Elspeth took the letter, opened it and read its contents. There was now a wicked grin on her face.

'You know what this is, don't you Scott? This is your chance to nail this fucking bastard. This is surely the final nail in his coffin!'

She handed it to DI Johnson. He read its contents, nodded grimly, then placed the letter back in its envelope, slipped it in his jacket pocket and left the room.

* * *

Scott took his seat opposite James Ledbetter and his lawyer - a certain Michael Garland. DI Scott knew Garland. He was a very experienced, well-connected and shrewd lawyer.

Ledbetter could not have chosen a better advocate. This was going to be a tough session, thought Scott.

'I would like to start, Dr Ledbetter by asking you what you know about a novel by Georgina Cousins. Its called *The Gilded Cage*.'

At this point Scott took from his briefcase a hardback copy of the novel and handed it to Ledbetter. Ledbetter took it and looked at it, somewhat disdainfully. He then carefully placed it back on the table.

'Can't say I have read it, Inspector. Why do you ask?'

'Because I think you have read it. I also think you know whose photograph is on the back of this novel. Please pick it up again and look at the image on the back cover.'

Ledbetter did as he was asked. He took a brief glance at the photograph of Caroline Wear (purporting to be 'Sarah Daniels') then placed it back on the table, face down. His face remained absolutely emotionless.

'So, who is that photograph of, Dr Ledbetter?'

'I have no idea, Inspector. I have never seen that young woman before. I take it to be a photograph of Sarah Daniels, the author of this work of fiction.'

'Well you would be wrong.'

Here Scott again picked up the book and held it in front of Ledbetter's face, with the back cover towards him. Elspeth, watching closely on the CU camera in the observation studio next door, detected a distinct flicker of fear on Ledbetter's face but it passed in a moment.

'This, Dr. Ledbetter, is your daughter - Caroline Wear.'

'Nonsense. I have no daughter. This is more rubbish. Really! Where do you get your information from, Inspector Thompson?'

Scott then took from his pocket the letter Elspeth had given him earlier. He handed it unopened to Ledbetter.

'From you own Forensic laboratory, as it happens Dr. Ledbetter. Open the envelope. Look inside if you do not believe me.'

Ledbetter stared at him for a moment in astonishment then opened the envelope and took the letter out and read it slowly.

Elspeth, watching enthralled from next door, saw Ledbetter then crumple before her eyes. The letter fell from his hands back onto the table, his head fell forward and his shoulders dropped. So alarmed was his lawyer at this sudden transformation in his client that he immediately stood and placed his arms protectively on Ledbetter's shoulders.

'This letter proves that you are Caroline Wear's biological father. It also means that the young woman you so cruelly rejected all her life is the one whose sad story is given fictional expression in this novel you claim not to have read.'

'Stop, Inspector', said Ledbetter's lawyer. 'Can you not see that my client is not well. I must ask you to stop this interview, here and now.'

'Not yet, Mr Garland. Your client has the right to know that it was his daughter who told Georgina Cousins what kind of man he really was. It was Caroline who enabled Georgina to finally identify the serial-killer she had been hunting. It was Caroline who - rejected all her life, befriended briefly by Georgina Cousins - finally died neglected and unloved in some sordid street In Edinburgh with a knife in her chest. That, Dr Ledbetter, is who that photograph is of. Look at it. That young woman was your daughter.'

With that Scott shoved the book back under Ledbetter's nose. For a long moment he stared at it then raised his head slowly. His face was ashen, drained of all colour. He could barely speak. It was as if he had aged within moments. He was, as Elspeth saw with utter astonishment, a broken man.

'I wish to make a statement, Detective Inspector Thompson. I wish....'

Garland immediately interjected but Ledbetter pushed him aside and with a wave of his hand silenced him.

'I wish to confess to the murders of Georgina Cousins, Alison Rutherford and two others whom I killed on the Isle of Skye.'

36
Monday, 28th May

Fiona Ledbetter (nèe Pawley) was arrested later that afternoon at her house on the outskirts of Aberdeen. She made no attempt to resist.

'Come in, gentlemen', she said as she opened her front door to five uniformed policemen, all of whom were armed. 'I have been expecting you'.

She was then cautioned and taken to Police HQ in Aberdeen for questioning by Detective Inspector Scott Thompson. At this stage, Fiona Ledbetter did not know that her husband had just signed a written statement in which he confessed to the murder of four people on the Isle of Skye between the 20th and 22nd April, 2012.

It would be some days before she was told about this confession.

The Ledbetters' house proved to be large, expensively furnished and in immaculate taste. There were 18th Century prints on the wall in the hallway, several signed prints by Peter Blake in the study and a fine collection of 'Ruralist' paintings by David Inshaw in the large, sumptuous living room. Curtains, fittings and carpets were all of the highest quality. Upstairs, in the five bedrooms and three bathrooms (including a Jacuzzi and sauna), the décor was similarly refined and of exceptional quality.

Not only were the Ledbetter's obviously rich, they clearly had expensive tastes. While Consultant Pathologists are well paid, this house showed that they either had private incomes - or that Ledbetter was supplementing his official income in some other way. The police were pretty sure which it was they favoured and were quick to seize computers, laptops, memory sticks, discs and the contents of James Ledbetter's large filing cabinet.

Later that evening, two white vans full of boxes of evidence and several hard-drives, set off down James Ledbetter's manicured drive and out past his large wrought-iron gates towards Aberdeen

Police HQ.

The police also found a battered green Land Rover in the garage. Forensic spent several hours examining this vehicle. They were particularly interested in the large (empty) ice-box they found in the boot.

* * *

When she arrived at Police HQ in Aberdeen and was ushered into an interview room, Fiona Ledbetter's lawyer was already waiting there patiently for her. He was a young man, unconnected with Garland's legal offices. His name was Bentham, Nicholas Bentham.

'Detective Inspector Scott, my client here would like it be known that she has every intention of helping the police throughout their enquiries. She has already prepared a lengthy written statement, copies of which I have with me for you and your colleagues.'

At this point Bentham handed Scott a beautifully typed statement running to eighteen pages. It was dated Friday, 25th May - the same day Ledbetter had been brought in for questioning.

Scott took it, utterly fazed by this opening gambit.

'My God!', he thought immediately, 'she's going to turn Queen's evidence! She's going to tell us everything!'

He was pondering the significance of this dramatic development and starting to read Fiona's statement when her solicitor took from his briefcase a CD-Rom.

'My client', he said quietly, 'would also like you to have this.'

Bentham handed the CD-Rom to a bemused Scott.

'She thinks', he added, 'that it will help you establish Dr. Ledbetter's guilt and her active involvement in the filming, editing and distribution of obscene material over a number of years.'

* * *

And so it proved.

Not only did her signed statement contain reference to every obscene or degrading image that the Ledbetter's had ever made but revealed the exact nature of their distribution methods, income and expenses (properly audited), together with a list of the websites and dealers they had used.

It also showed in some detail their methods of laundering the extensive income their 'snuff-movies' had generated since 1995.

There was, however, no mention of Florida or any indication of similar activities committed abroad.

The investigating officers in Aberdeen and technicians from the Obscene Publications Unit in London were both shocked and staggered at the amount of information the disc also contained. The digital images - both stills and moving footage - were truly horrific and sufficient in themselves to convict Ledbetter on at least seven counts for murder. The most horrific of all were the moving pictures of Ken Sutton being tortured to death with a blowtorch.

What they had on that disc were the original digital 'rushes' in which Ledbetter's face was often clearly visible.

Even images from the murders on Skye were present in their unedited form. Those of 'Alison Rutherford' having her arm amputated while she hung by her ankles from a pulley were some of the worst images hardened veterans of the OP Unit had ever seen or would ever want to see again. They proved that Alison was partially conscious throughout the entire process. For weeks afterwards, those that viewed this part of the disc, found it difficult to forget the screams of that young woman as her assailant methodically amputated her arm. Images of Ken Sutton being burned to death with an acetylene torch were simply too grotesque to watch for more than a second or two.

* * *

Scott Thompson, armed with all this information, interviewed Fiona several times over the next few weeks. She knew now of her husband's confession. Ledbetter had denied any connection with these other, earlier murders, confessing only to the four killings on Skye. Yet the disc Fiona had given to the police provided all the proof they needed. Ledbetter and his lawyers now knew that Fiona had turned Queen's evidence and that her disc would surely seal her husband's fate when it came to trial, scheduled for August.

Why then had Ledbetter continue to deny any involvement with Sutton and the other, earlier murders?

It made no sense. Elspeth had puzzled over this for weeks.

It was clear now that husband and wife had acted in unison and that the moment he had been arrested Fiona began to gather and coordinate the evidence the police would need to convict him. The disc itself would have taken many days to compile and her eighteen page statement would appear to have been written long *before* he was arrested. It was as if his arrest had not only been prepared for but 'rehearsed'. His phone-call to his wife on the morning of his arrest was an encoded message to tell Fiona to prepare for her own arrest. It was as if Ledbetter had given up there and then, even before his second interview. Elspeth found this extraordinary behaviour, even for someone as deranged as James Ledbetter. Somehow, he wished to control even his arrest and the inevitable consequences that followed. James Ledbetter was meticulous in everything he did - including his own, inevitable demise.

He was *managing* events - as one might 'manage' a suicide.

While Elspeth wrestled with these behavioural conundrums, Scott tried to unravel Ledbetter's online involvement with Georgina Cousins and why he had always felt so threatened by her. It had, after all, brought him to Skye in the first place - with dire consequences for all concerned.

How, for example, did he discover that Georgina was investigating a number of unsolved murders in the region, including the horrific killing of Ken Sutton near Perth in 1998?

'It was me who first noticed her online research into the Sutton murder. I had no idea who she was then but I sensed danger for Jim. Together we monitored her progress, all the while trying to identify who he (or she) was. We could see that somehow she had hacked into police records and that she had information that had never been released to the press. That meant that she was a real threat. We clearly had to do something about that.'

'But how did you find out that it was Georgina Cousins?'

'We didn't. In the end it was she who contacted us - or rather a 'Sarah Daniels' who contacted us, sometime in 2010. That was very alarming. Suddenly, out of the blue, we received an email from this author claiming that she knew that Jim was a serial-killer and that she was about to expose him. While Daniels was widely known as a novelist we assumed that she wrote under a pseudonym. We never found out her real name or where she lived until much later. For months she taunted us and then, in 2011 published a novel that purported to tell the story of Caroline Wear whom she claimed was Jim's illegitimate daughter. The photograph on the back was confirmation of that. Circumstantial, of course, but damaging all the same. There was, she threatened, worse to come.'

'Tell me about Caroline Wear. It is difficult to see where she fits in. Did you know that she was your husband's illegitimate daughter?'

'Not at first. It was when some slut of a girl started calling Jim and demanding money that he told me that he had had a relationship with some nurse when he was a young doctor. This woman was sleeping with a number of men at the time so Jim was never convinced that he was Caroline's father. For the first year or so he sent money to Wear, then living in Edinburgh I think. When he discovered that she was using the money to buy cocaine Jim stopped helping her. For the next year or so he heard nothing from her and assumed that she was dead. Years later some girl suddenly rang him up at work claiming that she was his daughter. This was Caroline. She threatened to 'expose him' if he didn't send her money. She kept calling him for months. Each time he refused. Eventually she stopped harassing him. That would have been sometime in 2010.'

'Then what happened?'

'One day we got an email from someone called 'Sarah Daniels' telling us that her new book - called *The Gilded Cage* - had just published and showed Jim for the 'uncaring bastard that he was'. Her story was based on Caroline Wear's life - or so Daniels claimed. We were horrified. While Jim was not named in her trashy novel he felt that it was still very damaging. He was now Consultant Pathologist to the police here Aberdeen. If the press discovered that he was possibly related to some prostitute who had been murdered on the streets of Edinburgh then that could have been very damaging to his career. When - a year or so later - 'Sarah Daniels' threatened us with *The Hunter* we knew we had to do something to finally stop her.'

'How? How could you stop her? You had no idea who she really was. Not even her publisher knew the real 'Sarah Daniels'.'

'It was difficult. Very difficult, even with my computing skills. The break-through came when we stumbled upon Alison Rutherford. Her online 'address' cropped up on a number of internet sites that we sometimes used to sell our images - including one 'sponsored' by 'Sarah Daniels'. That was the link we had been searching for. Perhaps, we thought, Rutherford would lead us to Daniels. And so it turned out. Even though Rutherford used different names at different times I managed to back-track one of these 'names' and came up with Alison Rutherford from Portree. It turned out that Jim had actually met an Alison Rutherford in Portree. That was our lucky break.'

'But how did you find out her connection with Cousins? Even Daniels' publisher did not know her real identity, let alone her relationship with Rutherford?'

'Oh, it was quite easy to find out where she lived. I hacked into Rutherford's computer and very quickly discovered her connection with Georgina Cousins. It was also clear from their emails to each other that Cousins and 'Daniels' were one and the same person. Bingo! We had finally found the woman who had been threatening to expose my husband as 'Scotland's most dangerous, most pernicious serial-killer'.'

'Then what happened?'

'What happened next is that tracked them down in Portree and killed them both - starting with Georgina on the beach and then Alison in the lighthouse. The other two merely got in the way.'

* * *

While Fiona Ledbetter's testimony did not explain all the details of her husband's complex, largely online dealings with 'Sarah Daniels' during the period she was hunting her serial-killer, it did explain how Jim Ledbetter had turned the tables and tracked her down and killed her.

It was indeed Fiona who had stolen Jennifer Chancellor's severed arm from Dr. Sutherland's laboratory. She also confessed to the idea of using the damaged watch as the 'signature' for their next series of mutilations and killings; an idea eagerly adopted by Ledbetter himself. Thereafter, 'three-thirty' became the way internet dealers would identify their work - just as they had used the 'torch' motive in the late 90's for images also destined for the darker side of the web.

What Scott Thompson could not stomach, however, was the calm way Fiona confessed to being the camera operator on each of her husband's gory outings. She appeared utterly unaware of her gruesome contribution to his 'work' and devoid of all remorse. She was as cold as ice when recounting their editing sessions together. It was as if she were describing the editing of family footage rather than snuff-movies and hard-core porn. Her entire attitude towards her husband's secret life as Scotland's most dangerous serial-killer was chilling in its mundane, almost banal insouciance.

If anything, Scott found Fiona Pawley (as she now insisted on being called) more scary than her deranged husband. The idea that, because she had turned Queen's evidence, she was already a free woman made the hairs on the back of Scott's neck rise.

What continued to puzzle both Scott and Elspeth was the way in which husband and wife had mutually agreed what both of them should do if arrested. It was clear that it had been agreed from the start that Fiona would give Queen's evidence, and thereby escape prison. Perhaps that way her revelations would give Ledbetter even greater notoriety. Perhaps too it ensured that Ledbetter's trial would be the sensation that it ultimately became, finally giving him the kind of notoriety serial-killers frequently crave. Perhaps it was simply to do with Ledbetter's pathological need to control his life - even when, to all intents and purposes - it was over.

37
23rd. August, 2012

Poppy was curious. There were aspects of the Ledbetter case that she simply did not understand. She needed to tie up a number of lose ends and anomalies, for her own peace of mind. She was a tidy woman.

She had, naturally - being a detective's wife - read everything Agatha Christie had ever written and was fully aware of that author's predilection for final gatherings of the more obvious suspects - usually everyone who had appeared in the story. It was during these tense gatherings that Hercule Poirot or Miss Marple would dramatically expose the killer, having provided a lengthy but enthralling exposition.

To that end Poppy had gathered two of the key players in the recent Ledbetter drama - her husband, Detective *Chief* Inspector John White and the redoubtable Dr. Elizabeth Grant, PhD.

They were lounging in deckchairs on Poppy's lawn, close to the river, and enjoying an early evening Pimms. It was now late summer and the last rays of the sun were glancing off the River Tay as off a dragonfly's iridescent wing.

'So, how did he do it?', Poppy asked, with the enthusiasm of a schoolgirl asking if Brad Pitt really was in town. 'How on earth did he murder Georgina on an open beach?'

'How did *they* do it, you mean', said John. 'Fiona was involved right from the start. I think it was she who drove Ledbetter to Portree that Thursday afternoon. We found an old, green Land Rover in their garage in Aberdeen. What better vehicle to use if you want to merge on Skye - or most parts of the Highlands, for that matter. She dropped Ledbetter off then probably waited round the corner in case they needed to make a quick escape.'

'How did they know where Georgina lived?'

'I'm not sure they did know exactly where she lived. Ledbetter knew that Georgina and 'Alison' were lovers so he probably assumed that they lived together. Since Portree's Assistant Librarian was the more 'visible' of the two women, it would not have been difficult for him to find out where she lived. He knew that 'Alison' was at work so he expected to find Georgina alone at her desk. But the cottage was empty. Anyway, he got in somehow and searched the place for manuscripts, files, notes, memory sticks - anything that might have something to do with the new book. When he checked the computer - Alison's computer, as it turned out, he found that it had been virtually wiped. He found nothing, thanks to Teddy!'

'So, what did he do then? Sit and wait?'

'Exactly. He would have had a problem if both women had returned to the cottage together but that was not the case. When 'Alison' walked in at about five-thirty he probably just stepped out from behind her kitchen door and overwhelmed her, possibly with chloroform. I assume he then bound and gagged her. By now he would have had a really good look round the cottage and seen that Alison lived there by herself. That meant that Georgina must be somewhere else. I guess that Fiona had now joined him in the cottage. I assume they then forced 'Alison' to reveal the whereabouts of Georgina's cottage and give them a spare key. He then left 'Alison' tied up in a back room perhaps with Fiona keeping guard. He then set off to find Georgina in her cottage. Dressed, as he was, as a bearded hill-walker no one would have looked twice at him.'

'Emma must have been terrified', added Elspeth. 'Both for herself and for her lover. She knew who this man was and what he was capable of. His presence now in Portree was the one thing both women had always feared. Their false names and anonymity had failed them. And here he was, about to destroy their lives and everything they had achieved together.'

John took another sip of his Pimms, then continued.

'Ledbetter found Georgina's cottage empty. He let himself in and rapidly searched the place. No manuscript. When he opened up her laptop he found that it had been virtually wiped in the same way as Alison's. He probably guessed that they were covering their tracks, just as he and Fiona had always done. Maybe they were even expecting him. He needed to act decisively. He had seen framed photographs in Alison's cottage so he now knew what Georgina looked like. It was now just a matter of waiting for her return or picking another opportunity to kill her. He chose the latter.'

'He chose the latter, added Elspeth, 'because of his love of the melodramatic and the 'grand gesture'. This was not just to do with the potential commercial exploitation of his snuff-movies but because it served some darker, psychotic need.'

'He also needed Fiona', John added, 'to help him in his grisly activities. So, he left Georgina's cottage and returned to Alison's. I'm not sure what he would have done had Georgina phoned Alison that evening. Maybe she did. Maybe he forced 'Alison' to say on the phone that she was OK. Anyway, he and Fiona spent the night in Emma's cottage planning their next move.'

'The murder on the beach?'

'Exactly. I'm not sure I know quite how that trap was set. If indeed it was a trap. It feels more like opportunism to me than anything planned. My only explanation is that he and Fiona started to stalk Georgina. It was now Friday morning. They parked near Georgina's cottage but out of sight and kept watch.'

'Why did they not abduct her there and then?' asked Poppy

'I'm not sure. Remember, this was the first time either of them had seen the real 'Sarah Daniels'. Maybe they just wanted to get the measure of their opponent. We know that Georgina was seen in Portree that Friday morning at about 10.30 so they probably watched her leave her cottage at about 10.15, and followed her into the village. I think they then followed her back to the pub. They may even have been there in the pub while she ate her lunch. If they were, the police never traced them, not surprisingly.

Dressed as hill-walkers, maybe even disguised, neither would have stood out.'

'How on earth did they know that she was about to go for a walk on the beach?', asked Poppy.

'They didn't. When they saw her leave the pub they probably followed her out into the car park and got into their own car ready to move off behind her. However, when she locked her handbag and coat in her car and set off across the grass on foot towards the sea they realised that this was their chance. They then drove off up the sandy lane that runs parallel with the beach and got well ahead of her. Ledbetter knew this beach. By the time Georgina spotted a man at the water's edge Fiona and the land Rover had disappeared and Ledbetter had planted the severed arm - an arm that they must have kept in an ice box in the back of the Land Rover.'

Elspeth poured herself another Pimms and took a long, contented swig before she spoke.

'Serial-killers like Ledbetter act spontaneously but only within clearly defined parameters. They are control-freaks and 'seizing the moment' is not natural to them. Dragging someone's frozen arm around in the boot of your car is not normal either but for Ledbetter he needed his 'signature'. When an unsuspecting Georgina actually joined him at the water's edge he probably could not believe his luck. He then strangled her and swiftly amputated her arm.'

'So where was Fiona while all this was happening?'

'I suspect that she hid the Land Rover several hundred yards away and then positioned herself amongst the rocks to film the murder and amputation. One of the cameras we found at their home in Aberdeen had a zoom lens capable of close-ups from that distance. Murdie Monro had said that the man he sold diesel fuel to on Soay was bearded. The unedited tape of the murder and mutilation of Georgina shows a bearded man. Although there are graphic close-ups, the wide shots show that the camera must have been some way away.'

'My God, what ghastly people!', said Poppy. She then took a long, calming swig of Pimms and poured another for John and Elspeth.

'Thank you, darling. She and Ledbetter then escaped in their car, having popped Georgina's arm in ice in the cool-box. On the way back to Alison's cottage Ledbetter, adopting a 'northern' voice, told the police of the severed arm on the beach.'

'Yes, that's all very well but what about the *time* on Jenny's watch? Three-thirty. That's far too much of a coincidence for anyone to swallow! Come on John, how do you explain that?'

'Well, for a while I couldn't - until I realised that no one had ever *said* it had stopped at that time. Indeed, if it had stopped on the impact of the crash it should have been saying four o'clock and not three-thirty. The two eye-witnesses to Jenny's crash had said that it was nearer four when it happened. When we checked at the hospital, the paramedics remembered nothing about a watch. They were too busy trying to save Jenny's life to take note of a watch that might have stopped. Because the watch on Jenny's arm now said three-thirty we all assumed that that was what it had read originally. It never occurred to any of us that it might have been changed subsequently!'

'So, where does this three-thirty come from?'

'I think Ledbetter took the watch off the severed arm, adjusted the time to three-thirty and then put it back. The actual time of the murder was probably nearer two-thirty. They then waited until it really was three-thirty before calling the police in Portree. That way they had already left the crime-scene and were probably safely back in Alison's cottage.'

'Wow! So mere chance had supplied him with his next 'signature' - not just the severed arms that he had planned for but a 'three-thirty' motif. Very bizarre. Very clever, what?'

'Very Ledbetter!' added Elspeth, lighting up another cigarette.

Because it was now starting to get cool and because Elspeth was complaining about being bitten alive by midges, they retired indoors to continue their discussion in the comfort of Poppy's spacious lounge.

38
Conclusions - Part Two

On reflection, Poppy found it hard to remember either Hercule Poirot or Miss Marple actually sipping Pimms as they prepared to reveal the murderer in their midst but here, in the warm comfort of her lounge, it seems perfectly natural. She could hardly wait for part two!

Elspeth and John were already sat in cosy armchairs. The last rays of the setting sun was casting deep shadows across the lawn, visible through the conservatory windows. With the golden glow of three large table lamps adding a touch of warmth, the scene was now set for the next thrilling instalment.

Or that, at least, was how Poppy saw it as she placed a tray of gin-and-tonics before them.

'So, darling Detective *Chief* Inspector Plod, tell us all about murder at the lighthouse!'

'I do wish you would stop calling me that. Even Elspeth does it now - which is a bit rich from someone whom Mother often called 'Elliebob'!'

'It was an intimate term of affection', said Elspeth rather coyly. 'But we don't talk about *him*, do we folks. On with the motley, John!'

'Well, I think they had always planned something dramatic at the lighthouse. It's a beautiful, remote spot in a dramatic setting to the far north of the island. Ledbetter must have been there many times as a hill-walker. It would serve their purposes well, particularly at that time of the year when there were no tourists about. However, I think they had always planned to kill 'Sarah Daniels' there and not 'Alison Rutherford'.'

'Interesting theory, John', said Elspeth. 'Please elaborate.'

'Well, the beach killing had been opportunist but had worked for them in the end. The watch was also an elegant touch, something I am sure Ledbetter had planned once he heard about Jenny's arm being within reach, as it were. The idea that her watch had stopped at the very moment of her death (not true, as it turned out) was a beguiling thought for a sadistic killer. It appealed to his sense of the dramatic. I think I'm right is saying that it was originally Fiona's idea but it was certainly one that Ledbetter readily endorsed. No, the problem now was what to do with Alison, still held captive in her own cottage.'

'So what did they do?'

'They kept to their original plan - except that this time it would be poor Emma Butterworth they would torture to death in the lighthouse and not Georgina Cousins. The problem was getting to the island. I suspect that they had always planned to steal a boat to get to the lighthouse but that afternoon the weather deteriorated rapidly, with storm clouds moving in from the west. By Friday evening they were in the middle of thunderstorm. Thunder and lighting. Gale force winds. The lot!'

'In short, they were stuck!'

'Exactly, Poppy. I think they sat out the first part of the storm but could then wait no longer. It was now late Friday evening and Ledbetter was due back at his lab on Monday. Later that night they took the bold decision to drive down to the harbour, park the Land Rover somewhere not too obvious and smuggle an unconscious 'Alison' on board Neil McPherson's fishing boat - the one nearest to the dock. Ledbetter then cut the moorings of two others and let storm and tide do the rest. 'Bloody dangerous', as Sergeant McGregor eloquently put it to me - but it bloody-well worked.'

'I'm amazed no one saw them', said Poppy.

'I agree but all this was done at dead of night when people are usually tucked up in bed. I checked the high tide for that particular night. It was due at two-forty-five in the morning. I think that's when they must have left. Maybe they both wore their disguises while in the village, just in case they bumped into someone. Anyway, once out of sight of Portree, Ledbetter started the engine and headed for the island.'

At this point Poppy refreshed their glasses and fetched some 'nibbles' from the kitchen. John then resumed his account.

'An hour or so later they landed at the little jetty beneath the lighthouse, after what must have proved an alarming crossing. It was now about four-thirty Saturday morning. The storm had abated somewhat. They carried 'Alison' into the lighthouse and up to the first floor gallery. I think Ledbetter then took Neil's boat and moored it just out of sight round the headland. That would explain why George McClure did not see another boat at the lighthouse when he dropped 'Gibbons' off later that morning. Ledbetter then walked back to the lighthouse. They needed light to film their grisly activity so they then waited until morning before starting work on poor Alison.'

'Enter Trevor Burns, alias Charley Gibbons!'

'Precisely. No one had expected him to arrive that morning. When 'Charley' climbed those stairs, the first thing he encountered was Ledbetter. I think Ledbetter must have seen McGregor's boat arrive and was already lying in wait for whoever came into the lighthouse. When Trevor reached the first floor gallery, Ledbetter leapt out and grabbed him while Fiona probably applied the chloroform with her usual deft touch.'

'So then what?'

'Well, according to our Consultant Pathologist (you can guess who that was!) the internal damage done to 'Charley' was so extensive that one fall alone could not have caused it. I think a bearded Ledbetter threw 'Charley' from that upper gallery while Fiona filmed it all from below. Worse than that, I think they did it *twice* before 'Charley' was dead.'

'Oh my God! That's terrible!' cried Poppy. Even Elspeth was

shaken by this new interpretation of events in the lighthouse. John continued, grimly.

'This now raises the matter of the suit. To dress 'Charley' in a suit from Three-Thirty Couture could not have been part of any plan. My theory is that Ledbetter had that suit with him so that he could travel back to Aberdeen on Sunday night and go straight to work the next morning. However, such is his devious mind, it suddenly occurred to him that here was yet another chance to 'sign' his work. So, they undressed 'Charley' and put him in the most expensive suit he had ever worn. Sadly, he was no longer alive to appreciate it. Later, on their way to Soay, they dumped him overboard knowing that he was sure to end up somewhere on Skye. Sinclair's crew saved them the trouble by fishing Trevor out of the sea in their fishing nets and 'landing' the poor bugger at Portree.'

Elspeth and Poppy sipped their drinks in silence for a minute or two, trying to absorb the horror of the events John had been describing. It was Elspeth who was the first to speak.

'Serial killers and their accomplices are seldom emotionally engaged in murder in the way conventional killers are. Most murders are acts of anger, passion or vindictiveness. Cold-blooded murder is exactly that. Cold. Deliberate and calculating. It also requires meticulous planning. Although their victim this time was not whom they had originally intended - that dire fate would have been Georgina's - what followed had clearly been thought through very carefully already.'

'Indeed. That is why I still find what they did to Emma Butterworth beyond comprehension. I will spare you the details but as soon as 'Charley' had been disposed of somewhere in the lighthouse, they stripped Alison, tied a rope to her ankles and suspended her from the pulley above the stairwell. The pulley is normally used for lifting machinery.'

'Do you think, John that she was conscious? That she knew what was happening to her?' It was Elspeth who asked this question.
'Sadly, I think she must have been aware - even if she was still

sedated enough for them to manhandle her into position on that pulley. I cannot begin to imagine the horror of that situation. Fiona then went back half-way down the stairs and started video-taping what followed. We measured the width of the stair-well level where Emma's shoulders would have been. It was ten feet across. That means that they must have tied a rope round Alison's chest and pulled her to one side, tying the rope off on the stair rail. This left her suspended but within reach of Ledbetter's scalpel.'

Elspeth continued the account at this point.

'The fact that Alison was still alive when Ledbetter amputated her right arm is just too horrible to imagine. I hope that at this stage she quickly passed out, to save her from the agony. They then left her to bleed to death. That must have taken about thirty-minutes, according to our Consultant Pathologist. He should have known. He was there!'

A long silence ensued before John continued.

'The 'three-thirty' motif presented Ledbetter with something of a problem when it came to Alison. This they had definitely not prepared for. The fact that it took even Elspeth here some time to fathom it out is indicative of the crudeness of Ledbetter's 'solution'. Tying Alison's remaining arm to the rail to make it look like her head was pointing to 6 and her arm to 3 (three-thirty) was crude in the least but it was the best they could do in the circumstances.'

'Then what?'

'Well, they packed up, checked for any clues they might have left, fetched the boat and bundled 'Charley' on board, plus Alison's severed arm. They then damaged the mains supply to the lighthouse light, causing the main beam to go off. They then headed out to sea. They wanted Alison to be found, but not before they themselves had vanished. Once out at sea they chucked Charley overboard, as described earlier, followed by Alison's arm. Thanks to Wing Commander Finlayson's skill as a sea-angler, the arm was recovered a day or so later. They then headed for Soay where they bought fuel and then turned back towards the Strathaid peninsula where they planned to dump the boat. It must now have been late Sunday afternoon. I suspect Ledbetter realised that they had been spotted by the RAF jet. Tom thought that he had been monitoring radio traffic, including our own, so it was imperative that he and Fiona got off that boat as soon as possible. The unexpected arrival of young Gabriel at the sea cave complicated matters but he was despatched with Ledbetter's usual efficiency. As a photo-opportunity expedition, this was turning into an unexpected triumph.'

'And so they got back to Portree?'

'Yes. Fiona might have found the night trek across the Coullins a trial but she had with her an experienced mountaineer who knew the area backwards. Early next morning I think they simply took the six-thirty local bus from Sligachan back to Portree, picked up their land Rover and drove home to Aberdeen. We found someone on that bus who vaguely remembered two hill-walkers, a man and a woman. The man had a beard so that could well have been Ledbetter. Consultant Pathologist James Ledbetter would have been back at work that morning in Aberdeen not later than ten o'clock.'

'Thank you, darling', said Poppy. 'Absolutely fascinating. I'm not entirely sure I can eat anything after that but there is roast beef and potatoes in the oven. Elspeth, will you join us for supper?'

'Yes, of course, but who killed Caroline?'

39
The Hunter

Georgina's book was published the week after Ledbetter's sensational trial in August, 2012. It was called *The Hunter* and widely promoted as the last, posthumous novel of Sarah Daniels who, it would seem, had died peacefully in her bed in Chlomotiana, Corfu earlier that year.

Some cynics might argue that this was commercialism at its worst but it certainly benefited from the publicity that attended Dr. James Ledbetter's conviction for the murder of seven people, not least Georgina Cousins.

At the book-launch in London, news of 'Sarah's' premature death was met with disbelief and disappointment by her fans but her literary 'demise' was eventually accepted. They were compensated, however, by the re-release of six of her most popular novels from previous years - including *The Gilded Cage*. This expensive box-set subsequently became something of a collector's item.

The new book itself was an enormous success, selling a 250,000 copies within the first week. Subsequent reprints resulted in sales that year alone in excess of 700,000 and was quickly translated into seven languages. It received very mixed reviews from the literary press but then 'Sarah Daniels'' work had never received much positive critical acclaim. That had never actually bothered Georgina Cousins, nor indeed her agent and publishers - all of whom benefited from her enormous sales.

Few readers made the connection with the Georgina Cousins that had featured so much in Ledbetter's trial with the author of the book they were now reading in their thousands. This was not as remarkable as it might seem for the name 'Sarah Daniels' never actually cropped up at trial. Whether this was by design or mere chance we shall never know.

Either way, 'Sarah Daniels' simply faded out of the literary world and her alter ego, Georgina Cousins, retained her secret identity to the grave.

What is remarkable, however, is that one chapter in 'Sarah Daniels'' last novel almost anticipates her own death in a disturbingly prescient way. In this particular chapter, near the end of her book, the central character - a writer of trashy 'lesbian-chic' - lures to his death on a Greek beach in Ithaca the serial-killer she has been threatening to expose. It was this particular chapter that had both startled and disturbed Detective Inspector John White and his team when they first read it. Although in reality it was Georgina who had died on a beach (not in Ithaca, but Scotland) it was this chapter that had first alerted the police to the autobiographical elements within her new and, at that time, unpublished book. It was her new book that also provided the police with vital clues in their investigation into the links between Georgina and her killer.

It was almost as if Georgina Cousins *knew* that by exposing a serial-killer she risked becoming one of his victims - which is exactly what happened.

The central narrative thrust of the new novel focussed on the death of Ken Sutton, the blow-torch murder victim whom we now know Ledbetter had tortured to death in 1998. In Georgina's novel all the names had been changed and the entire action moved from Scotland to Los Angeles and later Greece but it was still essentially Ken Sutton's tragic story. The fact that somehow Georgina's latest novel was an exposé of the serial-killer behind that ghastly murder also played a central role in shaping the Prosecution's case against Ledbetter. The novel had indicated that Ledbetter's real motivation for murdering both women had been to protect himself from being linked with previous murders, not least that of Ken Sutton.

While it was clear to the police that Georgina Cousins had successfully identified an active serial-killer from as early as 2000, it was never properly established whether or not she knew his real identity until much later.

She just knew that he was out there.

At trial no one was able to satisfactorily show how Georgina had known Caroline or, indeed, how she had obtained the girl's photograph. Perhaps they had met in the two 'missing' years in Caroline's tragically short life - between 2008 and her death in 1010? Perhaps they were friends or even lovers? This was certainly the view held by the 'Gang of Five' who had closely examined Georgina's two last novels. There again, maybe Caroline was someone Georgina simply came across in her research into Ledbetter's past. The 'Gang of Five' had come up with a number of possible scenarios, partly based on fictional accounts within certain novels by 'Sarah Daniels'. In the absence of concrete facts, this 'literary evidence' was discounted in court.

It was also established at trial that Georgina had taunted her prime suspect from moment she identified him - the very year in which Caroline Wear herself was savagely stabbed to death on the streets of Edinburgh. That same year Georgina placed Caroline's photograph on the back of her latest book in which Caroline's own tragic story featured. This photograph was meant to be a genuine photograph of the author 'Sarah Daniels'. It was as if Caroline herself were now taunting her cruel father. It was both a gesture of defiance by Georgina and a challenge to the serial-killer whom she intended to expose.

It said: 'I know who you are. You are responsible for your daughter's tragic life. For that I will finally expose you as the serial-killer I now know you to be. Watch this space, you degenerate bastard!'

Either way, from the day Caroline Wear fell within Georgina Cousins' remit she became, unwittingly perhaps, a significant player in Georgina's secret conspiracy to expose Ledbetter as Scotland's worst serial-killer.

Both Ledbetter and Georgina Cousins moved in the murky waters of hard-core porn. For Georgina, it was her lover Emma (alias Alison Rutherford) who had the computing skills to both find the sites and people that turned her on. It was also Emma's IT skills that enabled her to eventually trace Ledbetter and hack into police files on murders that they thought he had committed. In the end, it was this online activity that led Ledbetter back to the woman he had only known as 'Sarah Daniels' and whose real identity and location had until then been such a successful secret.

Ledbetter and Cousins communicated, if at all, online and under assumed names. The evidence on Fiona's hard-drive was that they circled around each other like dangerous, predatory animals for at least three years - from 2008 when, with Caroline Wear's help, she had positively identified James Ledbetter as the man she had been looking for since Sutton's murder in 1998.

From the evidence Fiona gave the Crown Prosecution, it was clear that Ledbetter's 'snuff-movies' alone generated hundreds of thousands of pounds and indirectly fuelled his innate need to kill, again and again.

At trial it was shown conclusively that images from almost all of Ledbetter's murders had appeared at one time or another on the 'dark side' of the internet. Indeed, they went a long way to secure seven of the nine convictions against him. It was also clear from this evidence that he had, with Fiona's help, established a hugely successful hard-core business in which he had turned his own dark, psychotic nature to commercial gain. His work, clearly 'signed' in a series of bizarre ways, commanded very high prices with dealers.

The unexpected emergence of Elspeth's fabricated, somewhat melodramatic 'death' on the internet not only alerted Ledbetter and his wife to the fact that they had been discovered as purveyors of hard porn but effectively damaged material already out there. If 'Three-thirty' products were fakes, then all Ledbetter's gruesome work was in vain.

For them, it was the beginning of the end.

Georgina Cousins - aided and abetted by Emma Butterworth - had exploited vulnerable women, extracting their stories of abuse to flesh out her novels and to obtain her own kind of sexual gratification. Her two-year relationship with Caroline Wear had revealed, rather unexpectedly, that the serial-killer she had been hunting since 1998, was Consultant Pathologist Dr. James Ledbetter.

That he should also turn out to be Caroline's father was one of those absurd coincidences that frequently occur in fiction but seldom in real life. That it happed for real in this case belies that truism - obviously a clear and remarkable exception to the rule.

Somewhere in this dark and murky process, James Ledbetter and Georgina Cousins crossed virtual paths.

It was then only a matter of time before they established some kind of vicarious, online interaction in which Georgina the 'huntress' regularly taunted her devious prey, threatening exposure at any moment. His awareness that she was about to publish her findings in the form of a new novel only hastened his resolve. Thus cornered, Ledbetter had in the end no other choice than to find both women (now hiding on the Isle of Skye) and destroy them.

He managed to do that and obtain his savage revenge but in so doing he invoked the full force of the law and was himself destroyed.

Ledbetter's 'confession' during questioning by the police and his subsequent decision to plead guilty to all nine counts made the trial a great deal easier than had been originally anticipated by the Crown Prosecution Service. Ledbetter steadfastly denied that there were other killings for which he was responsible but the FBI is currently investigating a series of similar, unexplained deaths - some with mutilation - that took place in Florida between 2000 and 2012.

It was in Florida that he and Fiona regularly spent their vacations. Ledbetter, therefore, may face further charges from America.

Postscript

James Ledbetter's trial lasted six weeks. He was convicted on seven out of the nine counts against him. He is now serving life-imprisonment at HMP Barlinnie. It is said that he has so far written three historical novels, none of which have been published. To most people he is probably one of the cruellest and most dangerous psychopaths ever to have walked this planet. He remains Scotland's worst serial-killer.

Georgina Cousins was a predatory lesbian who preyed on vulnerable young women and exploited even those she loved. For nearly twelve years she devoted her life to hunting and exposing a dangerous serial-killer. It cost her her own life and that of her partner. After the revelations at trial, neither women will be remembered with affection in Portree and beyond.

Fiona, Ledbetter's wife, obtained immunity from prosecution by turning Queen's evidence against her husband. She cooperated fully with the police right up until his trial. She was not, therefore, bought to trial herself and the nine counts originally against her, including trafficking in obscene images, were dropped. Once James Ledbetter was incarcerated she sold the large family home just outside Aberdeen and moved to Fort Lauderdale, Florida where she now deals in real estate, selling and buying holiday bungalows for ex-pats. She has gone back to her maiden name, Fiona Pawley.

It is said she has taken up golf.

Detective Chief Inspector Paul Elliott was generally regarded as the mastermind behind the successful identification, capture and indictment of Scotland's worst ever serial-killer. He was rapidly promoted - twice - and is now Deputy Assistant Commissioner with the Metropolitan Police in London. He has special responsibilities within their Counter Terrorism Command.

Paul Elliott has given up golf.

John White is still based in Inverness but has been promoted to

Detective Chief Inspector. His handling of the 'Gang of Five' was regarded by his masters as exceptional. He is still very happily married to Poppy.

The celebrated 'Gang of Five' remained together until Ledbetter's trial, throughout which period they spearheaded the research element in the last phase of that investigation, based not in Portree but in Inverness.

After Ledbetter's successful conviction, they all went their separate ways.

Detective Sergeant Tom Watson was given further training and then promoted to Detective Inspector, in which capacity he returned to Ullapool. He is now married to a young English girl called Penelope Jones.

DC Paul Mills and PC Nick Fellows were both promoted to Sergeant. Both returned to their respective operational bases in Oban. Both are currently applying to become detectives.

WPC Janice Ward became Sergeant Janice Ward and was transferred to the Public Protection Unit in Strathclyde where she deals with rape cases on a daily basis. WPC Charlotte Stephens left the police force and with her new girlfriend now runs a help-line and community centre in Edinburgh for abused women - a genuine one. WPC Deborah Saunders of the Portree Constabulary is back in Portree, working beside Sergeant Albert McGregor. Two weeks ago she became engaged to Portree's one and only postman.

As for the celebrated Dr. Elspeth Grant, she is still very active. She continues to divide her time between All Souls College, Oxford (where she is trying to complete her second PhD - something about the function of multiple 'tells' within the Limbic system) and her flat in Edinburgh. Mother is no longer there with her in her exotic 'Moroccan' apartment. He left Edinburgh two months ago to continue his work as a cosmologist at the European Organisation for Nuclear Research (CERN) in Switzerland. Although clearly upset that her relationship with 'Mother' was over, Elspeth was recently seen executing cartwheels on Poppy White's lawn - just for fun!

The End

If you enjoyed this book then why not try the others in this series

Volume 1
But who killed Caroline?
By
Mike Healey

Volume 2
The beasts of Rannoch Moor
By
Mike Healey

Volume 3
Cri de Coeur
By
Mike Healey

Also by Mike Healey

Tales of Odd
Twelve short stories similar to Roald Dahl's celebrated 'Tales of the Unexpected' but darker. Much darker!

Journey to the dark side of the Moon
Surreal, science fiction story set in Victorian times

All these titles are available on Kindle/Amazon

Printed in Great Britain
by Amazon